P9-BYV-607

Praise for Leann Sweeney's Yellow Rose Mysteries

"As Texas as a Dr Pepper–swigging armadillo at the Alamo. A rip-roaring read!"
—Carolyn Hart, author of *Death of the Party*

"*Shoot from the Lip* is full of emotions! Anger, sadness, fear, happiness, laughter, joy, and tears . . . they are all there, and you will feel them along with the characters in this book!"
—Amanda Shafer, Armchair Interviews

"I adore this series." —Roundtable Reviews

"A welcome new voice in mystery fiction."
—Jeff Abbott, bestselling author of *Collision*

"A dandy debut . . . will leave mystery fans eager to read more about Abby Rose."
—Bill Crider, author of *Of All Sad Worlds*

"*Pick Your Poison* goes down sweet."
—Rick Riordan, Edgar® Award–winning author of *The Battle of the Labyrinth*

"A witty, down-home Texas mystery . . . [a] fine tale."
—*Midwest Book Review*

The Yellow Rose Mysteries
by Leann Sweeney

THE CAT, THE QUILT AND THE CORPSE

A CATS IN TROUBLE MYSTERY

LEANN SWEENEY

AN OBSIDIAN MYSTERY

OBSIDIAN
Published by New American Library, a division of
Penguin Group (USA) Inc., 375 Hudson Street,
New York, New York 10014, USA
Penguin Group (Canada), 90 Eglinton Avenue East, Suite 700, Toronto,
Ontario M4P 2Y3, Canada (a division of Pearson Penguin Canada Inc.)
Penguin Books Ltd., 80 Strand, London WC2R 0RL, England
Penguin Ireland, 25 St. Stephen's Green, Dublin 2,
Ireland (a division of Penguin Books Ltd.)
Penguin Group (Australia), 250 Camberwell Road, Camberwell, Victoria 3124,
Australia (a division of Pearson Australia Group Pty. Ltd.)
Penguin Books India Pvt. Ltd., 11 Community Centre, Panchsheel Park,
New Delhi - 110 017, India
Penguin Group (NZ), 67 Apollo Drive, Rosedale, North Shore 0632,
New Zealand (a division of Pearson New Zealand Ltd.)
Penguin Books (South Africa) (Pty.) Ltd., 24 Sturdee Avenue,
Rosebank, Johannesburg 2196, South Africa

Penguin Books Ltd., Registered Offices:
80 Strand, London WC2R 0RL, England

First published by Obsidian, an imprint of New American Library,
a division of Penguin Group (USA) Inc.

First Printing, May 2009
10 9 8 7 6 5 4 3 2 1

This book is for Maddie

Acknowledgments

A huge thanks to my critique group for their inspiration and keen eyes: Kay, Amy, Laura, Bob, Charlie, Millie, Dean and Joe, as well as Susie and Isabella. I am grateful to Felicia Donovan for her wonderful computer forensic knowledge and to the online "cozies" who have carried me along as a friend—you know who you are and I love you. My family—Mike, Shawn, Jillian, Jeffrey, Allison, Maddie, and to my sister Candy and my great friend Lydia—thank you all for your love and support. To my agent, Carol Mann— I am so glad you keep sticking by me. And to my editor, Claire, who encouraged me to write this book and stood by patiently during a year of challenges—I can never thank you enough. You are amazing.

Curiosity is lying in wait for every secret.

—RALPH WALDO EMERSON

One

My cat is allergic to people—yes, odd, I know—so when I came in the back door and heard Chablis sneeze, I stopped dead. Why was she sneezing? This couldn't be a reaction to me. I use special shampoo, take precautions. Chablis and I are cool.

Besides, she hadn't been near any humans for more than twenty-four hours, since I was just arriving back from an overnight business trip to Spartanburg, a two-hour drive from my upstate South Carolina home. I'd left her and my two other cats, Merlot and Syrah, alone in the house, as I'd done many times before when I took short trips out of town. So how did human dander, better known as dandruff, find its way up her nose?

I released my grip on the rolling suitcase and started for the living room, thinking there could be a simple explanation for a sneezing cat other than allergies. Like an illness.

The thought of a sick Chablis pushed logic down to the hippocampus or wherever common sense goes when you have more important matters to attend to. I dropped my tote on the counter and hurried past the teak dining table. Since my kitchen, dining area and living room all blend together, the trip to where I'd heard Chablis sneeze wasn't more than twenty feet. But before I'd taken five steps, I stopped again. Something else besides a sneezing cat now had my attention.

Silence. No background noise. No *Animal Planet* playing on the television. I always leave the TV tuned to that station when I go away. If the cats were entertained by *The Jeff Corwin Experience* or *Heroes* or *E-Vet*, I'd convinced myself, my absences were more tolerable. Okay, I'm neurotic about my three friends. Not cat-lady neurotic. At forty-one I'm a little young for that. But cats have been my best friends for as long as I can remember, and the ones that live with me now have been amazing since my husband, John, died ten months ago. They take care of me. So I try my best to take care of them.

Could the TV be off because of a power failure?

Glancing back at the microwave, I saw that the clock showed the correct time—one p.m. Perhaps the high-def plasma TV blew up in a cloud of electronic smoke? Maybe. Didn't matter, though. Not now. I'd only heard from Chablis, and none of my cats had shown their faces. I was getting a bad vibe—and I can usually rely on my intuition.

"Chablis, I'm home," I called. I kept walking, slowly now—didn't want to panic them if I was overreacting—and went into the living area. "Syrah, where are you? Merlot, I missed you."

I breathed a sigh of relief when I found Chablis sitting on the olive chenille sofa, her blue eyes gazing up at me. Himalayans look like long-haired Siamese cats and Chablis was no different. Her gorgeous crystal blue eyes and her champagne fur were accented by deep brown feet, and she had a precious dark face and a fluffy wand of a tail.

Her nose was running and she seemed awfully puffed out—even for an already puffy cat. Was she totally swollen up by an allergen other than dandruff?

I knelt and stroked the side of her cheek with the back of my fingers, ran my hands over her body, looking for the mass of giant hives I was sure I'd find.

Nothing. She was simply all bloated fur and loud purrs.

"I am truly sorry for leaving you overnight. Are you telling me you have feline separation anxiety?"

Chablis blinked slowly, opened her mouth and squeaked.

How pitiful. She'd lost her voice. She *had* to be sick. With a virus? Or leukemia? Cats do get leukemia.

Quit it, Jillian. Call the vet.

When I stood to pull my phone from my jeans pocket, I heard Merlot's deep, loud meow and saw him perched on the seat cushions that line the dining area's bay window—a spot that provides a spectacular view of Mercy Lake. He knows the entire lake belongs to him, despite never having been closer than the window. But he hadn't been sitting there when I first came in, and he wasn't gazing out on the water. No, Merlot was looking right at me and his fur was all wild and big, too.

Since he isn't allergic to anything, dumb me finally realized that they were both scared.

And then I saw why.

Broken glass glittered near Merlot's paws—paws that could each substitute for a Swiffer duster.

My heart skipped. Broken glass ... a broken *window*. "Merlot! Be careful." Fear escaped with my words. I attempted to mask my distress by smiling as I walked over to him.

Yeah, like Mr. Brainiac Cat would buy this fakery.

I petted his broad orange and white tiger-striped head while making sure none of his paws was bleeding. He seemed fine other than that he reminded me more than ever of one of those huge, shaggy stuffed animals at a carnival.

I hefted him off the cushions—he's a Maine coon, a breed that weighs four times more than the smallest felines. Merlot stays lean, usually hovers around twenty pounds. I was hoping to keep him clear of the glass, but he was having none of that. He squirmed free and jumped right back on the window seat and proved himself amazingly nimble by staying away from any shards. While I examined the damaged window, he intently examined me as if to ask, "How will you rectify this now that you're finally home, Miss Gadabout?"

The jagged hole in the lowest pane was large enough for a hand to reach in and unlatch that window. And it *was* unlatched.

"Someone's broken in. Someone's been in our house." But stating the obvious couldn't help them explain what had happened. Figuring this out was human territory. For a millisecond, I wondered if this—this *intruder* might still be here. I shook my head no. My cats are not fools. They'd be in the basement or under a bed if any danger still remained.

And exactly where was Syrah? My Abyssinian hadn't made an appearance yet. I supposed he could have been frightened enough to stay in hiding, but no. He was the alpha cat of my little pack.

Okay, I decided. This break-in had upset him. That was why he wasn't making an appearance. Either that or he was so angry I'd left him and his friends to be threatened by a burglar that he was hiding to teach me a lesson.

The thought of a thief frightening my cats produced anger and fear and the sincere wish that I'd had a human friend who could watch out for things just like this while I was away. Since my husband's death, though, I'd been caught up in my own troubles and too proud to reach out to anyone. But making friends, getting to know my neighbors, might have prevented this whole episode.

I inhaled deeply, let the air out slowly. *You can change that, Jillian. But right now you need to find Syrah.*

That was what John would do if he were here. Hunt for the cat in a methodical, logical way. Solve this problem quickly. But I wasn't John and my calm began to crack like crusted snow before an avalanche. Between the silent TV, the scared animals and the absent Syrah, fear now claimed top billing.

"Where are you, baby?" I called, my voice tremulous. "Come here, Syrah."

I hurried toward the hallway leading to the bedrooms, Merlot on my heels. Poor Chablis would have been on his tail, but was stopped by a fit of sneezing. I began the search through all three thousand square feet of my house, the house that was supposed to be our dream home, the one John and I had designed ourselves.

But this was no longer a dream come true. John, at fifty-five, had been far too young to die of a sudden and unexpected heart attack. Though I was coming to terms with his death, letting go day by day, thoughts of him always seemed to flood my brain when I was stressed. And a broken window and a missing cat were certainly enough to produce that state of mind.

I rushed from room to room, but didn't find Syrah hiding behind my armoires or beneath the dressers or under any beds. He wasn't in the closets or the basement, either. I went outside and checked the trees and the roof for a third scared cat. After all, the intruder might have let him out when he made his escape. But leaves had been falling for weeks, and spotting Syrah's rusty gold fur against the reds, browns and yellows of the oak, hickory and pecan trees in my yard would be difficult.

Syrah, however, is my most vocal cat, and when I didn't hear any meowing in response to my calls, I was sure he wasn't nearby. Cats have such good hearing that they can detect the sound of a bat stretching its wings, and I was nearly shrieking his name.

I finally gave up, and when I came inside I found Merlot sitting by the back door. I was trembling all over as I crouched next to him. He rubbed against my knees and purred while I took my cell phone from my pocket, ready to report the break-in.

"Are you trying to comfort yourself or me?" I asked as I dialed 911. The last time I'd had to do that—when John collapsed—had been the worst day of my life. This event certainly wasn't as horrible, but punching those three numbers again made it seem like John had died only yesterday.

My big cat circled me lovingly as I stood, nudging me, trying to comfort me as best he could. He knew how upset I was.

"What is your emergency?" said the woman who answered.

"Um . . . um . . . my cat is missing."

The dispatcher said, "Ma'am, this line is for—"

"I've had a break-in. There's a shattered window and—" My mouth was so dry, the words wouldn't come.

"Your name, ma'am?"

"J-Jillian Hart. I live at 301 Cove Lane in Mercy." Merlot and I walked back to the living room and I picked up the cable and DVR remote. I hit the MUTE button to kill the audio before I turned on the TV. The Sony plasma worked fine and was tuned to *Animal Planet* as it should be. I jabbed the OFF button, wondering what kind of thief would break into my house and turn off my expensive TV.

"Ma'am. Are you there, ma'am?" It came out like "Ah you there, ma-aaam?" Very Southern, reminding me that I was far from our longtime Texas home and far from anyone who really understood what an emergency this was for me.

"Yes. I'm here."

"I see this is a cellular numbah, but are you callin' from inside the home?"

"Of course. My cat is gone and—"

"Officers are on their way. Do you feel safe or do you believe the intruder might still be inside or in the immediate vicinity?" Her South Carolina drawl was so thick and I was so distracted by worry that she might as well have been speaking a foreign language.

I closed my eyes, processed her question. "I-I've searched the house. No one's here but me and my two babies."

"But you do fear for your safety, ma'am?"

"I fear for my *cat's* safety and—" Tears sprang unexpectedly to my eyes and I bit my lip.

"Ma'am, is something happenin' right this minute? Is this intruder back?"

"No. It's just that . . . I don't know where he is. I can't find him." How pathetic I sounded. Syrah was a cat, after all.

"I fully understand your concern. My name is Barbara Lynne. May I call you Jillian?"

"Yes. Of course."

"Tell me about these babies you mentioned. How old are they, Jillian?"

"Chablis is about five and Merlot is probably around eight. They're fine. Well, not exactly fine because Chablis is having an allergic reaction and—"

"Oh my. Should we send an am-bu-lance?" Her previously unruffled tone was now laced with concern.

"I have medicine. She'll be okay in an hour or two. I haven't had time to give her an antihistamine. I've been busy searching—"

"Exactly where are your children, Jillian? I don't hear them, but I assume they're with you, with their mama?"

"Oh. Oh no. You're confused. Chablis and Merlot are my two other cats."

A pause, then, "Is that so?" Sweetness and concern had now left the building. She couldn't have sounded any colder if she'd been standing in a blizzard in North Dakota.

I stayed on the line as instructed—I was "ma'am" again—and no longer felt any love from the dispatcher. She offered only an occasional "Are you still there?"

Meanwhile, my panic worsened as I waited for the police. Possibilities ran through my head. The person who broke in obviously let Syrah out. My beautiful, wonderful cat could be lying dead by the road after being hit by a car. He could have fallen off the dock into the lake and drowned. He could have— *No. Stop this.*

I decided to do something constructive rather than continue to conjure up worst-case scenarios. To make sure Chablis and Merlot wouldn't run out the door if they got the chance, I put my cell on speaker and set it on the coffee table, then dragged their travel carriers out of the foyer closet. For once, crating them wasn't like trying to bag smoke. They were compliant, perhaps unnerved enough themselves to want the security of their carriers right now.

Not wanting them out of my sight, I kept them with me in the living room. I dreaded the arrival of sirens and uniformed strangers. It would only add to their trauma.

It didn't take long for the cops to show. Five minutes later I heard the cruiser's engine in my driveway, and the dispatcher quickly disconnected when I told her they had arrived. But the car had come without a siren—I guessed because this wasn't an emergency that required one.

Mercy is a small town—teensy compared to Houston, where I'd lived with John for the six years we'd been married. Seemed like you could get anywhere in Mercy in five minutes. I ran to the foyer and answered before the police officers could even knock. I was sure glad I'd put Merlot and Chablis in their carriers because, as expected, they freaked out and started up with a cat duet best suited for an opera: loud, mournful and tragic.

Two officers stood on the porch, one male, one female. The man said, "Deputy Morris Ebeling. Are you Jillian Hart?"

"Yes. Come in." I stepped back.

"Deputy Candace Carson," the other one said as they came inside.

She looked to be in her twenties and Morris had to be about sixty, his face round and pasty. His stomach hung over his equipment-laden uniform belt, his gut reminding me of a sack of potatoes under his brown shirt.

I led them into the living room, and Candace immediately went to the carriers, knelt and murmured to Merlot and Chablis in a comforting voice. They quieted at once. She was an animal person, thank goodness.

"What exactly happened here, ma'am?" Morris's accent made me think he could have been dispatcher Barbara Lynne's daddy.

"I don't know," I answered. "I was on an overnight business trip and came home to find a broken window. And my other cat is missing. He's an Abyssinian. Sort of amber with—"

"Is he an expensive cat?" Morris asked. "I mean, could someone have broken in to steal him because he's worth buckets of money?"

"No way," I said with a laugh. "He was a rescue. After Katrina. So were Merlot and Chablis. They're all purebreds, but without papers."

"What kinda papers?" he said.

"A pedigree. The papers that show who their parents were and that they are truly purebreds. He doesn't have those, so no one would consider him worth a lot of money."

"Anything else gone missin'?" Morris said.

"Nothing that I could tell from the quick run-through I made. But who cares?"

"Um . . . sure," Morris said. "Who cares?"

The sarcasm wasn't lost on me, but even with his attitude, if he could help get my cat back, I'd be grateful.

Candace rose after one last "It'll be okay, sweetheart" to Chablis. "May I search the premises, Ms. Hart?"

Shiny blond hair was coiled at the nape of Candace's neck, and her eyes were as blue and intense as Chablis's, which I found comforting in a way.

"You might want to start there." I pointed out the broken glass on the window seat cushion.

"I'd like to search from the basement up, if you don't mind. The stairs?"

"I've already looked everywhere," I said. "If Syrah were here, I would have found him."

Candace, even though she was young, reminded me of the principal at my elementary school who'd admonished me for chewing gum when I was about eight years old. Maybe the pine green uniform made her look like an authority figure to me.

"That means we've got a contaminated crime scene," she said. "But I can work around that."

Morris raised his eyes to the ceiling. "Not this crime scene rigmarole again. A damn cat is missing, Candy. Did you hear the lady say anything about missing valuables? Did you notice how her fancy TV and stereo are right here?"

"My name is *Candace*," she answered through clenched teeth. "And—"

"Bet this event was some kid workin' on a dare." Morris took a tin of Skoal from his pocket.

Candace said, "You ever consider that this lady is so distressed about her missing cat she might not realize valuables are gone? Some folks don't care about money and diamond rings above everything else."

"Oh, for criminy sake. Then puh-leese, go find every piece of lint you can, *Candy*." Morris pinched some tobacco and mashed it between his lower teeth and lip.

Candace's cheeks colored. She took a pair of latex gloves from her pocket and put them on. "That's exactly what I intend to do. The basement, Ms. Hart?" she said.

I pointed to the kitchen. "Through there. You'll see the door to the stairs."

Morris was shifting his weight from one foot to the other. Seemed to me like he wanted back in his police cruiser as quickly as he could manage it. "I need to start the paperwork, Ms. Hart. Excuse me for a moment."

He went out the front door and took his time before coming back with a clipboard. In the interim, I'd filled a dropper with Benadryl, unzipped the top of Chablis's carrier and given her a dose. Poor baby's nose was running like a faucet now. I checked out Morris's shoulders for any dandruff when he returned, wondering if he'd made her allergy attack worse. I mean, it was obvious that this reaction was caused by an intruder with dandruff.

Morris, whose graying hair seemed dandruff free, sat on the reclining wing chair across from the sofa, a simple, normal action that jolted me. That leather recliner had belonged to John and no one had touched it since his death.

It's okay. It's only a chair.

But anxiety mixed with grief made my stomach knot.

I would have preferred to pace off this unwelcome emotion, but instead I sat on the edge of the sofa, hands clasped in my lap. Merlot and Chablis were already worried about their friend Syrah. They needed me to at least act like I was in a stable emotional state.

"You live alone, ma'am?" Morris said.

"No, sir. I live with my three cats—Chablis, Syrah and Merlot." Maybe I could make him understand through some sarcasm of my own that cats are as important as people.

But he didn't bother to write their names down. He just stared at me with tired brown eyes. "No gentleman residing here with you? Because I heard tell you was married."

"You heard tell?" I said.

"No secrets in Mercy, Ms. Hart."

"Apparently there are," I said softly. "My husband died unexpectedly not long after we moved here. Heart attack."

His forehead wrinkled in confusion, as if to say, "Why didn't I know this?" Then he said, "I'm sorry for your loss. Sorry indeed," and at least he sounded like he actually meant it.

Candace returned to the living room and, without saying a word, focused first on the window and then on the glass still lying undisturbed on the cushions. At least I'd done something right by leaving it there.

She took out her phone and snapped off a few pictures before removing a folded brown paper bag from her uniform pocket.

"Candy, what the hell do you think you're doing now?" Morris said.

"*Candace* is collecting evidence," she said, carefully picking up the pieces of glass and putting them in her bag.

"'Cause a cat ran off? I know you take your job real serious, and I try my best to respect that, but I'm thinking the county crime lab won't be happy about this particular evidence."

Candace said, "Someone invaded this kind lady's private property, so I disagree. And can we assume the cat ran off? Maybe the bad guy took him."

Morris sighed heavily. "Took the cat? Why in heck would someone break in to steal a cat? You can go the SPCA or— Forget it." He refocused on me. "For my report, exactly when did this happen, Ms. Hart?"

"I got in at one o'clock. Did I mention that this . . . this *person* turned off my TV?"

"Huh?" Morris said. "Don't you mean turned *on* your TV?"

"No. I leave it on. I like people to think I'm home when the cats are alone." For some reason I felt a little embarrassed about this, so I added, "Obviously that tactic didn't work."

"Can I offer a piece of advice, Ms. Hart?" Morris said. "Get yourself a dog. A real dog, like a German shepherd. A dog with a big bark and a bigger bite."

"Sorry. I love dogs, but my cats don't."

"Okay, then get yourself a nice state-of-the-art alarm system. We got a guy in town who does that stuff. Name's Tom. Tom Stewart. Nice fella and—"

"Did you *touch* the television when you came in, Ms. Hart?" Candace interrupted. She was on her knees by the window seat, staring intently at the cushions, her tweezers poised and ready to collect more evidence.

"I used the remote," I said. "I thought maybe the TV wasn't working."

"Gosh darn," Candace muttered, getting to her feet. "Okay, we might still get prints off the TV if the perp shut off the television without touching the remote."

"The *perp*?" Both of Morris's bushy gray eyebrows were working. "We don't have perps in Mercy. We got dumb drunks and outta-control kids who should eat dinner with their mama and daddy more often. This is about a broken window, Candy."

"And you have no idea when this break-in occurred?" Candace continued, seemingly unflustered by her partner's lack of interest in what had gone on in my house.

But I sure appreciated her interest. "I left yesterday afternoon for a quilt show in Spartanburg. I make and sell small quilts for cats."

"Figures," Morris said under his breath.

I shot him a look. "I also make quilts that I donate for the children of the men and women in the military who have been killed in Iraq and Afghanistan. I had a meeting with a charitable group this morning, gave them pictures of my designs and took their order for a hundred children's quilts. Anyway, I left here around eight a.m. yesterday and I've told you when I returned."

"You mind if I dust your TV and remote?" Candace asked. "I'd also like to see if I could lift prints off the window latch and the outside molding."

Morris rose abruptly, his patience spent. "Candy, quit with this *CSI* crap. We're leaving." He offered me the best smile a wad of Skoal allowed. "You catch sight of any teenage boys lurkin' around or peekin' in your windows, you give us a call. And Billy Cranor can fix that window for you. He works at the hardware store."

Morris turned and marched toward the foyer, waving a hand for Candace to follow.

But before she left, she took my elbow, leaned close and whispered, "I'll be back when my shift's over. I've got my fingerprint kit with me at all times and I know how to access AFIS—that's this big old fingerprint database. This bad guy's not getting away with this. Try not to disturb the scene too much until I get back here."

What a pair, I thought, once I'd closed and locked my front door. But Candace was certainly dedicated, and even crotchety Morris Ebeling's eyes told me he was a decent guy.

I let Chablis and Merlot out of their carriers and said, "Come on, you two. We have flyers to make about our lost buddy."

As soon as I said the word *lost*, tears threatened again. I walked to my office, Merlot and a wobbly, sleepy Chablis right with me.

It was only after I'd printed out fifty copies with Syrah's best picture prominent in the center, only after I'd stopped feeling sorry for myself, that I realized I'd never told Candace about Chablis's human allergy, how the intruder must have had dandruff. From watching her work, I was certain she might be the one person in Mercy who would consider dandruff important.

Two

Once my flyers were ready, I duct-taped plastic wrap over the broken window to keep insects out of the house. That was about all duct tape could accomplish in this case. I was painfully aware that my home was unprotected from a second break-in. A call to security guy Tom Stewart was definitely on my to-do list. Good thing I'd sold ten quilts at the show yesterday. At a hundred bucks a pop, that meant some extra cash for a security system—one John and I had never thought we'd need in this sleepy lake town.

I thought about his hunting rifle and briefly considered pulling it out of the closet. But I don't care for guns and have no clue how to shoot a rifle. Maybe I should plan on learning. Surely Mercy had somebody who could provide that service, too. Morris seemed to know everyone's skills; if he could give me a name or take it upon himself to teach me to shoot, then I could protect myself and my furry friends.

Shoot? What are you thinking? You don't step on ants or spiders. You couldn't even shoot Hannibal Lecter if he came calling.

Pushing these thoughts aside, I called my vet, Dr. Jensen.

"This is Jillian Hart," I said when the cheery lady at the front desk answered. Her name was Agnes if I remembered right.

"Hey, Ms. Hart. How's those three little darlings of yours? Nothing wrong, I hope."

"Syrah is missing and I wondered if anyone's brought in a lost cat. You remember him? The sorrel Abyssinian?"

"I surely do remember that handsome boy. But we haven't seen Syrah. I don't recall—did you take us up on having the microchips inserted when you were in last? Because, of course, you know that helps when our darlings get themselves lost."

No, I didn't get the chips, I thought. *Probably because I am as stupid as the excuse I will not be making.* "No microchips."

"I am so sorry, Ms. Hart. Maybe we can put in the chips for your other two. I can make that appointment right now," she said.

"I'll get back to you on that. I'm busy looking for a cat." *Microchips. Add that to the to-do list.*

I had to get moving, but I wasn't about to put Merlot and Chablis at risk by leaving them home. I wrangled them into their carriers again and took them out to my minivan.

Stoic Merlot tolerated my trip around the nearby neighborhoods as I hammered, stapled or taped my lost-cat flyers to telephone poles, street signs and even the FOR SALE signs at a few houses. I might have appreciated the crisp late-afternoon air if not for Chablis. She hated every minute of this exercise. Even Benadryl didn't keep her from howling her displeasure. I hoped a revenge hairball on my pillow wasn't in my immediate future.

After covering the areas close to home, I headed for downtown Mercy. It's a cute town that attracts tourists who'd probably first visited more interesting places like Atlanta or the Biltmore Estate but weren't ready to give up on Southern charm and go home yet. There's a restored town center where green, gold and red awning-ed antiques stores, bookshops and little restaurants line the main drag. A brick courthouse and other well-cared-for old buildings mark the horizon. I'd never had much chance to shop in Mercy aside from my frequent trips to the fantastic quilt shop, the Cotton Company.

I decided that posting lost-cat flyers on the live oaks that lined the pristine street would be a giant no-no. Yup, Main Street was as tidy as a kitchen floor you'd see in a TV commercial. No flyers would fly here.

The local Piggly Wiggly might be an excellent option for advertising my problem. When I pulled into the parking lot, it was close to five p.m., and the cool fall day allowed me to leave the cats in the van, something I never could have done in hell-hot Houston during unpredictable October. I'd loved that city, but had not experienced near the level of humidity here—at least not this past summer.

David, one of the sackers, allowed me into the store ahead of his train of grocery carts, saying, "Hey there, Ms. Hart." He was maybe in his late teens, had this odd lopsided head and a friendly, guileless expression.

"Hi, David," I said. "Can I talk to you after you get those carts stowed properly?"

"Stowed?" David grinned. "Now that there's a new word. You're always giving me something to think on, Ms. Hart."

He parked the carts and met me at the store bulletin board.

"What can I do fer ya?" he said.

I resisted the urge to calm the blond cowlick that had my attention. "One of my cats is lost and—"

"Not the one who only eats salmon? 'Cause that could be a problem out there where you live. No salmon in Mercy Lake that I've heard tell."

Oh my gosh. I hadn't even thought about Syrah's food. He *was* the one who ate only salmon. Whether it was Fancy Feast or Friskies, he didn't care, but there had to be salmon in his dish or he'd turn up his nose.

"That's the one," I said. "Syrah is out there somewhere and he's never been outdoors since he lost his first family during Hurricane Katrina." I shook the handful of flyers I held. "Can I put a few of these up in the store?"

"Anything for a pretty lady. You could be a movie star, you know."

I felt the heat of a blush. "I'm old enough to be your mother, David."

"No, you ain't. My mother's got white hair. She says I gave her every one of them, too." He smiled again and held out his hand for the flyers.

David stared at Syrah's picture for a few seconds. "So this is the salmon cat. Mighty nice-lookin', just like you always say. If he caught one of those bass out of Mercy Lake, he might change his mind about salmon. My mama always says look at the good side. He could come back with a whole new appetite."

I smiled. David *was* an angel. "I hope you're right. Think I'll pick up a rotisserie chicken for dinner and get on home. My other two cats are in the van."

David's face lit up. "They are? Can I visit with them when yer done shopping?"

"Um, sure." I was a little surprised at how excited he seemed.

But as we walked out to my van ten minutes later, with David carrying my dinner, he explained how his mother thought cats were bad luck. "When I get a place of my own, I'm getting me a cat. I love my mama, but she's gotta let me grow up and move out sometime. And when I do, I'm having a cat—maybe a dog, too."

I opened the back of the van. When David set down the grocery bag, Merlot turned his head away. Not happy. Chablis started up with her dismal mewing again.

I pulled her carrier closer and unzipped the top just enough so David could fit his hand in to pet her.

"She don't bite, does she? Grandpa Nagel had a cat that was so mean he could run a dog off a meat wagon."

"She doesn't bite. And she'd love a scratch on the head."

David stuck his hand in and did just that. Chablis closed her eyes and starting purring. "Wow. She likes me, huh?"

"If she could talk, she'd say 'yes.' Look how she's closing her eyes." If only more people knew what a cat can accomplish with a purr. David was beaming.

A few minutes later I was on my way home when my cell rang. The caller ID read MERCY POLICE.

"Did you find him?" I said when I connected. "Where was he?"

"Sorry, Ms. Hart," Candace said. "I'm at your place and I haven't seen your cat anywhere. Think you'll be home anytime soon?"

"I'm five minutes away." I wanted to add, "This is Mercy. Everything is five minutes away," but I was too disappointed even to offer a smile as I made that all too true observation.

"Good. I took the liberty of calling up Billy and he says—"

"Billy?"

"Hardware store guy," she said.

"That's right."

"Anyway, he's meeting me here to get your window fixed. Can't be sleeping in your house with a broken window, can you?"

"Thank you, Candace. See you in five." That was a kindness and now I managed a smile as I drove on home. Small towns have their advantages—like genuine concern from a relative stranger.

Turned out, Billy looked familiar. Where had I seen him before?

Candace hovered near him as he fixed the window. If I read her smiles and body language right, she was flirting with the guy. He had dark brown hair, muscles that told me he could pry the lid off a nuclear reactor and just enough scruffy facial hair to remind me of that nameless actor on some crime show I watch. But where had I seen him before? I mean, I hardly knew anyone in Mercy.

While Billy measured my window, Candace went to work with her fingerprint kit. As I watched them, I decided she'd planned this all out. What better way to be that close to a hunk like Billy than to be dusting while he was measuring? And it worked. They were ear to ear.

She kept glancing his way and he kept ignoring her. Guess putting in new windows is a fascinating occupation. When he left for his truck to get the new pane, her gaze never left his butt with its weighted-down tool belt.

Candace said, "What is it about a tool belt that just fills my mouth with spit?"

"That's not exactly an attractive thought, Candace." I smiled. "Besides, it's more what holds up the tool belt that has your mouth watering."

"You got that right. Now, back to business. I got nothing off that window. Perp musta worn gloves. I'll dust the TV, but I'm thinking I won't find anything."

And she didn't. By the time she was finished, Billy had cut the glass to size under Candace's adoring eyes, and I soon had a brand-new window.

"How much do I owe you?" I asked when he was done.

"Five bucks oughta cover it," he said. "The pane itself only cost a buck fifty."

"Is that all?" My purse was sitting on top of Merlot's carrier. He was sound asleep and Chablis had worn herself out, too. I took out my wallet.

"There might be one thing you could help me with," he said. "I'm a volunteer fireman and we put together this calendar. I know it's late in the year, but if you'd be so kind as to buy one, that would sure help our charity. We donate the money to kids all over South Carolina who've been burned in house fires or accidents."

That was where'd I'd seen him. "I bought one of those calendars way back when we first moved here. And aren't you, um . . . *featured*?"

His cheeks colored to almost strawberry. "Ma'am, it's for the kids."

"I want two more calendars, then," I said. "And by the way, I make quilts for charities. Children's quilts, so I could—"

"I need another calendar, too," Candace said quickly.

Billy's eyes met hers for the first time. "Now that's real nice of you two ladies."

I caught a lingering gaze between them. Candace was catching on about how to make Billy pay attention.

"What I started to say was that I have some quilts in the other room looking for small bodies to keep warm," I said.

"You'd give us those?" he said.

"That's why I make them. Let me get you a few."

As I left the room, I heard Billy say to Candace, "She's one sweet lady, isn't she? Young to lose a husband, though. Dan Meade caught that 911 call last January. Couldn't do a thing for the man."

I swallowed hard and picked up my pace. John's death would always leave a wound, but the constant grieving had to end—and I'd been making progress. He would have wanted me to move on with my life. And I was trying my best.

When I returned, quilts in hand, Candace was busy dusting the rest of the entertainment center for prints.

"I thought you said the intruder wore gloves?" I said.

"I know." She faced me. "I guess I'm as stubborn as my daddy always says. Bad guys leave things behind, even the smart ones, and I want to find something this one left."

Just then Billy came back into the house with three calendars. We paid up and he left, again with Candace admiring him every step of the way.

As soon as he was gone, she flipped the calendar open to July and said, "Now here's what I'm talking about. Can't have enough of this."

Billy was shirtless and wearing his volunteer fireman pants, suspenders loose over broad shoulders. The man was oiled, bronzed and had muscles Superman could only wish for.

After we stared for a few seconds, Candace wiped a damp strand of hair off her forehead—she was a bit sweaty even though the evening was beginning to cool the house down considerably. She said, "Let's get back to work."

"Obviously you think there might be a clue here, so tell me how that will help find my cat. If I don't get Syrah home by dark . . ." I'd been distracted for a time, but now my eyes burned. I willed back the tears. Tears wouldn't help anything.

"You really love these cats, huh?" Candace said.

"They're all I've got."

She nodded, as if to tell me she understood. "I collected a clump of what looks like cat hair out near the end of your driveway—can't say that's what it is 'cause I got no hard evidence, but you want to take a look? If it belongs to your missing cat I can surely find a match here in the house. Plus there were tire tracks. I took a picture, but matching the tire to make and model probably won't happen. No way the town's gonna pay a nickel to search for a match since they'd be with Morris—decide nothing was taken. But that missing cat is as good as gold to you."

"Syrah might have simply run off. That's what most people would conclude. But he wouldn't go with a stranger," I said. "He's too smart for that. This voice in my head is telling me he was stolen. But why?"

"That's what we need to find out—why he's gone and where he is. Doesn't matter to me if your Syrah ran off or was catnapped; I plan to help you," Candace said.

"That means so much—you helping me on your own time."

"I like you, Ms. Hart. Plus I need to practice my evidence-collection skills if I'm ever gonna get out of Mercy and get me a real police job. Sure, this is my home, but they're not so hot here on using all the new scientific stuff that can help in police work. Just want to keep everything the same old same old."

"Help me understand how any evidence you find will help you get a lead on Syrah."

"Don't rightly know. But you collect stuff, then you hope and pray the evidence leads you down the right road."

I nodded. "I'll buy that. Let me see what you've found so far."

She'd brought in a little satchel that held her fingerprint

kit and now took out a small brown envelope. "Haven't sealed it yet. Wanted you to take a look first. But don't go touching it, okay?"

She squeezed the stiff pouch open so I could look inside.

"Syrah is a sorrel color, so if it's his hair it should be coppery ticked with chocolate ... and the base of the hair should be a bright apricot. Together all these colors make him look amber."

"Sorrel? Ticked? What's all that mean?" Candace asked.

"Syrah is an Abyssinian cat. His color is sorrel. And 'ticked' means that chocolate is his second tabby color besides copper. He's really just a fancy tabby cat."

"Ah. I get it. But you sound like some kind of expert cat person. Are you?" she said.

"I know a lot about cats, but I wouldn't call myself an expert. I like to learn things—just like you do, right?"

"You got that. Anyway, here's what I found. Your cat's hair look like this?"

I stared down into the envelope, but couldn't see very well, so we moved closer to the window. Then I knew. "Yes. See the chocolate ticking? Cats can lose clumps of hair when they're stressed, so that's proof to me it's his."

"Let me tell you about proof. In my line of work, it's not proof until it's evidence of a crime. As of right now we can't prove whether your cat slipped out when the perp came or left, or was in fact stolen. And if he was stolen, why leave the other two cats?" Candace said.

"Maybe the thief couldn't find the other two? They know how to hide from me, that's for sure," I said.

"This Syrah—I remember you said he's not expensive because he doesn't have his papers to prove he's a purebred. But maybe some idiot thought he was worth something even without these papers you're talkin' about," she said.

"He'd be most valuable to me," I said, realizing exactly

how valuable even as I spoke the words. "Do you think the thief will call and say he or she has Syrah? Ask me for money?"

"That's possible. Or whoever it was simply fancied your cat and decided he wanted him. You can't tell what a person figures they can steal if they so desire. We had a perp once who stole Christmas lights right off people's houses. I always thought it was Lewis Rainer 'cause his house is always lit up like New York City during the holidays. No way he could afford all those lights and snowmen and reindeer on the roof."

"Let me guess," I said. "You couldn't prove it because you couldn't get the evidence?"

"You are catchin' on." Candace smiled and it made her face even more attractive. "Anyway, you never hear about those animals lost during Katrina so much anymore, but lots of folks did lose their pets, huh?"

"That's for sure. My husband and I took in foster cats after the storm and we fell in love with the three I've got now. No one ever claimed them."

"You got yourself some beautiful cats. I love animals but my mom's allergic."

"Allergic! *That's* what I forgot to tell you. Chablis was sneezing when I came home and she's allergic to dandruff—human dandruff. The perp must have left some behind." She had *me* using TV cop lingo now.

"Gosh. I wonder if there's human DNA in dandruff." She pursed her lips, looking thoughtful. "Dandruff is dead skin, after all. Could be useless. But it could be something."

"You don't know?" I said.

A determined look took over. "Nope. But I intend to find out."

Three

I slept poorly without Syrah curled near my head like he loved to do. Plus Chablis purred as loud as a fan all night. I think I hushed her about a dozen times, but the Benadryl was still in her system. Outside the bedroom, I kept hearing Merlot's mournful calls for his friend Syrah.

Yeah, sweetheart. I miss him, too.

Last evening Candace and I had ended up on a first-name basis—but there'd been an almost immediate bond between us from the minute she took the time to comfort my stressed-out cats. After I mentioned the dandruff, she spent an hour to find four flecks on the window seat cushion and carefully placed them in one of her little evidence envelopes. Then we shared deli chicken and a salad.

I drink sweet tea by the gallon and it turned out that Candace did, too. We had another thing in common besides a definite admiration for firemen posing for calendar shots. I was surprised how nice it felt to share something silly with her. My husband had been smart and handsome and funny, but definitely not calendar material. I felt a tad guilty enjoying such careful examinations of every page of that calendar, but maybe a little fun was one of the things I needed to help me move on.

The cat hairs Candace collected from Syrah's favorite spot on the couch resembled what she'd found outside, but she wasn't making any promises that they *were* a match until she looked at them under a microscope. She was definitely dedicated when it came to her evidence obsession; maybe Morris didn't like this, but I sure appreciated it.

She also gave me the number of a small local no-kill shelter. If I didn't find Syrah hanging around outside looking clueless and pathetic in the morning, maybe he was lost and had been dropped off there. The nearest SPCA was about ninety miles away, in Columbia, and this shelter was the closest thing they had in Mercy.

I'd awoken filled with the hope that someone had done exactly that, since I'd had no response to my beautiful flyers—yeah, after less than a day, I know. Before I made a call to that shelter or any other rescue organization I could find within fifty miles, I went out back to look for him again.

In the morning light, Mercy Lake looked more huge and scary than it ever had before. Maybe the strong breeze and gray clouds made the water seem more like an enemy than like the friend it had been since John's death. I'd spent hours by the water this past summer, listening to the gentle lap of waves against the dock, appreciating the birds and squirrels so busy with their simple pleasures. This lake and my cats had helped my heart heal.

But now Syrah could be in that water.

No. No. Don't think that way, Jillian.

I walked straight toward the lake, refusing to believe he could be dead. "Syrah," I called. "Come home, kitty. We miss you."

No cat.

Then I checked out all the trees, as I had yesterday. Many were shedding their leaves with each gust and showering me with their inevitable passage into winter. If Syrah were anywhere near, he would have answered my call—he loves to talk back—but I heard only the wind and the angry water.

I wrapped my arms around myself—it was a lot chillier than yesterday—and went back inside. After three cups of French roast coffee, the clock finally ticked its way to nine a.m. and I called Tom Stewart, the security guy. He agreed to come over in late afternoon and see what he could do for me.

Next I called the shelter—the Mercy Animal Sanctuary—but the line was busy. And though I pressed REDIAL over and over for ten minutes, I got the same result. Didn't everyone have call waiting these days? Well, maybe not in Mercy. I'd simply have to go there. My cell number was on the flyers, so I could be reached if someone found Syrah.

Candace had given me her private mobile number, and I called her for the address and directions. As expected, the place was five minutes away. But it took me longer than that to round up Chablis and Merlot, who after yesterday were not eager to get back in their carriers and the car.

I found the place easily, set back in the woods on the opposite side of the two-lane highway that ran along the lakefront properties. The Mercy Animal Sanctuary was housed in a long log cabin with two hurricane-fenced runs on the side farthest from the entrance. Four dogs barked their greeting when I pulled into the small parking area.

I rolled the windows down an inch or two for Chablis and Merlot's comfort and climbed out of the van. But before I even made it to the shelter door, a young brunette wearing jeans and an oversized sweater met me outside.

"Hey there," she said. "Allison Cuddahee. How can I help you?"

"Jillian Hart. I've lost— " I took a deep breath. "L-lost my cat." I wasn't about to cry again. Stupid tears. You'd think I would have used them all up in the last year.

Allison opened her arms and came to me. "You need a hug, Miss Jillian Hart."

She was a tiny thing, maybe three inches smaller than my five-foot-six and at least ten pounds lighter, but Allison Cuddahee provided one monster hug. It felt wonderful to have a caring human touch, and all the tension seemed to leave my body. I closed my eyes and enjoyed the calm in my center.

She broke away a second later but kept her hands on

my upper arms. "I want you to tell me about your kitty, but let's go inside. Winter has apparently arrived on this fine Saturday morning."

That hug seemed to have infused me with determination—the kind I'd been famous for before John's death. I would find Syrah. I was certain I would. And I had a feeling that Candace, and now this young woman, would help me do just that.

We entered an office area and were met with a loud "Hey there," by an African grey parrot. There was also a cage full of chirping canaries, a fish tank bubbling away with plenty of colorful swimmers and a glass case with the biggest tarantula I'd ever seen. A chill ran up my arms. I'm not a fan of spiders.

I focused on the bird, with its gorgeous scarlet tail. "Hey there," I said.

"What can I do ya?" came its response.

I laughed and said, "This is obviously a Southern African parrot."

"Snug loves his buttermilk biscuits, so I guess you're right." Allison took a seat behind a cluttered and rusted metal desk, gesturing for me to take the folding lawn chair opposite her. "Money goes for the animals, not the decor, so sorry about the chair."

"A chair's a chair, and I like your philosophy," I said.

"I'm sorry to say we haven't had any cats turned in recently, but let me get every bit of your information. We have a strong network in Mercy—we use old-fashioned word of mouth. We'll help any way we can."

Allison and I spent the next few minutes talking about Syrah, the break-in, the police coming out, but when I mentioned the flyers, she shook her head sadly. "Those won't do you any good."

"But why? I thought—"

"Sign ordinance. They're probably all snatched up already. I'm surprised the cops didn't tell you. Who came out to take your report? Morris?"

I nodded. "Morris and Candace."

"Morris needs to retire—and that's me being nice. Candace is a whole other story. She was probably too busy looking for cigarette butts or picking up pebbles to tell you about the sign thing. But you're saying no jewelry or computers or electronics were taken?"

"Taken from where?" The door that I assumed led to the shelter area had opened, and a tall redheaded man who looked to be in his early thirties joined us with this question. He put a freckled hand on the back of Allison's neck and rubbed gently.

"Jillian, this is my husband, Shawn. He does the heavy lifting around here." She smiled up at him. "Someone broke into Jillian's house, and one of her cats is gone."

Shawn focused his hazel eyes on me. "I heard about a break-in. Lake house on Cove Lane?"

Seemed the network was alive and pumping out information. "That's the one."

"And nothing was taken except your cat?" he said.

"I didn't say he was taken," I said.

"But that's what you think, right?" Shawn said.

"I guess I do," I said. "Candace found a clump of his hair out by the road and tire tracks nearby. Am I stupid for thinking someone would steal my cat?"

"Course you're not. Don't go beating yourself up, girl," Allison said. "I can tell you've had enough stress in the last twenty-four hours."

I smiled. "That's for sure."

"Maybe we can help get your cat back," Shawn said. "What's he look like?"

"He's a sorrel Abyssinian. But why would someone steal a cat?" I said.

Shawn nodded toward the parrot. "I asked myself the same question after we had a break-in here. Lost two cats and a dog. Snug told us all about it. But think about it. Pretty cat sitting in your window? Person decides they want him? Wouldn't put it past some jerk."

That was when I noticed the camera in the ceiling corner facing the entrance. "You have security cameras?" I said.

"Yup," Shawn answered. "That's why you're sitting in a folding chair. You skimp in some areas so you can have the best equipment in others. Listen, you need security, so call up—"

"Tom Stewart?" I said.

Shawn smiled for the first time. "Tom does fine work. We haven't had any trouble since he did his thing here. Ask Snug. He'll tell you. No trouble, huh, Snug?"

The parrot walked back and forth on his dowel, bobbing his head. "No trouble. No trouble, Snug."

I shook my head and smiled. He sounded so human. Then I looked at Allison. "I have my two other cats in the van. I'm not leaving them home alone until I see Mr. Stewart about a plan to protect my house."

Allison said, "Two more? Why didn't you say so? Let's bring them in. Then maybe you'd like to see some of our clan. They need good homes. You could become a part of our very important network and help find them places to live."

I stood. "I'd be happy to do that. All three of my cats were rescues."

Shawn helped me bring in Chablis and Merlot and after a good fifteen minutes of visiting—with Merlot far more interested in Snug than any of the people—the Cuddahees were ready to show me the shelter.

As we started for the door that led to the rest of the building, I said, "If I can't put up flyers, what can I do?"

"You came here. That's what will help the most," Shawn said.

"Come visit our friends. It's good for the spirit," Allison added.

They led me to the lost or abused animals that had found sanctuary with these kind people. I counted ten cats and the four dogs I'd seen earlier. Every cage was clean, every dish full of food and every water bowl brimming. The dogs—two Labs and two mixed breeds—seemed happy. But I did notice that the cats had clean but tattered blankets to curl up on. I needed to fix that. Each cat should have a quilt of its own. I had some in my van and would give them to Allison before I left.

I cuddled with a few kitties, their soft fur soothing beneath my touch. When one after the other closed its eyes and purred, I wanted to take all of them home. But that wouldn't work. I couldn't seem to hang on to the three I had. After I petted the four exuberant dogs, we started back to the office.

I said, "When was your break-in?"

"Last spring," Shawn said.

"Do you think they were stolen because someone thought they could make a buck?" I asked.

"Snug would have been the one to take, then. He's worth a lot of money. I have to say that the missing dog was a handful of trouble. Pretty yellow Lab, but way too full of herself."

As we reentered the office single file, I still had those kittens on my mind. "What's your adoption fee?"

"The cost of altering," Allison said.

"That's all? Then how do you keep this place running?" I asked.

"The kindness of strangers," Allison said. "Plus Shawn makes furniture. We have a Web site business and word of mouth has drawn customers from plenty of places." She smiled at her husband. "He is an extraordinary craftsman."

Shawn's ears reddened and he focused on the floor, obviously embarrassed by her praise.

"But where do you build?" I said. "I don't see—"

"A shop at the house. No room here," Shawn said.

"Duh. I should have figured you had another place," I said. "But back to your break-in. You ever get any clues as to who the culprit was?"

"I had my suspicions, but old Morris didn't much care to follow up. I'm guessing you got the same treatment."

I nodded my agreement.

Allison said, "We think Flake Wilkerson took the cats. See, only the two purebreds were gone. He was always coming around here looking for purebreds. Since the break-in, we don't let him near our place."

"*Flake?* Is he a local?" I asked.

"Local hermit," Shawn said with disgust. "Who knows how many poor cats he's got holed up in that big house of his. You think I could get anyone to check him out? No, ma'am. Know why? He pays a lot more taxes than we do."

"He's wealthy?" I said.

Shawn's jaw tightened. "He—"

Allison rested a hand on her husband's arm. "Calm down, baby. We don't know anything about Mr. Wilkerson except that he eyed the purebreds with . . . well, *lust*. Gave me the creeps. We pay close attention to prospective owners, and no matter how many times he came here, we never let him adopt."

"Pissed him off royal, too," Shawn said with a smile.

"You're saying he could have seen Syrah sitting in my window and broke in?"

"Maybe," Shawn said. "Don't know if he trolls neighborhoods looking for cats, but I wouldn't put it past him. He doesn't have a job in town that I know about. I figured he was living on his pension."

"Where does this man live?" I asked.

Allison's sweet face grew tight with concern. "Wait a minute, Jillian. We shouldn't have said anything. He's a weird guy, and you shouldn't go knocking on his door. Besides, we don't know for sure if he took our cats."

"This is the only lead I have. I want my cat back. I'll go anywhere, do anything—"

"Okay, then, I'll take you there." Shawn picked up my cat carriers. "Come on."

"Baby, do you think that's a good idea?" Allison said.

"Wouldn't be going if I didn't." By the steely look in his

eyes, it seemed as if Shawn was on more of a mission than I was.

I handed Allison the half dozen quilts I had in the van and she fingered them lovingly and thanked me several times. After we hugged good-bye, I followed Shawn's beat-up Ford 150 as we took off toward Wilkerson's house. If not for a traffic delay on the one-lane bridge that ran over a stream feeding into the lake, we would have made the trip in five minutes.

The Wilkerson house was set back in the trees on a lonely dead-end road. Dry leaves flew in the wake of Shawn's truck, and pecans were tossed around by our approach. Bet the squirrels had a field day out here.

The house was very odd-looking—a giant Victorian painted a dull pink. It looked old, with graying gingerbread trim and sagging eaves.

I parked behind Shawn in the driveway and we walked together toward the front door.

"Does Mr. Wilkerson have a big family?" I said.

"Nope. Lives alone. Has a grown daughter who lives somewhere else."

A knot of sadness filled my throat. Being alone in a house meant for more than one person was something I was far too familiar with.

Then I saw a cat in an upstairs window. My heart skipped. But I quickly realized this cat was much smaller and darker than Syrah.

Shawn noticed what I was focusing on and said, "Tortoise exotic shorthair."

"Exotic shorthair?" I said. "They are so cute. My cat breeder friends say they shed as much as a Persian or Himalayan, though."

"That's because they're just Persians with short hair. Sweet cats," he said.

We'd reached the front stoop and Shawn said, "Welcome to the famous Pink House, one of the first houses built in Mercy." Shawn pressed the doorbell.

The dampness and chill of the day seemed to inten-
sify as we waited for Wilkerson to answer, and I pulled
my sweater tighter around me. When we got no response,
Shawn pushed the bell again and didn't take his finger off.
I was a little surprised by his determination, but it matched
my own. Finally we heard footsteps accompanied by mas-
culine curses. The door opened a crack.

"What the hell—oh, it's you, Cuddahee. Shoulda known."
The door opened about six more inches.

Flake Wilkerson's face was lean and roughened by
weather, his gray eyes small and narrow with suspicion. Not
a pleasant face, that was for sure.

"See you got a cat upstairs, Flake. Where'd you get it?"
Shawn said.

"SPCA in Greenville—not that it's any of your business." Wilkerson moved one bony blue-jeaned knee into
the open door space. Maybe he didn't want that little exotic
shorthair to escape.

For some reason I noticed his foot. He wore a leather
slipper and I think he had the smallest man feet I'd ever
seen.

"How many more cats you got in there?" Shawn said.

"You still looking for those fe-lines you lost? Still whining about that break-in months ago? Get over it, man,"
Wilkerson said.

"I know it was you, Flake," Shawn said. "Prove me
wrong."

"I don't have to prove nothing to you." For the first time
his gaze fell on me. "Who's this? The Pet Patrol?"

"You don't need to know," Shawn said. "You need to
deal with me once and for all. Invite us in, Flake. Show us
those cats of yours, the ones you claimed to love so much
when you visited the Sanctuary."

But Wilkerson didn't seem to be paying attention. He
was looking me up and down. "Like those green eyes of
yours, lady. Like a cat's, only softer."

I was creeped out by his comment, but he didn't seem

to notice. He turned his gaze on Shawn. "She's pretty puny muscle if you intend to push your way in here. I say go ahead and try. Then we'll see who'll be accusing who of what. Only this time I'll have you for trespassing. Maybe I already got you—"

But Wilkerson was interrupted by a long, lean tuxedo cat that had slipped around his barrier leg. Before he could bend over to catch the cat, it streaked away from the house and into the trees.

Wilkerson's cheeks infused with color and he got in Shawn's face. "Now look what you done, you ass."

Wilkerson stepped outside, closed the door behind him and shoved Shawn aside. Then he took off after the cat. The man had to be sixty if he was a day, so I was sure his pursuit would be futile. That was one fast cat, one that seemed determined to escape.

"Should we help him?" I asked, even though I was certain I didn't want to return a cat to this man.

"Are you crazy? Let him run himself right into a heart attack." Shawn was as angry as the man he'd just confronted, and I was beginning to regret coming here. Obviously Wilkerson wasn't about to cooperate and let us inside. And he surely wasn't about to admit he'd stolen my cat. Why should he? I had absolutely no proof that he had Syrah. This dispute was between Shawn and a strange man, and it was an old dispute at that. My desperation had put me in the middle.

"I think we should leave," I said. "He *could* charge us with trespassing—especially now that he's pissed off that one of his cats escaped."

"He won't charge us with nothing. Don't you see he's hiding something—like maybe more than the four pets the town allows? I could lie. I could say we saw five cats in the windows. That would get someone's attention."

"Come on. Let's go." I took Shawn's elbow. "You don't want to lie and get yourself in trouble. I am so grateful to you for helping me, but I've learned a thing or two from

Candace in the short time I've known her. We've got nothing but suspicion. We need evidence."

Shawn closed his eyes and took a deep breath. "Guess you're right. It's just that I know there's something wrong with this guy. He's not a cat person. He's too mean-spirited."

"Maybe Candace will help us get evidence. She seems to know a lot about the folks in town. Wilkerson would be hard-pressed to turn the cops away if I could convince her to question him."

I glanced toward the woods to the left of the house and caught glimpses of Wilkerson's red plaid shirt weaving between the trees. At least he wasn't yelling. Nothing like screaming profanities to send a cat in the opposite direction. "He wants that cat back in a bad way. But you're sure right about him. It's not about love."

We started toward the driveway, Shawn's head hanging in defeat. "I'll get that bastard another day."

I thanked Shawn and then we both climbed into our vehicles. But we hadn't gone a hundred yards when Shawn's brake lights came on up ahead of me. I had to stop quickly to keep from slamming into him.

But then I saw why. He was out of his truck in a flash and soon kneeling by the side of the road. The tuxedo cat, its tail in the air, was rubbing against a slim maple. Shawn held his hand out, and soon the cat came to him. Wearing a satisfied expression, he swept up the kitty, turned and smiled at me. He gave me a thumbs-up before he put the cat in his truck and we took off again.

Uh-oh. I believe I'm a witness to a catnapping.

Four

After I'd arrived home and released Merlot and Chablis from their crates, they took off as if their tails were on fire. Seemed they'd had enough of traveling around town. Their absence while I ate made me a little sad. I needed to discuss today's events with them. No, I don't hear their voices while I jabber on, but they can be attentive. And sometimes they've helped me see things I might otherwise have missed. Maybe later on I could advise them to never go near any pink houses.

I'd picked up a bag of boiled peanuts from a roadside vendor, and now I made a lunch of sweet tea and nuts. Only quasi healthy, but great comfort food. I wondered whether what I'd seen Shawn Cuddahee do—grab that tuxedo cat off the side of the road—was exactly what had happened to Syrah. And would I ever get an answer to that question?

The tuxedo would fare well in Shawn's care, and the cat hadn't been on Wilkerson's property when Shawn had found him, so maybe that didn't qualify as catnapping. I still felt guilty about what I'd witnessed, though, and for the next several hours I kept busy picking out quilt patterns and fabrics for recent orders rather than think about it.

Merlot and Chablis finally joined me in the sewing room. Peanuts and tea didn't interest them, but fabric sure did. I engaged them in my one-sided chat about all that had happened and how much I missed Syrah. Every time I said his name, Merlot meowed and Chablis blinked. They knew I was sad, and I was betting they were, too.

Tom Stewart, the security expert, arrived in his van about three p.m. When he got to the house, I saw that he was about my age and had dark hair and pale blue eyes. The combination was strikingly handsome. He was holding a large to-go coffee from Belle's Beans, the Mercy answer to Starbucks—an establishment I'd wanted to visit more than once but never had.

I welcomed him inside with a smile and said, "Boy, do I need your help."

"Had a break-in, I hear," he said. "That's pretty rare around here."

"Rare?" I said, leading the way into the living room.

"I say rare because nothing was taken. I mean, we have the usual amount of vandalism and petty theft in this area. Crying shame kids have nothing better to do than sneak into people's houses when they're not home."

I wasn't sure how to react to his knowledge that nothing of material value was missing. "H-how . . . I mean, where did you—"

"You're fairly new in town," he said. "You'll get used to everyone knowing your business soon enough."

"Something important *was* taken, though," I said.

"Forgive me, Ms. Hart. Didn't mean to imply your cat isn't important. You wouldn't have called me if you didn't think so. Now, if you'll show me around, I can determine what equipment can protect you from this happening again."

"You know about my cat, too?" I said.

"Yes, I know about your cat," he was saying, "and I know about your husband's death—my condolences, by the way. I'm also aware you're making a go of it with a home business. Cat quilts. Luxury items for pets are big business these days. Smart idea, if you ask me—which you haven't."

"Thanks," I said. I realized then just what a recluse I'd been. Clearly everyone in town knew these things about me, but they didn't know if I was smart or crazy or just plain ordinary because I'd met almost no one. It was time for that to change. "Even in a small town, I'm impressed you know all this."

He said, "Well, it's my habit to pay attention to things. I do some private eye work, so I have to keep my ear tuned to the town buzz. Good thing you've decided to protect your investment with what I have to offer. I install alarms, cameras and—"

I held up a hand. "I'm not a fan of sales pitches, especially since you already have my business. But tell me this. Who would need a private detective in Mercy?"

"You'd be surprised how many rich people like you live in this part of South Carolina. The town of Mercy may be small, but the area around the lake is getting more and more populated. They require my services for all sorts of things—most of them involving the tawdry, the nasty and the downright stupid."

"I am *not* rich by any stretch, but I do have a missing cat and a house that needs protecting. Let's get busy." The house was paid for and I had inherited John's retirement account, but it was untouchable if I wanted a secure future. For now, I lived on my savings and what I could make off my quilt business. But if I told him all this, I feared the entire town would know everything by tomorrow. And I didn't really want that to happen.

We started with a tour of the house, and if the two hours that followed didn't confuse the heck out of me, nothing could. "Security speak" is a foreign language, and I understood little of what Tom was telling me aside from the words "wireless cameras" and "motion sensors."

After his careful scrutiny of every room, we went outside into the dreary, cold dusk and he examined the gutters, the roof and all the windows. As we stopped at a corner of the house that faced the lake, I wondered if I could put a wireless camera there or if it would be damaged outdoors. But lots of places had outdoor cameras—like convenience stores and other businesses. Though I had questions, I kept quiet since Tom was consumed by studying angles and possible mounting points. I just shivered alongside him.

Finally he said, "I have what I need." He held up the cardboard coffee cup he'd been sipping from throughout his appraisal of the property. "Except for this. I'm empty. Would you happen to have any coffee?"

"Sure. I could use a cup myself," I said.

While I brewed a pot of Italian roast, Tom scribbled on clipboarded forms. He took his coffee black, and his eyes widened in appreciation after his first taste.

"This is damn fine coffee, Ms. Hart. Not everyone knows how to make a decent cup of java."

"Please call me Jillian." I glanced at his clipboard. "And tell me what you've learned and how we can do this."

Just then Chablis jumped on the table, carefully avoiding our hot drinks. She settled on the clipboard and raised her crystal blue eyes to Tom. He rubbed his knuckles on the top of her head and she began to purr.

I said, "How did you know she loves to have her head rubbed? And don't tell me Mercy is talking about that, too."

He laughed. "I have a cat. Dashiell appreciates exactly the same treatment."

He had a cat? And Chablis had quickly given him her approval? Why did that make me want to smile? I stood and lifted Chablis from her spot, saying, "You'd sleep on the man's paperwork the rest of the day if I let you, sweetie." I held her close and we rubbed noses. Then I sat and offered her a new spot in my lap. Never thwart a cat, though. She ran off to sulk, since she'd had other plans.

"First," Tom said, "I need to know your budget. Cameras are pretty cheap these days, but if you want to be wired to my security service, that will cost more."

"Do I need to be set up with your service?" I asked.

"Not necessarily. I can rig your phone to alert the local police if there's another break-in. And you can check your own wireless cameras for anything suspicious, both inside and outside of your house. I can even set up a feed to your cell phone when you're out. We'll call it your cat-cam."

I smiled. "I like that. Cat-cam."

"Is your computer networked?"

"I have two computers, a desktop in the office and a laptop that I take with me on business. Do I need a network?"

"You do—to monitor your cameras. But that's part of what I do. Set up the computer network for you. I can use your desktop as the hub. And since the town is so small, the police hookup is probably all you need rather than a line directly to my security service."

"You're turning down money?" I said.

He smiled. "It's not that much." He went on to tell me what everything would cost, a figure that was higher than I would have liked. Tom assured me he would mount the cameras to capture everything going on inside, as well as motion detectors with floodlights outdoors that would scare away man and animal alike, and told me that was what I needed. But when he said he'd get started tomorrow, I balked.

"No. Today. You have to do this today." I gave him my best tight-lipped determined expression. I couldn't haul my cats around town all the time, and I had to get busy on the quilt orders I'd taken at the Greenville show—especially since this system would cost more than what I'd made the other day. I would need at least an hour at the Cotton Company tomorrow to purchase fabric, and I didn't want to cart Merlot and Chablis along with me or leave them here without safeguards in place.

Tom and I stared at each other in silence for a few uncomfortable seconds. He finally said, "If not for your amazing coffee I wouldn't agree to a Saturday-night job. Hope you have plenty of java. This could be a long evening."

And it was. Tom didn't complete his work until almost one a.m. He'd finished off two pots of coffee and a delivery pizza while he worked. But I was grateful, and he must have known my thanks were sincere, because he gave me a kind and engaging smile when he finally said good night.

After he was gone, I sat in John's recliner with my laptop. The network was working fine, and I practiced all the skills Tom had taught me—how to do split-screen monitoring, how to check the cat-cam feeds from the half dozen wireless cameras and even get the live picture on my cell phone.

My head was aching from all the new things I'd learned in such a short time. If the house alarm was triggered, it would alert the Mercy police—something Tom would inform them about in the morning. Seemed they needed my information and a code. That worried me a little. I could picture Morris Ebeling rolling his eyes if a call came from my house and then taking his time getting here.

One thing bothered me—the possibility that Syrah might return but be scared away by the motion lights. Cats like their environment to remain unchanged—but things had certainly changed around here in two days. If he came home, maybe it would be in the morning. That would be a dream come true.

After I'd brought up the feeds on the laptop over and over, I still wasn't the least bit tired. Besides the headache that wouldn't go away, I'd had too much coffee coupled with too much stress. I closed my computer and leaned back.

Merlot, who'd been asleep at my feet, raised his head, and his amber eyes seemed to ask, "Can we go to bed now where it's warm?"

Chablis, tucked beside me, didn't move a whisker. She was happy right where she was.

I ran my hands along the leather arms of John's chair, realizing how good it felt to sit in the same spot where he had spent so much time talking to me or reading or listening to Bach on the stereo. I'd be across from him on the sofa, hand-quilting a special gift or reading a mystery. Such a dull and wonderful life we'd had together.

Then I noticed with surprise that my eyes didn't fill with tears as I recalled these simple joys. I felt warm inside. I felt lucky to have known such a special man. I felt wrapped in love in his worn, comfy chair.

It was the best good-night kiss I could have had.

Five

Despite Chablis and Merlot remaining as close to me as possible, I spent another fitful night considering life without Syrah—my playful, agile, brilliant kitty. Even when I went to the kitchen at dawn to feed the other two, I was unable to push away those sad thoughts. As I opened cans of tuna and refilled their food bowl, I hoped I could consider the problem logically rather than with emotion leading the way.

If Syrah had left through the window and had been roaming outside, he would have come home by now. Cats, like birds, have homing devices that use the earth's magnetic field and the angle of the sun, so he could easily have found his way back. Yes, I know way too much about cats—a hobby of mine. Anyway, since he wasn't coming home on his own, that meant someone either took him on purpose or invited him in when he landed on their doorstep. With the kind of weather we'd been having, Syrah would have welcomed such an invite.

While Chablis and Merlot chowed down—and I hoped they wouldn't get used to breakfast at dawn—I took the pitcher of sweet tea from the fridge and poured a glass. I'd had enough coffee last night to wake up all of Mercy. The first cold swig sent a shiver from my gut to the top of my head. Who else but me would drink sweet tea at six in the morning when we were probably having the first freeze of the season?

"You think this will be the day Syrah comes home?" I said.

Merlot stopped eating and looked up at me, offering a sympathetic meow. Chablis left the dish and rubbed my ankles.

They didn't seem as upset as the previous two days, so maybe they knew something I didn't.

With Chablis at my heels, I walked into the living area and grabbed a throw quilt from an antique chest alongside the sofa. After I set my glass on the end table by John's chair, I wrapped myself in the quilt and again sat in his recliner. It felt just as welcoming as it had last night. Chablis was in my lap in an instant, and as I petted her I looked out at the rising sun bleeding scarlet onto the water. What a breathtaking sunrise. Maybe my two remaining friends were right—this would be the day we would find Syrah.

Revisiting what I had done in my search so far, I felt frustrated. It wasn't enough. But what else could I do? Friday I'd placed an ad in the *Mercy Messenger*, the small weekly paper, but that wouldn't even appear until Wednesday, and with the sign ordinance, how could anything— *But wait*. What had I learned about this town in the last two days? That everyone knows everything about everyone. The Mercy grapevine was a dynamic force, and that meant someone might know where Syrah was. The Cuddahees said they'd do what they could, but what if I became an active part of the grapevine? I might get a lead.

I sipped my tea and smiled down at Chablis. "Yes, my friend. I'll stop at Belle's Beans before I visit the Cotton Company for my fabric. I might learn a lot listening to the locals, don't you think?"

But Chablis was fast asleep.

The next four hours seemed endless. After a long shower, a litter box clean-fest, and an hour of machine quilting on outstanding orders, I decided that most of Mercy was up and moving by this time on Sunday morning. I set the security alarm as Tom had taught me to do, petted Chablis and Merlot and told them to be careful, then headed into town.

Once I reached Belle's Beans—an establishment that had the audacity to use the same green color for its awning that Starbucks liked so much—I checked the computer feed on my cell phone and grinned when I saw Merlot sleeping belly up on the window seat and Chablis curled on the sofa. I hadn't anticipated how much I would love being able to watch them from afar.

Thank you, Tom Stewart.

After last night I was sure I'd feel nauseated when I walked into the little café and smelled the coffee, but I was wrong. I closed my eyes and took in the aroma. What is it about the aroma of coffee that is so soothing and wonderful?

The high round tables were all occupied, but that wasn't about to stop me. After Belle—there really was a Belle because she wore a name tag pinned to her green canvas apron—made me a low-fat latte, I sat down with a woman reading the Sunday paper.

"Mind if I join you?" I said.

She smiled and said, "Course I don't mind, honey. What's your name?" I guessed she was in her sixties, with misapplied coral lipstick and too-white hair that she'd probably had colored and permed at the Finest Cut or Betty's Salon, the only two hair places in town.

"I'm Jillian Hart. Kind of new around here," I said.

"Oh, you're that young widow. I am so sincerely sorry for your loss. I've been a widow for five years now." She took my left hand and squeezed. Her fingers may have been cold, but hers was a warm touch in a more important way.

Why hadn't I done this before—put myself out to make new friends? Is that what grief did, froze you up until you were ready to move on? Had Syrah's disappearance released my emergency brake?

The woman said, "I hear you make cat quilts—which

had me thinking you must be an old woman like myself. But here you are, looking like a freckled teenager." She reached up and touched a loose strand of my hair. "Is this your natural color? Such a lovely shade, sort of like mulling spices."

"It needs a little help from a bottle these days," I said with a laugh. "That seems to happen once you pass the big four-oh."

"Oh, don't I know, honey. I must say, I have never seen you in this establishment before. I am so glad to meet you."

"I didn't get your name," I said.

"I'm Belle Lowry, the owner." She smiled widely and I couldn't help but stare at her lips. Guess she didn't use a mirror when she put on that color.

I glanced back at the counter. "But—"

"Oh, they all have the same name tag. Little trick of mine. Didn't you feel pleased as punch when you thought the owner was taking care of your coffee needs?"

I laughed again. "I did."

"Course that only works with the tourists and the new customers like you. Everyone in town knows me and my tricks. I do like a joke. I say if you can't laugh, don't come around here."

"I intend to come around here more often, that's for sure. I'm on my way to the Cotton Company, but they don't open until eleven on Sunday. Do you know Martha, the lady who works there?"

"We play bridge together, as a matter of fact. Are you picking out material for your cat quilts? Good idea, by the way—those quilts for cats."

"I love fabric hunting, and Martha is so helpful." I liked this lady and could only hope she knew something about my situation, but I felt so awkward bringing up my problems. This wasn't as easy as I'd thought it would be.

Belle closed her newspaper. "I have never been inclined to sit in front of a sewing machine. I like to talk too much, and machines simply won't talk back." She laughed and I so wanted to mention the lipstick problem, but she went on, saying, "I must tell you, I was ready to purchase one of your cat quilts when Martha told me about what you do, but then poor Java disappeared. Broke my heart, too. So you see, we have something in common. I understand you've recently lost a cat, too."

So she already knew. "Yes. His name is Syrah. Tell me about Java," I said.

"Cute thing. How I do miss that cat."

"What happened?" I asked.

"Foolish Belle left the back door open. And you know what amazed me? That cat had never in her young life been outdoors before. Guess her feline nature took control. She had to explore. I was sure she'd come back, but she never did."

"When was this?" I said.

"Few months ago. I've been thinking about adopting another kitten from the Sanctuary. Have you been there to see if your cat's been turned in?"

"I was there yesterday."

"Those are some mighty fine people, the Cuddahees. Shawn made me a dining room table and chairs that will last for centuries. Making a perfect piece of furniture or even a perfect cup of coffee is a lost art. You think Starbucks is good? You taste from that cup you've been clinging to for dear life, Miss Jillian. Then tell me what you think."

I sipped and discovered she was right. "This is fabulous. No wonder I see everyone carting your cups around town."

"Thank you, ma'am," she said with a smile.

"I know you didn't get your cat back, but maybe you could give me some hints to help me find mine. Tell me what steps you took."

"First off, I went to that silly town council and asked them to change their ridiculous sign ordinance so I could put up flyers. Got nowhere fast. Those folks are so hard-headed you could turn them upside down and use them all for rock crushers."

I laughed out loud and gosh, did it feel good.

Belle smiled, too, and said, "I'm guessing you haven't let out a belly laugh in a very long time. I am privileged to give you the opportunity. Old Belle is good for something besides coffee."

"Thank you, Belle. I'm so glad I chose this table."

"I am, too," she said.

"What else did you do to find your cat?" I asked.

"Talked a lot—real hard for me, don't ya know? I have the opportunity to see most everyone in town on one day of the week or another," she said. "And no one could keep me from putting up a flyer in my own establishment. I'd be glad to tack up a picture of your cat in here. Just fax it to me. Sandy up at the counter will give you one of my business cards. Maybe you'll get lucky."

A few minutes later I left for the Cotton Company feeling as if I'd perhaps taken an important first step in joining the Mercy community. Time would tell. The fabric store was down the block, and I wrapped my peacoat tighter around me as I walked in that direction. The wind was up today, and the temperature must have been hovering close to forty.

Martha was cutting fabric for a customer when I walked in. Bolts arranged by color filled the store, and bright finished quilts hung on the walls of the high-ceilinged old building. She also sold folk art, candles, pottery and other things that a quilter might enjoy, and this month she was ready for Halloween and Thanksgiving with an orange and brown color scheme. There were also racks of patterns, old-fashioned wooden mailbox cubbyholes filled with folded fabric fat quarters and stands with every color of thread imaginable. Quilt stores and libraries rank as my top two places to spend time, and I could already feel the tension melting away from my neck muscles.

"Hey there, Jillian," Martha said. "You find your cat yet?"

"No, I'm sad to say I haven't," I answered, heading for the prints for children's quilts. I was no longer surprised to find that everyone knew about Syrah. Indeed, now I was counting on it.

"Which one was it?" She was intent on her work, a large rotary cutter slicing through several layers of the fabrics her customer had picked out.

"Syrah." I saw a fabric with bunnies and frogs in pastel colors. The Halloween designs seemed a little intense for sick children, but I did snatch up a Laurel Burch cat print.

"Syrah is the one who only eats salmon," Martha told her customer, an older woman resting heavily on a three-pronged cane.

"I know. David at the Piggly Wiggly told me," the woman said. She didn't even bother to look at me, even though she was talking about my cat. "Poor David. You know his story, don't you?"

Martha started to speak, but the woman went on. "Heard tell his mama dropped him on his head when he was a baby, but neither me nor my friends can confirm or deny. See, every time someone asks her why his head is shaped so funny, she starts up cryin'. And we don't want to be upsettin' her, so we just leave it be."

"Is there anything else I can help you with?" Martha asked.

"No, my dear. One quilt at a time, I always say."

Martha walked with the woman to the register in the middle of the store while I continued to pull bolts for the patterns I had in mind.

Martha helped the lady out of the store after the purchase and then came over to where I was appraising the flannels. "What does Syrah look like again? Because I can describe him to my customers. Who knows? Someone might have found him already."

I reached into my bag for my phone. "I can show you. I took several new pictures of him before . . . before . . . Anyway, I have this fancy new security system so I can even show you the other two."

I'd brought up the live feed and saw neither Chablis nor Merlot. But what I did see was my overturned lamp, its ceramic base shattered on the floor.

I stared, wide-eyed. No way could this be happening again.

Six

Five minutes later, I swerved into my drive, sped up to the garage and slammed on the brakes. Everything seemed so quiet, so normal—*normal* meaning the front door wasn't broken down. Maybe I was overreacting. Maybe Merlot had knocked the lamp over and the noise had sent him and Chablis running for cover. Merlot—who could pass for a jungle animal—had certainly knocked over things before.

Just as I got out of the car, a Mercy patrol car pulled up behind me. Candace and Morris. I'd called Candace's cell on my way home, hoping she was the one who would respond to the alarm. When she'd told me she was on her way, I felt a small bit of relief. Not bothering to close my car door, I started for the house. "There's a lamp knocked over. Something's happened again."

Morris's hoarse whisper stopped me from taking another step. "You stay right here while we investigate."

Why wasn't I hearing the alarm? I couldn't remember if Tom told me the noise cut off on its own after the system called the police station. And how did this new thing send the alert anyway? A phone call? A buzzer? What? Why couldn't I remember?

Candace motioned she wanted to go around to the back of the house, so I walked ahead and pointed out the gate. As she ran by me, I saw no one racing away down the slope toward the lake and heard no sounds coming from the house.

Morris reappeared and whispered, "Your key?"

I gave it to him, thinking that at least that meant the lock wasn't broken.

Then I stood impatiently in the cold, trembling more from fear than from the weather. Were my cats all right?

After what seemed to be hours, Morris and Candace came out the front door, guns holstered, expressions relaxed.

Morris said, "I don't see any problem 'cept for a broken lamp. Bet that big old cat knocked it over."

"You saw my cats?" I said.

"Both of them," Candace said.

"And the alarm went off, right?" I looked at Candace. "That's why you said you were on your way when I called you from the quilt shop?"

"What alarm?" Candace said.

"You didn't get an alert at the station about a break-in at my house?"

"Um, no. I sorta always say we're on our way when upset folks call me." She looked embarrassed. "That's how I calm them down. You said you'd seen evidence on this cell phone doodad that someone was in your house, but you never mentioned an alarm."

"There's an alarm?" Morris said. "We didn't get no notice from Tom that you had a phone hookup to the station," Morris said. "Did he fiddle with your telephone line when he put in the system?"

"I—I don't know." Gosh, did I feel stupid.

"Then you're not hooked up straight to us yet," Morris said. "Sometimes Tom calls us right when he finishes the work, but sometimes it takes a day or two."

"Wish he would have told me that important piece of information, but if my cats are okay, then so am I. Can I go in?"

"Sure. You're spooked after that broken window the other day, is all," Morris said. "Bet everything is fine."

"Um, maybe not," Candace said. "Like I told you, Morris, the back door wasn't locked." She looked at me. "Did you have your new system turned on?"

"Of course. I locked every window and door. If you found the back door open, someone must have broken in after all." Now I wanted to see my cats more than ever. I retrieved my keys from Morris on the way to my front door.

Then I heard Candace's footsteps behind me. "Where's the control box for your alarm?" she asked.

I opened the door and stepped inside, calling for Merlot and Chablis before I answered her. "Inside the pantry by the back door."

"I only checked to make sure no one was hiding in here. But if you locked your door, something's not right." She took off in the direction of the kitchen while I crouched to greet Chablis and Merlot as they came into the foyer. Both of them were wide-eyed, their coats puffed out in fear again. Was that because there'd been another break-in? Or just because Morris and Candace had been inside looking around?

I took Chablis in one arm and drew Merlot close with the other. "What has been going on here, you two?"

Merlot was quickly done with cuddling and went off in the direction Candace had gone, watch-cat that he is. I soothed Chablis for a few more seconds, then picked her up and closed the front door with my foot. I wasn't surprised that Morris had gone back to his squad car.

I found Candace staring at the new control box. Or what used to be a control box—and now was a mangled mess.

Candace looked pretty disgusted.

As for me, I was stunned. The alarm must have gone off and made someone very angry to do this much damage.

"I'll need my fingerprint kit," Candace said. "I'm guessing someone took a hammer to this after they picked your back door lock."

"How can you pick a lock that has a dead bolt?" I said.

"All you need is a thin, strong piece of metal and a pin tool for a basic dead bolt like yours. Happens all the time."

"I need to start researching criminal behavior rather than cat trivia," I said. And make sure I was hooked up to both the police and Tom Stewart's security service. Doubly safe was obviously the way to go.

Chablis jumped out of my arms, but didn't run off. She leaped onto the kitchen counter, her blue-eyed gaze switching from me to Candace and back to me as if to say, "What are you two planning to do about this situation?"

But I had no answer. I was bewildered. "Why would this person break a window one time and then enter through the back door the next?"

"You're assuming the same person did this. Never assume." She might as well have added, "Haven't I taught you anything?"

"Oh," was all I could manage.

"Course the perp could have seen all your brand-spanking-new cameras and thought they could hide their identity better coming through the back door. Breaking a window is a whole lot quicker than picking a dead bolt, but bad guys adjust to the circumstances."

The microphone attached to Candace's uniformed shoulder spewed static, and then I heard a female voice say, "We got a house fire at 808 Westwood Drive. Children in the home. All units respond. All units respond."

"Sorry." Candace whirled and sped out the back door, yelling, "I checked and there's no intruder here now, so you're fine. Just try not to touch anything that might be evidence. I'll call you." She disappeared.

I was alone with my cats again. Alone and worried about human children who needed help in a burning house. Plus I was a little frustrated. I understood why Tom couldn't get me hooked up to the police station when he finished the job at one a.m., but I sure wished he'd been able to do so this morning. He probably felt entitled to sleep late after working into the wee hours. Just my luck.

I took a calming breath and then remembered the cameras. They weren't connected to the alarm box. And unless this malicious person had smashed all my cameras, too, I might find something important on my computer. Yup. My cell phone feed was limited, but the computer kept the recordings of everything.

I hurried to my office. Merlot loped ahead and beat me there, with Chablis not far behind. Whatever had gone on apparently hadn't upset them as much as last time, and I was thankful for that.

Both cats jumped on the double-stacked barrister-style bookcases to get a good view as I sat at my desk. It was set catty-corner to the case—and it needed to be catty-corner so the kitties would have a place to watch me. Otherwise they'd plant themselves on top of the hard-drive tower or the other tall bookshelf. But Merlot wasn't happy sharing space and swatted poor Chablis on the nose. She jumped from the table onto the keyboard. I'd just started booting up, and her landing did strange things to the start-up screen.

I was forced to turn off the computer, put Chablis in my lap, start the whole procedure over and still try to stay composed enough to remember all the steps to bring up the camera feeds.

At first I couldn't figure out how to get to the stored video rather than the live feed currently recording my empty living room. Chablis was ready to help, and I had to grab her playful paw right before she shut me down again. Then I remembered the file Tom had set up on my computer desktop. I clicked on the icon and chose the last hour's worth of video, hoping I could discover exactly what went on when my poor control panel met the business side of a hammer.

And there it was. On feed number two. First the alarm shrieking, then the back door opening. But the stupid camera was positioned too low and too far to the left. I must have moved it inadvertently when I made coffee this morning—it was in a potted plant right by the coffee canister. Then I saw a dark-clad figure taking a mallet to the control panel. The time stamp read 10:37 a.m.

I'd been chatting with Belle while this—this miserable excuse for a person broke into my kitchen. Trouble was, all

I could see was an arm and a gloved hand. Small hand. A woman? Why had I been thinking all along that the perp was a man? *Perp?* Candace's influence was creeping into my vocabulary again.

But I was getting excited. Surely I hadn't missed every shot of this person—not with all the cameras Tom had installed. I switched to the living room—feed number four. Merlot came into the small video square at full speed, and behind him raced the intruder complete with ski mask.

What? This is crazy.

I watched the lamp crash to the floor when the person knocked it over with an elbow as he or she chased my cat. Then they came back into view running from the other direction, Merlot not even at full speed.

The scene reminded me of something Charlie Chaplin or Jackie Chan might have choreographed. I glanced over at my hero Merlot and gave him a thumbs-up.

He closed his eyes, his expression saying, "I am a ninja warrior. My evasive actions are quite effective."

Seeing the stranger in relation to Merlot, I decided the height as well as the stride was definitely male. But those small hands . . .

Wait a minute.

I rewound and looked at the intruder's feet. Small feet, too. Feet very much like I'd seen yesterday.

I stood so abruptly that poor Chablis ended up hanging on to my thighs for dear life. I hardly felt the pain of her claws digging into my flesh.

I pried her loose, held her to my face and kissed her nose. "I have to see a man about a cat. Right now. A man who must have gotten greedy after he'd had time to think about two more beautiful cats living here."

Minutes later, I was in the minivan on my way to Flake Wilkerson's house. But after only a few seconds on the road, I thought twice about confronting him alone. He'd had the audacity to break into my house not once, but probably twice, and as was evidenced yesterday, he was a hateful man. Plus the police were definitely tied up and might be for a while.

But I wanted my cat back in the worst way, and I was sure I knew where to find Syrah.

I reached over and grabbed my phone. Tom Stewart answered on the second ring.

"Guess what," I said.

"I know," he answered. "You called the police and figured out you're not connected yet. I'm sorry I didn't get the hookup done. I planned to call you as soon as—"

"We can sort through that later. Meet me at Flake Wilkerson's house right now. I'm certain he has my cat, and I need you to help me deal with this situation. I'd already thought about hiring you to find Syrah anyway and now it's settled. We can talk about money later. Do you need directions to the Pink House?"

"I don't, but—"

"This is important. Five minutes."

"Can you give me a little more time than—"

"Five minutes." I snapped the phone closed.

I took a deep breath and smiled, certain I was about to be reunited with Syrah. But the time it took to get to Wilkerson's house seemed like forever. I was hoping Tom would beat me there, but his van wasn't in the driveway when I arrived. I parked on the street close to the ditch, not willing to walk up to that front door alone.

Be smart, Jillian. You can wait.

But something changed my mind.

Syrah.

My gorgeous Syrah came walking down the driveway away from the house, his distinctive meow—the one I hear when he gets himself stuck behind something or locked in a closet—loud and clear. He was calling for me.

Worried that I might spook him, I left my van as quietly and carefully as possible, crouched at the end of the driveway and whispered his name. He stopped and looked at me, all thirty-two muscles in his ears working. He cocked his head, meowed again. I know every single one of his special sounds, but I didn't recognize this one. He sounded . . . well, demanding.

Then he turned and scurried back toward the house.

What? No!

"Syrah. Come here, baby," I called, running after him.

At the open back door, Syrah had stopped, back arched, his body pressed against the doorframe and his wonderful big ears twitching. I reached out with both arms, thinking he would jump into them like he always does, but instead he slipped inside the house.

I stood there, surprised. What the heck was going on?

Better question, Jillian: Why is the door open?

The shiver of fear that ran up both arms almost stopped me, but rescuing my cat overrode common sense. I went up two concrete steps leading to the door, halted on the stoop and used one finger to open it wider.

"Mr. Wilkerson, your door is open," I called.

Always the well-mannered Texas girl. Even though this man stole your cat.

I knelt and called Syrah's name, hoping he'd come back. Then I could grab him and race to my van. But instead of seeing Syrah coming back to me, I saw a few tiny, rusty-colored pawprints on the kitchen tile in front of me.

Blood? Oh my God. Was Syrah injured?

Those sticky-looking pawprints drew me into the kitchen when Syrah did not come bounding back. Where the heck had he gone? He knew I'd help him if he was hurt.

The kitchen was gloomy gray, and the fear that had taken hold in my gut felt like a hand twisting my insides. Announcing my presence wasn't exactly the most brilliant thing I'd done today. I looked back at the open back door. Where the heck was Tom? I needed him this instant.

Leaving might have been a wise choice, but I couldn't. Not before I found Syrah. I wished I could call Candace,

but she was definitely tied up. Besides, why would the police be interested in an injured cat whose feet bled a little
on an eccentric old man's kitchen floor?

I kept whispering Syrah's name as I scanned the
room. The kitchen, though tidy, smelled sour—like an old
sponge—and then I heard the plaintive call of what was
surely a trapped or injured cat. Not Syrah's voice, but some
other cat in trouble.

How serious was this problem I'd stumbled upon? An
animal was bleeding, and I was certain that through either
neglect or intention Flake Wilkerson had something to do
with it. I listened hard and decided that the cat noises were
coming from the second floor.

Find Syrah first and then worry about the other cat.

Sidestepping the pawprints, I made my way around a
rolling butcher block island with a cracked top covered
with knife marks. Slices of apple just turning brown and
half a glass of fizzing Coke sat abandoned on its surface.

I kept my eyes on the floor, still whispering for Syrah,
and reached an arched entry. I heard a clock somewhere
farther inside the house chiming the half hour. I stopped,
hoping I would come upon my cat so I could grab him and
run. Then I'd call animal control. Yes. That was what I'd do.
They would want to know if cats were being abused here.

Wishful thinking.

My jaw dropped and my stomach roiled simultaneously
at what I saw in the dining room beyond.

It wasn't an injured cat.

Flake Wilkerson lay sprawled on the floor, a butcher
knife sticking out of his flat belly like a gruesome flag.

Seven

Though I didn't take my eyes off Wilkerson's still body, I detected movement to my right. My heart skipped a beat before I realized it wasn't a killer but rather a small dark cat running across the front hallway. Not Syrah. Maybe the one I'd seen in the window yesterday?

I closed my eyes, trying to gather myself. Then I stared at the man lying on the floor. So much blood had been spilled that it drenched his shirt and pooled around his center. His cloudy, fixed eyes told me he was most certainly dead.

And whoever had done this could still be in the house and come after me next. I should run. Get out. But I couldn't seem to move. Aside from the sounds of wailing cats—yes, more than one now—coming from upstairs and my own heart beating wildly in my ears, I heard nothing.

I was afraid, yes, but running didn't seem like the right thing to do, perhaps because John's death was so fresh in my mind. I had tasted my husband's still warm, lifeless lips not so long ago. I understood that being in the presence of the dead could make you scared and brave all at once.

That brave part pushed me forward toward this strange old man's body, propelled by the thought that no matter how he had lived his life, he needed someone to care for him now, someone to do right by him.

The blood was a problem. I circled his body to avoid stepping in the glistening puddle near his left side, its symmetry marred by little cat feet. Probably Syrah's. That was why there'd been pawprints in the kitchen.

I ended up at Wilkerson's head, knelt and searched for his carotid artery. He skin was still warm. I bent my head to feel for any hint of breath against my cheek. No pulse. No breath. No life. He wasn't cold yet, but he was very dead.

Sadness filled me then. A life cut short, this one by manmade violence. Why did I feel so sorry for him? Especially after our encounter yesterday? Didn't matter now.

I sat back on my heels and reached into my pocket with a shaky hand for my cell phone, surprised that a sheen of tears blurred my vision. I couldn't even seem to find the number nine, but finally I managed to make the call. I blinked hard, fighting back tears. But the dispatcher wasn't answering, and while I was waiting I heard a tiny meow. A softness brushed my wrist; a whiskered face nuzzled my hand.

I looked down and saw Syrah.

When I touched him, he raised his head to meet my fingers. Seemed both of us were looking for comfort.

That tender moment was cut short when I heard, "What the hell happened?" in a deep baritone—a sound that made my stomach jump because it wasn't coming from the phone.

I started and dropped my cell phone. It closed and disconnected. Tom Stewart stood in the arched entry.

"He—he's dead," I managed, picking up my phone and gathering Syrah into my arms. I stood, clutching my cat close.

"No kidding."

I held out my phone. "I—I was trying to call 911, but—"

"I'll do that. You take a seat." He nodded at the furniture in an adjoining parlor that seemed about a mile away. "And stay where I can keep an eye on you."

I had trouble processing what he'd said, but then made my way to a settee in the parlor. Once I sat down, it dawned on me that he'd told me to stay put. Why? My God, did he think I'd had something to do with Mr. Wilkerson's death?

"Don't worry. I'm not going anywhere. This man is dead and his house is full of cats that need help."

"Good, because you'll have plenty of questions to answer once the police arrive." He jabbed at his keypad, then started tapping his foot and muttering, "Come on, come on."

"There's a house fire. The entire town probably went to help. See, that's why I was depending on *you* to arrive—in *five minutes*."

"I tried," he said. But then the dispatcher apparently answered, and he gave her the unfortunate news about Flake Wilkerson.

While he talked, I decided I couldn't wait around with those cats calling for help. With Syrah still in my arms, I started for the hallway where I'd seen the streaker a few minutes ago.

Tom barked at me to stop.

But I couldn't. Once the police arrived, they would clear the house. I might be the only one who cared about those cats, and right now I had a window of opportunity to help them.

I reached a large foyer and saw a fluffy tail disappear into the hall closet. I calmly called, "Here, kitty. Come on, baby."

Syrah wiggled, probably anxious to help out. But I held on and he didn't resist much, no doubt appreciating the safety of my embrace. I didn't have to wait more than two seconds before a small Persian peeked out from behind the cracked door beneath the stairs. Not the cat we'd seen yesterday in the window. Then Tom's "What do you think you're doing?" sent the poor scared thing retreating into the safety of the closet.

He entered the foyer, his cell pressed to his ear. "No, not you," he said into the phone. "It's the person I told you about, the one I discovered by Wilkerson's body."

The person? Discovered? Like he didn't know I'd be here? "I have a name, you know," I said, heading for the closet.

"Quit moving around, Jillian." This time he held the phone pressed against his thigh.

"I saw a cat. And there's more of them. Can't you hear?"

Tom cocked his head and finally tuned in to the sounds coming from upstairs.

"Wilkerson had a bunch of cats," he said. "Everyone knows that."

I crouched in front of the closet and whispered, "Here, baby. It's okay."

Persians are friendly and affectionate, and I figured this one would come out again with a little coaxing. But Syrah might not like sharing me during this stressful time, so before I rescued the little one, I put Syrah in Tom's free arm. He sputtered, but I gave him no chance to refuse.

I went back to the closet, knelt and soon gathered up the scared cat. I sat on the floor to better examine the animal's paws with their long, matted fur. The blood on the floor was probably from Syrah walking around the dead man, but I had to make sure this one wasn't hurt. Didn't seem to be. And I couldn't tell if this was a boy or girl—too much hair. The cat purred through my examination, probably more out of stress than from feeling affectionate.

Then I rose and went toward the stairs, Persian in arms.

"Come on, Jillian," Tom said. "Stop walking around. We're in the middle of a damn crime scene."

I halted on the bottom stair. "But the man is dead and obviously the cats upstairs are not." I felt much calmer now that he was here. "Someone else might be hurt. And I'm not talking only about animals. What if another person has been stabbed or injured?"

"Please wait," he said, sounding more like himself rather than the control freak he'd been acting like since he got here. "The police will arrive any minute. You're a smart woman, so be smart about this," he said.

"The police are busy dealing with an emergency. You

have no idea how long it will take for them to get here. Ask Billy Sue or whatever that dispatcher's name is." I nodded at the phone still pressed against his leg.

He brought it to his ear, and it immediately started blaring a country song I did not recognize. Must be his ringtone.

"Damn," he muttered before answering the phone. "Guess I lost you, Barbara. What's our status?" He listened for a second before saying, "Yeah, I promise to stay on the line."

"How long before they get here?" I cast an anxious glance toward the landing, where I could still hear mournful cat music.

Tom said, "Don't know. The chief is on his way since everyone else is at the fire. And a county sheriff deputy's been called, too."

Yup, just as I thought. Chaos would soon reign. I was certain no one would let me upstairs then. Nor would anyone care about the cats. So I bolted before Tom could even blink.

The Persian did not appreciate being held by a running woman and told me so by digging its claws into my shoulder and leaping from my arms. It took off back down the stairs. Since I would probably find it in that closet in a few minutes, I wasn't too worried.

I made my way toward the cat meows coming from a room at the end of a long, dark hallway. One cat was surely a Siamese; one of their sounds mimics the cry of a human infant, and that was what I was hearing.

The door was ajar, and inside what was once a bedroom I found three anxious cats in individual cages on a large table. There seemed to be more cages disassembled and propped against a wall papered with what looked like a 1930s design.

Each of the cats offered its own distinct and loud voice when I walked in. I murmured, "It's gonna be okay" over and over, and they seemed to calm a little. As I approached,

I noticed two black canvas carriers—the kind that zip at the top. They were both partially open. Could have been how Syrah and the Persian escaped.

At that point I noticed something that had somehow escaped my first glance into the room. I stared in disbelief, not at the cats but at what was with them. Each had a quilt to lie on—one of *my* quilts.

Where had Wilkerson gotten them? Had he stolen them from my sewing room when he snatched Syrah?

But when I took a closer look I saw that the quilts were made from fabrics I'd purchased months ago. I fingered one quilt corner through the wire cage—a log cabin design. I hadn't made that pattern since right after John's death. I'd been doing nine patch and crow's nest designs lately.

The exotic shorthair in that cage rubbed against my fingers, and I scratched its small head. "You'll be okay, smoosh-face," I whispered. "I'm here to help you."

I bent and peered into one canvas carrier. I could see a quilt in there, too, one that appeared to be covered with Syrah's amber fur. The other carrier was coated with long dark hairs. Syrah must have figured out the zipper and helped the Persian escape. Persians are one of the sweetest breeds, but some of them aren't exactly the brightest matches in the box.

"Jillian, get back down here," shouted Tom.

"You come up," I called back. "I need to check the other rooms."

"Please don't do that," he answered. "Every step you take up there might compromise evidence."

I've already compromised plenty, then, I thought. *Might as well make sure no other person or animal was hurt, or worse, dead.* I ran from one room to another—big house, lots of musty bedrooms—all of them filled with ancient furniture. I found no people and no more cats—unless they'd found excellent hiding places.

I returned to the caged kitties. Besides the exotic there was a Tonkinese—could have been a show cat with its platinum mink points—and of course the louder-than-loud lilac-point Siamese. I was about to reach my fingers inside the Tonkinese's cage and offer some much-needed reassurance, but a man's voice stopped me.

"Mercy Police. Don't touch anything, ma'am."

I turned and briefly took in the dark green uniform before the gun he held in his right hand grabbed the better part of my attention. I pressed my back against the cages and gripped the scarred table the cat prisons sat on.

"I *told* you not to touch anything." He sounded calm despite my mistake, and I looked up into a face that seemed far kinder than that huge gun. He was about Tom's age, with sandy hair and warm brown eyes.

"Then put the AK-47 away," I said. "You might accidentally shoot a cat." Though I sounded flip, I was scared out of my gourd. I mean, I'd never had a gun pointed at me in my life.

"This is no AK-47, and if I were to shoot anything, it wouldn't be an accident. Put your hands where I can see them," he said. "It's Jillian Hart, right?"

I intertwined my fingers in front of me. "It is. But do you honestly believe you have to defend yourself against me?"

"Let's go downstairs, Ms. Hart," he said evenly.

I heard several voices in the other rooms shouting "clear" over and over. Meanwhile, I seemed stuck to the spot like someone had superglued the soles of my shoes.

"I'm Chief Baca of the Mercy Police. You're looking chalky, Ms. Hart. We need to go downstairs, okay? Then you can sit down and tell me exactly what went on here."

Now that I was sure the cats were all right, I decided this was a reasonable request—and his delivery was a lot gentler than Tom Stewart's had been initially. But I hated leaving these terrified cats.

"What about the animals?" I said.

"They'll be taken care of," he said.

"By whom?"

"SPCA or—"

I shook my head vehemently. "No. The SPCA is too far away. Call Shawn or Allison at the Mercy Animal Sanctuary. Please?"

Through the open bedroom door I saw several more green-uniformed people disappearing down the stairs.

"Come with me and then we'll make arrangements for the cats," he said.

"C-could you put the gun away?" I had begun to tremble, the pick-me-up power of adrenaline suddenly abandoning me.

He holstered the weapon. "There. Now come on."

I put one hesitant foot in front of the other and made it across the room. Good thing, too, because then my knees buckled.

Chief Baca caught me before I hit the floor.

Eight

The house fire in town must have finally been contained because the Wilkerson property now became the hub of Mercy's police and paramedic activity. From my vantage point in the parlor that adjoined the dining room, I even caught a glimpse of Billy Cranor, the handyman and volunteer fireman. Apparently the fire department needed a presence here as well—why, I had no idea.

When Candace arrived she didn't seem to notice me. She began firing away with her camera before saying a word to anyone, moving around the crime scene with a constant whir of *click, click, click*. Next she knelt by the body, and I saw her tweeze something off Flake Wilkerson's pants.

Then Chief Baca spotted her and ordered her to "watch Ms. Hart."

I needed watching? Did he think I would head upstairs again after he'd practically had to carry me down? I still felt too stunned and sick to my stomach to do much more than sit here.

When Candace turned and saw me in the parlor, her blue eyes widened in disbelief. "What are you doing here?" she said as she took a spot beside me on the very uncomfortable gold satin settee.

The chief had put me here, and I suddenly wondered if maybe he thought I wouldn't faint again if I sat in the most uncomfortable spot possible. "I already told your boss, but you need to know, too. First, though, I understand I never should have come inside this house. But Syrah was here. I found him outside in the driveway and then he ran back inside. I couldn't help myself. I had to follow him." As I spoke, I was again consumed by worry. Tom had let Syrah go, and I could only hope my boy hadn't slipped out an open door. He surely would have had the opportunity, since this place was crowded enough to remind me of a departure gate at Houston Intercontinental Airport.

Syrah's disappearance wasn't a priority to anyone except me, and my emotions had been running wild—I was glad I'd found him, but now I was desperate to find him again. Plus I'd gotten the distinct feeling as I'd related what had happened to the soft-spoken Baca that he actually suspected I might have had something to do with the murder.

I was more at ease explaining the situation to Candace. She seemed receptive and kind as I summarized the morning's events.

"You're trembling," she said when I'd finished. She placed a hand on my forearm and said, "You gotta calm yourself."

"If I promise on Syrah's life not to leave this poor, unfortunate seat, will you look for him? I'm going crazy wondering where he's got to now. He might be in the closet with the Persian. I could show you—"

"No way," she said. "We're waitin' on the coroner's deputy and her investigator before any of us disturb the crime scene any further. That means we're stuck here."

"But I didn't kill that man," I said. "So why do you need to practically sit on me?"

"Because I have to follow orders. Besides, you can't be wandering around this house like you did earlier," she answered.

"Look at me, Candace." I twisted in my chair so I could see her face. "I didn't mean any harm going upstairs."

She said, "Don't you see how this looks? Flake Wilkerson had your cat, and I know how much you love that little guy. By the way, how did you recognize Flake Wilkerson on that video? That's why you came here, right?"

Uh-oh. That visit here yesterday was about to come back and bite me. "I've been talking to people, trying to figure out who would want to steal my Syrah. Mr. Wilkerson was known to have an interest in cats—especially purebreds. But you don't suspect me of anything more than coming into a house uninvited, do you?"

"No, but exactly who have you been talking to? Shawn?"

"Yes. Is that a problem?" I said.

"You're dodging the question. How did you recognize Wilkerson? No one sees him much, except at Belle's Beans. Is that where you met him?" she said.

"No. Shawn told me about Wilkerson, and I came here yesterday. Needless to say, the man didn't admit to stealing my cat." I wasn't about to mention that Shawn had come here, too, not before I knew if they'd enlisted Shawn to take care of the imprisoned cats. But I had a renewed uneasy feeling in my stomach. Shawn hated Wilkerson, and I was guessing Candace knew as much.

"You came here *yesterday*? That's not good, Jillian." She was shaking her head. "What happened?"

"Nothing. You have to know I would never kill another human being in a million years," I said.

She sighed. "I do, but these other folks don't. Our training as officers of the law makes us think the worst of people."

"So you don't believe I killed him?"

"Of course not. But you say anything to Morris about that and my cred is gone. I'm the evidence queen, remember?"

For the first time in the last hour, the knot in my gut loosened. Seemed I had one human friend after all. "That means a lot. Thanks."

This tender bonding was interrupted by the arrival of a woman who hollered, "What we got here?" so robustly that her words lifted me an inch off my seat. I resisted the urge to cover my ears. She gave *shrill* a whole new meaning. Southern shrill at that.

"That's Lydia Monk," Candace whispered from the side of her mouth. "Deputy coroner."

"Why are you whispering?" But I'd toned it down, too. Maybe we were both compensating for her.

"'Cause she's in charge and I don't want her hearing me talk to you. That might not look good for either of us."

"A deputy coroner's in charge? Where's the coroner?" I asked.

Candace quickly explained that the county had an elected coroner. He was an administrator and pretty much stayed in his office. This woman was the county's investigating officer when there was a suspicious death.

"But she's a doctor, right?"

"No way. She went to the community college, I think. Now hush, okay?" Candace squared her shoulders and looked straight ahead.

This was so different from big-city life. Houston had a pathologist as a medical examiner and a highly trained forensic unit.

Unlike Candace, who was intent on looking like my official watchdog, I had no problem checking out this flashy woman now in charge. If I thought the low-cut shirts women wore on shows like *CSI* were Hollywood tweaking reality, Lydia proved me wrong. She had quite the twin girls and wanted everyone to have a good look. But even on *CSI* they never went to crime scenes wearing sequins on their scoop-neck turquoise T-shirts.

Candace glanced at me and whispered, "In case you're wondering, she's the product of one too many pageants."

"Beauty pageants?"

"Yup. You are lookin' at Miss Upstate Winnebago 1999," Candace said.

"You're kidding, right?" Lydia Monk may have had the fading glory of a beauty queen—a tall, bleached blonde with chin-up posture—but that voice? My cousin was a pageant junkie, and she practiced not only her walk but a sweet voice, too.

"Nope, I am not kidding. Word around town is that the judges might have been drunk when they crowned her."

Lydia had been conferring with Baca but now started talking to the crowd again, and it was impossible to ignore her.

She said, "Now that I have been briefed, ladies and gentlemen, we can officially classify this as a homicidal death. Any suspects?"

"We're still investigating." Baca glanced my way.

I stared right back, feeling defensive. But I *did* have a connection to the victim. I'd shown up here yesterday and again today. And I'd walked into the house on my own when I should have known better. Oh, I'd invited this trouble. That was for sure.

Lydia's hands were on her hips, one bright blue spike-heel tapping the oak floor. "Glad you left me the body, seeing as how it's my job to coordinate this investigation and purserve the evidence."

"Huh? Why wouldn't they leave the body?" I whispered to Candace.

"Quiet," Candace answered from the side of her mouth.

I caught Baca rolling his eyes. "We know what your job is, Lydia. Where's Bob?"

"He went over to that house fire. You folks got more stuff happening here in Mercy than we've had in the entire county all year," she said.

"No one died in that fire, so what is your assistant doing over there?" Baca wasn't bothering to mask his irritation anymore.

"Are you telling me how to allocate my resources?" She'd moved close enough to him that her breasts were an inch from his chest.

"Your *resources* happen to be one assistant—that is, unless the county's added staff that I don't know about. We need him here." He made a sweeping gesture. "Look at all this blood. You've got to collect specimens, cart stuff to the forensics unit and get this body out of here for autopsy so we can get going on this investigation."

"I see you are intent on telling me how to do my job, Mike Baca. Guess that means you've been to coroner school since we last crossed paths." She smirked at him and in her heels was tall enough not to have to look up. "Course we all know that isn't true, is it, Mike?"

Baca handed Lydia a pair of shoe protectors. "I believe you'll be more comfortable in these."

Indeed, those heels aren't exactly crime-scene-friendly, I thought.

She snatched the protectors. "I got my tennies in the truck. Now be a good boy and fetch them. And while you're at it, can you get me the crime scene kit, too?"

Billy Cranor piped up. "I'll go, Mike."

Lydia removed her shoes and handed them to Billy before he eagerly took off through the entry to the kitchen. A minute later she was wearing the tennis shoes, the protectors and latex gloves. She stepped toward the body, but then spotted me. "Who is she?"

"The woman I told you about. She found the body," Baca said.

Lydia's red lips spread in a smile. "Is that so?"

She slowly walked into the parlor, her eyes intent on me. "I'm Lydia Monk and you're . . ."

"Jillian Hart," I said.

"And you found this man dead? Must have been very traumatic for you, Ms. Hart." Her tone dripped with concern that I found bewildering.

Why is she being so nice? Is this some kind of trick?

"Yes . . . my cat . . . Well . . . it's kind of a long story and—"

"I'm sure it is. Did you know this man?"

"Not really. I came by because I believe he stole my Abyssinian and I—"

"That some kind of Egyptian artifact?" she said.

"Um, no. It's a cat and he's—"

"Whatever. You don't need to be staying here, Ms. Hart. You need to get away from this awful place. Candy will take you on home and get your statement there." She beamed at Candace, pageant style. "I'm sure she's spoken with you or the chief, but we need her statement in writing. You can do that, can't you?"

Baca walked over to join us. "But Ms. Hart is—"

Lydia jerked her head in Baca's direction. "I can read your mind, Mike Baca. You think this poor woman had something to do with that man's death. But unless she went home and changed her clothes, that's not what happened."

Mike tried again. "But—"

"Did you notice the interrupted arterial spray on that dining room wall?" she said.

"Yes, I did. But we were waiting on you to—"

"And I'm here now. You let me do my job or I might have to discuss this with my boss. See, I am a trained investigator—but then, you already know that. You know everything."

Oh, I was beginning to get it. She must have a history with Mike Baca. A history that probably had ended unpleasantly.

She went on. "Look at this woman. You see any blood all over her? No, you don't. You gotta find a messy suspect somewhere or discarded bloody clothes. See, that dead man took it in the abdominal aorta. And my, my, my, aortas do like to spread their wealth when you poke 'em with a knife."

Baca said, "I planned on taking Ms. Hart's formal statement myself after you arrived and—"

"Nope. You need to let her go home so she can gather herself. She's probably not your murderer, but she's your best witness. Candy can take the statement, and if you insist, she can look for any bloody clothes at Ms. Hart's home once we get a warrant." She smiled at me again. "And I apologize, but that's what we gotta do. Check your house for any bloody clothes or other evidence. Doesn't mean

I believe you did anything wrong. I can tell by those sad green eyes that this is just your worst nightmare."

Maybe it was, but I wasn't leaving without Syrah. "My cat might be in this house somewhere. Is there any way—"

Tom Stewart appeared as if on cue. "I got your cat. He was hiding in the closet with that other little ball of fur."

He'd just made up for his three crimes of not hooking my alarm up to the police, not getting here quickly enough and acting like he suspected me. I stood and took Syrah in my arms, nestled my face in his neck. "Thank you, Tom."

He'd smiled as he handed him to me, so I guessed he was glad to have made up for something. But before he could speak, Lydia was between us.

"And what are *you* doing here?" she asked Tom. Then she held up her hand. "Never mind. Mike can tell me after you leave. Now, Candy, please take Ms. Hart and her cat home immediately."

I snuggled Syrah close and he began to purr. It felt wonderful to have him in my arms.

Baca spoke again, addressing Candace and me rather than trying to get in an entire sentence with Lydia. "A warrant won't be required if you give permission for Candace to search your house, Ms. Hart."

"She can search all she wants. I do have video of—of—" I glanced toward the body. "Of Mr. Wilkerson chasing my other two cats all over my house this morning."

This news elicited a radiant smile from Lydia. "The chief mentioned that you came here about cats or something. I am sure delighted to hear about that bit of video. That could help me narrow the time of death. Now go on, you two."

But Baca wasn't done. "And your car? Can we search that, too?"

Lydia looked at him like he'd grown another set of ears. "You think she stashed bloody clothes in her car? Doesn't make sense. You said you found her upstairs with the cats. Everything you've told me about the timing—when Candace and Morris left her house and her arrival here—makes it pretty clear she didn't have time to kill a man, change her clothes and then take herself to a bedroom to visit with the animals."

Baca said, "Maybe you're right. But I'm sure you'll agree Mr. Wilkerson's orphaned computer monitor needs to be investigated. If it's in Ms. Hart's van, then—"

"What do you mean—*orphaned*?" Lydia seemed flustered now.

He said, "What's a monitor for without the rest of the computer? I don't think the missing parts and pieces walked off on little cat feet."

Nine

If I'd thought I would be home in five minutes, I was way off in my timing. Candace took a battery-powered hand-held vacuum from her squad car, put in a new filter, then took my van apart so she could suck up every lost M&M, toothpick and cat hair. She emptied this collection of junk into what I assumed was an evidence bag.

I stood beside Tom on the road, holding fast to Syrah and watching this meticulous deconstruction of what I'd thought was a fairly clean vehicle. Menacing clouds had assembled to the west, and I sure hoped we wouldn't get wet while we waited.

Tom had come outside with us and had been silently watching Candace work beside me. Finally he said, "I wouldn't blame you if you're angry at me for yelling at you in there. I'm sorry, but that was not a good situation."

I glanced over at him, touched that he wanted to apologize. "We were both stressed, and all I could think about was the cats. Easier to focus on the living rather than the dead, I guess."

"I never thought about that, but it does help me understand you better. You love cats. I'm saying you *really* love cats. I get that now. Anyway, if it's all right, I'd like to go back to your house and finish that phone connection."

"It's more than fine with me, but Candace might not agree," I said. "She'll be conducting her search, after all. And then there's the dreaded *formal statement* to contend with."

"Just tell her exactly what you and I told Baca earlier. The truth."

"Seems like people on TV always get in trouble for telling the truth," I said, thinking about Shawn. The truth might get him in big-time trouble. "Oh, by the way, Wilkerson took a mallet to the security system control panel."

"He *what*?"

By the bulging veins in his neck, I'd say I learned a little more about Tom at that moment. He loved his control panels. *Really* loved them. I'm sure that was what upset him, not the idea that it was *my* control panel that had been attacked. But I had to smile to myself.

He ran a hand through his dark hair and said, "I'll have to pick up new equipment. Meet you at your house." His van was parked near the ditch and he took off in that direction.

I watched him leave, grateful for his help and glad I'd be seeing him again so soon. The wind picked up, swirling fallen leaves around my feet and making Syrah dig his claws into my arm. I sure wished Candace would hurry up. It was getting colder out here by the minute. Then the sound of an approaching vehicle caught my attention. I looked down the road and saw Shawn's pickup rumbling toward us.

He pulled into the driveway behind one of the squad cars. After taking several pet carriers from the truck bed, he waved my way, offered a grim smile and proceeded to the house.

Good. They must have called him to take the cats. For a second I felt immense relief, but then I recalled Shawn's anger with Flake Wilkerson yesterday and how he'd snatched that escaped tuxedo from the side of the road. I had to tell Candace he was with me yesterday—as soon as I got the chance. And, God, I didn't want to.

Finally, after what seemed like a year since I'd departed on my mission to confront the man who'd stolen my cat, Candace and I left. We soon pulled into my driveway, with her in the passenger seat holding Syrah. She told me Chief

Baca would arrange for someone to pick her up in an hour or two. Tom Stewart arrived seconds after we did. As he gathered his tools, we went inside.

Syrah immediately leaped from Candace's arms. He looked up at her, arched his back and hissed, then ran from the kitchen.

"Don't take it personally," I said to the befuddled-looking Candace. "I've pissed him off myself by putting him through the torture of a car trip. And he's been through much more than that in the last few days. He'll get over it."

She smiled. "Then there's hope he and I can still be friends. And now—I've never searched a place without a partner, so I'm gonna ask you to stay with me. I don't think the chief would like it much if I left you alone in one room while I searched another."

"Because I might hide those bloody clothes I don't have?" This was all so ridiculous that I felt like laughing. But I didn't think Candace would appreciate it. I knew she was only doing her job.

She squinted at me. "Know something? You're not looking so hot. Bet you haven't had so much as a drink of water since those sips the paramedics gave you after you fainted." She patted my arm. "Come on. Let's get you something to bring the color back to your cheeks."

I nodded in agreement. "Tea. I need tea."

While Candace was opening the refrigerator, a three-cat speed race with Syrah leading the way nearly knocked me over. Chablis and Merlot hadn't been this happy in two days. Candace handed me a glass of tea. "Are your cats always this crazy?"

"Yup. That's my clowder for you," I said.

"Clowder?" she said, pulling her eyebrows together.

"That's what you call a group of adult cats. On the other hand, a group of kittens is called a kindle."

"Learn something every day. So, I think I'll start in the basement with the washing machine. As I said, I have to keep you near so that nothing gets moved or—"

I held up a stop-sign hand and smiled. "I completely understand."

"Let's get busy, then." Candace started for the basement, but Chablis came back into the kitchen before we'd taken two steps and sat at my feet. She looked up and sneezed, a reminder that I had neglected my duties as her mom.

"Darn. I was so frantic about that man invading my house again, I forgot he must have left behind more dandruff. She needs Benadryl. You may not want to put this in any formal statement, but Chablis can testify that Flake Wilkerson didn't get his nickname because he was goofy. He had a serious dandruff issue."

Candace sighed and then smiled. "By the way, I did my research and discovered you *can* collect human DNA from dandruff."

"Really?" I said.

"You're not the only one who likes to gather information. I'll wait while you give her some medicine. I feel bad for poor Chablis."

I did this as quickly as I could, considering how much Chablis *loved* to take medicine, but Tom interrupted us the minute I was done wiping up the floor where she'd coughed out several drops of bright pink liquid. He needed access to the control panel and the phone. Candace told him she wasn't willing to leave him unsupervised in the kitchen.

"You have got to be kidding," he said.

"Can't fool around when it comes to procedure, Tom. But I do have the flexibility to compromise. I'll search the kitchen first while you work."

And so she rummaged through every cupboard and drawer—all the while casting anxious glances at me as I teased the cats with a feather or at Tom fiddling with the wiring. Once he was done and promised me I would be hooked up to the police after one last adjustment outside, I thanked him for his patience and for helping me get through this tough day. Then he left. And this time I didn't know when I'd see him again. Surprisingly, that bothered me.

The basement search came next, followed by the rest of the house. When Candace was done peeking in every corner and opening every drawer to look for those infamous bloody clothes, another hour had passed. Then we sat in the living room and she took my formal statement.

After I'd told her every detail again, aside from Shawn's helping me, she said, "I'm glad you didn't bump into the murderer when you went up those stairs or you might be gone now, too." I saw her swallow hard. "That would have saddened me to no end."

"Guess I wasn't thinking straight." But the truth was, I probably wouldn't have done anything any differently. I could never ignore the cries of a helpless animal.

Candace placed her hands on the clipboarded statement and stared up at the high ceiling.

"I don't have a secret hiding place up there," I said.

"Oh, I wasn't even thinking about that. I was wondering who coulda done that to Mr. Wilkerson. He may have been a mean son of a gun, but a knife in the gut isn't exactly the best solution to a problem."

Though I didn't want to involve Shawn, I had to tell the whole truth. I closed my eyes and took a deep breath, then said, "I have something to tell you, Candace. It could mean nothing, but you—and I mean you as a *policewoman*—should know."

"Go ahead," she said.

But before I could say another word, all three cats joined us. I said, "They've been so busy playing, they've missed out on our conversation. Merlot especially likes human talk. And I have to admit I speak to the three of them all the time."

Candace said, "Then tell your friend Chablis to be careful."

The Benadryl was finally doing its job—she had a slight problem putting one paw in front of the other. She kept running into sofas and ottomans.

I swooped her up before she hurt herself, and she was happy to curl up in my lap.

Candace said, "Okay. What else do you need to tell me?"

"Shawn went with me yesterday—to see Mr. Wilkerson," I said.

"Jeez. Why didn't you say so before?"

"I didn't want to get him in trouble. He seems like a great guy, and he cares so much about his rescues," I said.

Candace leaned back against the sofa, looking depressed. "This is bad. Real bad. Shawn is the nicest guy you'd want to meet, but he has had his share of problems when it comes to his furry friends."

"What do you mean?"

"For one thing, we got this county dogcatcher who comes around once a week or so. Shawn gets a little, well, *passionate* about what he considers mistreatment of the animals at the hands of the dogcatcher. But some of those loose dogs are nasty. And the feral cats? I wouldn't want to meet one of them in a dark alley."

"Passionate how?" I said.

"Let's just say the guy's got a restraining order against Shawn."

"I had no idea. Any other, um, *issues*?" I was beginning to wonder if our visit to Flake Wilkerson had been the last straw, the one that could have led Shawn to kill the man.

Candace said, "I shouldn't be talking about any of this. It's police business and I have to tell the chief right away. But before I leave, let's take a look at this video you have of Wilkerson inside your house."

"You don't really need that for establishing a timeline." I reminded her that I'd looked at the video on my phone in the coffee shop and checked again when I got to the quilt store. That was a pretty tight window—no more than ten minutes—and Martha at the Cotton Company could verify the time I left the store.

But of course Candace wanted to see the video anyway, and so I took her to the office and she burned a DVD of Wilkerson chasing my cats.

When she stood up from my computer desk, disk in hand, she said, "Perfect. Time-stamped and everything."

How'd she do that? I certainly needed to start figuring out all my computer's features now that I had this video security system.

"Guess I'm done here," Candace said. "I'll phone the chief and find out when I can hitch a ride back to my car."

"I'd be glad to take you anywhere you need to go," I said.

"Nah. You look like you could use a day at one of them spas to relax. Someone will come and get me."

"You're looking pretty frazzled yourself." I tucked a wayward strand of blond hair behind her ear. We had become friends, and I now felt guilty for my self-absorption. She was stressed out, too. "Thanks for being so patient with me. And I'm sorry I didn't tell you earlier about Shawn. I wanted him to get those cats out of that place, and the chief might have stopped that process to question him."

She smiled. "Darn right he would have. I'll help the chief understand your reasoning—which he won't consider reasonable, by the way." She took out her phone and called Baca. Turned out he was already on his way to pick her up.

After she hung up, she said, "I know Baca upset you today. But he's a nice guy. He just needs to loosen up. Always so uptight. Even more so since he's been seeing that divorced woman from the rich side of town. My guess is she has him on a short leash."

"I wouldn't think a police officer, especially the *chief* police officer in town, would like to be on any leash, short or long."

Candace pointed at me. "That's what I'm talking about."

We walked into the foyer to wait, and Syrah decided to say good-bye by rubbing against Candace's calves and leaving plenty of his own brand of evidence on her green uniform trousers.

"I told you he'd forgive and forget," I said. "If he could talk, he'd be saying thank you right now."

I heard approaching footsteps on the walkway and opened the door before Chief Baca could knock.

But it wasn't Baca.

Shawn stood there with two cat carriers, and neither was empty. One held the Persian and the other the noisy Siamese.

"Um, Jillian, I hate to surprise you like this, but we're at capacity at the Sanctuary. These two have been bathed and vaccinated, so could you—"

"Tell me something, Shawn," Candace said. She sounded calm, but her tone was cold. "When you were over there at Wilkerson's with all those fine officers present, did you happen to mention your relationship to the vic?"

"The *vic*? Did I just walk in on a filming of *CSI: Mercy*?" Shawn grinned.

During the ensuing silence, the foyer seemed to grow as frigid as a winter night.

Shawn's smile faded, and his expression went from smart-ass silly to stunned. Then he turned a harsh stare my way. "Just what have you been saying about me, Jillian Hart?"

Ten

"Shawn, please understand," I said. "I had to tell them about—"

"I'll handle this, Jillian," Candace said. "But not here. As for these cats, they need a temporary home?"

Shawn's mouth was now white-ringed with anger. "After this kind of greeting, I should walk back to my truck and forget about asking you for help. But I'm strapped for space and these two cats need placement immediately."

The Siamese began wailing its head off, and my three ventured to the foyer entrance to check out the noise. Merlot took one look at those crates, hissed and hightailed it back to wherever he'd come from. But apparently Syrah wasn't bothered, and Chablis was too drugged to care about possible unwelcome visitors.

Shawn put the two carriers down, and Candace knelt to talk to the cats. Unlike my attempt at Wilkerson's place to calm the Siamese, Candace was able to quiet it by slipping her fingers through the door grid and letting it rub its head against her hand.

"I could take this one," she said. "If my mom comes over I'll give her some of that Benadryl that works for Chablis's allergy."

"Good. Jillian, you willing to deal with the Persian until we know what to do with her?" His tone was brusque.

"Sure. She and Syrah have already bonded."

Syrah, tail in the air, was inching closer to the crates.

Poor Chablis, apparently too tired to take another step, stretched out in the entry to the living room. Oh, to be that mellow.

Candace addressed Shawn. "Now that we have this cat problem settled, we need to talk about you and Mr. Wilkerson. My ride will be here in a few minutes, so the three of us can head to the station."

"You want me to tell you I'm not sorry the jerk is dead? I'll say that right here, right now." Shawn's temper still controlled him, reminding me of how he'd behaved yesterday.

"Shawn." I put a hand on his arm. "You don't mean that."

"He doesn't mean what?" Chief Baca said. He'd somehow arrived at my open door without any of us noticing his approach.

I picked up Syrah, who had been sniffing the Persian through the crate's door. "Please come in, Chief," I said. "This cold air is a bit much." I wasn't talking about merely the weather, and from his expression I think he understood.

He stepped inside and closed the door behind him. "What's going on, Candy?"

"I got some information from Ms. Hart about Mr. Shawn Cuddahee here and thought it was worth pursuing, Chief."

"Information you planned to share with me right away, I assume," Baca said. Then he focused on Shawn. "What might that be, Mr. Cuddahee?"

"Mike," Shawn said, "don't act like we're not friends. That freaks me out."

I held Syrah close, fighting the urge to take my precious cats—all of them—and retreat to my sewing room. That was where I'd spent the better part of the last ten months. That was where nothing bad happened. But my world had changed in the last few days—even in the last few hours.

I said, "Shawn, you have to tell them about yesterday. About what that man was like when we went over there."

Shawn stared at me, his hard eyes and his clenched fists

speaking more than words. "Sure. I'll do that. Then you can tell them how all those little quilts of yours ended up in Flake Wilkerson's house."

I blinked. I'd forgotten all about them.

Shawn went on. "I recognized them when I went upstairs to get the cats Wilkerson probably stole from God knows who. They're like the quilts you gave the Sanctuary. The police should certainly be wondering exactly how that man got hold of them."

Both sets of police eyes turned on me.

"I—I don't know. I forgot to mention that I saw them . . . b-because of all the chaos." I looked at Candace. "Once I had a chance to remember, I would have told you, though."

She stared at the floor and shook her head. "You had a connection to the vic that you never told me? Even when I was taking your formal statement?"

"I forgot. It's that simple." I was trying not to sound pleading but wasn't sure I'd succeeded because she still looked disappointed.

I said, "I have no earthly idea how my quilts got inside his house. But the quilts he had were ones that I haven't made for months. I can check my orders from the last year. I do most of my sales online and—"

"You check those orders, Ms. Hart. As for now, Mr. Cuddahee, Deputy Carson and I will be leaving. Shawn, you follow us."

"Mike, what the hell?" Shawn said.

"We're taking this discussion down to the station," Baca said tersely.

With that, the chief turned, opened the door and walked out. Candace, carrying the crate with the Siamese, followed. So did Shawn, but not before he shot me a cross look.

I fought back unexpected tears—I really liked Shawn, and I certainly didn't want him to be in trouble. I spent the next hour trying to forget this awful day by coaxing the Persian out of the crate, first with soft words and then with a can of Fancy Feast. Syrah kept his distance, maybe because he thought she might not be the same cat he'd been hanging around with for the last few days. After all, she'd been bathed and smelled like perfume—seemed like a totally different animal from the poor matted and obviously neglected soul Syrah had undoubtedly released from captivity at Wilkerson's place.

Merlot continued to pout, keeping his nose to the window facing the lake. Syrah closed in and sniffed the little Persian when she finally emerged to eat her roasted chicken entrée. He nudged her away from the saucer, took a few bites himself and then let her eat again. Oh, yes. Pecking order must be established. Chablis slept through the whole episode, but at least the sneezing had stopped.

Once I'd pointed out the litter box in the basement to our new friend—whom I dubbed Dove because she was a dark chocolate color—I grabbed a glass of tea and went to my desktop computer. If I'd sold quilts to Flake Wilkerson, I had no recollection of any order and didn't remember seeing his name on the hard-copy invoices I keep. But of course he probably didn't use the name Flake on his credit card.

When I'd seen him the day Shawn and I went to the Pink House, I certainly hadn't recognized him. But I could have met him at a cat show where I'd had a vendor booth. If customers paid cash at a show, I wrote the name on the receipt, but no other information. According to the Cuddahees, Wilkerson was always on the lookout for purebred cats. What better place to find them than at a cat show? Even if the ones for sale at those shows were darn pricey. Yes. That seemed like a possible explanation for where he'd obtained my quilts.

I set my tea on a coaster by my keyboard, Chablis at my feet, and began searching my files for his name. I came up with nothing.

Wait a minute. What about the business cards on the vet's bulletin board? I sat back in the swivel chair, and poor Chablis thought this was her cue to jump in my lap.

She didn't quite make it and ended up clinging to my blue-jeaned thighs. I hefted her onto my lap and stroked her silky back. As she started to purr, my mind began to hum with memories.

All three cats had needed their yearly exams and I'd taken them to the vet one by one on three successive days. That was when I'd tacked up a few business cards. Flake Wilkerson might have learned about my business if he ever went to the vet. Maybe he'd driven by my house, spotted Syrah in the window and decided he wanted him for his own. My card did have my phone number and address.

Could a business card have led to all that had happened this week? Would this be something that could solve the mystery of the cats found at the Pink House? Was the vet Wilkerson's source once he realized the Sanctuary wouldn't cooperate with him?

I wondered if my theory would be of any interest to the police. I did have another huge question that Baca might not consider important either: Why was Flake Wilkerson obsessed with cats, especially those that belonged to other people? I didn't know, but I wanted to ask Baca. Maybe my ideas might even help deflect suspicion from Shawn. Perhaps there was another victim of cat theft out there, a victim with a temper. A victim not named Cuddahee. *Oh, gosh, Shawn. Will you ever trust me again?*

Eleven

Hoping to put aside thoughts of my almost surreal day, I settled on my sofa at about eight p.m. to watch *You've Got Mail*, the movie John and I had rented on one of our first dates. Unexpectedly, I wanted to enjoy something we'd shared rather than immerse myself in grief at the end of the day. I even lit ylang-ylang oil and poured myself a glass of white wine. I smiled as I came to my favorite lines from Kathleen, where she ponders leading a "small life" and considers whether she does what she does because she likes it or because she hasn't "been brave." I'd been brave today. And gosh, despite the trouble I might be in because I could have messed up evidence, I felt good about making sure those cats upstairs in the Pink House hadn't been sick or hurt and had ultimately been taken care of.

My phone rang, and I mumbled, "Do I really want to talk to anyone?" as I hit the remote's PAUSE button. Dove, who had taken up residence in my lap, much to Merlot's chagrin, jumped off when I reached for my cell.

"Miss Hart, this is Lydia Monk. You remember me?" She sounded so tired.

"Sure." I didn't add, "Who could forget an encounter with you?"

"If you're at home, Candy Carson and I need to pay you a visit. And trust me, this is not my idea. The last thing I want to do is bother you any more today."

"I'm home, but what's this about?"

"Very kind of you to accommodate us this late on a Sunday evening. We'll be by shortly and explain." She disconnected.

Did they want another recitation of the events from when I arrived at Wilkerson's house this morning? Maybe. Didn't cop shows always have scenes with witnesses saying, "How many times do I have to tell you what happened?" This thought reminded me that my whole knowledge of police procedure came from watching television—not the most reliable source of information.

They arrived in less than five minutes, so they must have already been on their way when Lydia called. Lydia still wore her tennis shoes and smelled like her deodorant had failed her several hours ago. Plus, her makeup needed a re-touch. One false eyelash was coming unglued and her concealer wasn't concealing much of anything. She was older than she'd looked earlier—maybe late thirties rather than early thirties. But her breasts were as perky as the day the surgeon sewed them in, and I had to admit that her posture, unlike her face, revealed no fatigue.

I led the two women through the foyer to my living room, where they both refused my offer of a drink.

I caught a vibe from Candace that I interpreted to mean she wanted to pretend we weren't friends. Maybe that was something she had to do in front of the deputy coroner.

Lydia sighed heavily as she sank into one of the easy chairs near the picture window. A full moon reflected off the restless lake in the darkening sky.

Perfect setting for a repeat interrogation.

Dove reclaimed her spot on my lap, while Merlot decided to play "I can love others, too" by jumping onto Candace's chair back. He stretched out and Candace reached around to scratch his head. Chablis and Syrah curled up next to me. Chablis closed her eyes, but Syrah seemed alert and ready for conversation.

"I haven't worked this hard since Frank Donnelly shot his sorry-ass self and his stupid girlfriend took off thinking we'd blame her," Lydia said.

I don't know if my confusion showed on my face, but perhaps that was why she went on with this odd opening statement. "Truth is, that woman would have driven anyone to suicide, but you can't make a case for that in court. Had to follow her trail all the way to Oregon in two frickin' days because I needed her version of what happened. See, families want answers."

"And Mr. Wilkerson's family wants answers, too?" I said.

"Oh, I wasn't talking about him. I tend to ramble after looking at blood all day. Not that I don't appreciate a nice bloody crime scene that might offer a wealth of information."

I swallowed. I didn't need to hear about that. "So how can I help?" I *had* initially omitted that Shawn and I visited Wilkerson yesterday. Maybe they wanted more details after speaking to Shawn. And then there was that tuxedo cat. I'd forgotten all about Shawn's roadside rescue. Maybe Shawn told them about the tuxedo and they wondered why I hadn't mentioned it. Problem was, so much had gone on, I'd pushed it to the back of my mind. But now I was concerned that if they didn't know, and I told Lydia and Candace about the catnapping, this might lead to the Sanctuary's being shut down. I sure wouldn't want that to happen.

Candace cocked her head. "Did you leave something out earlier today?"

My stomach tightened. That was it, all right. How much to say? What if none of this mattered and I'd get Shawn in more hot water? I certainly had to say something, because Candace was apparently learning to read every one of my expressions. "I forgot to mention that a cat escaped while we were talking on Mr. Wilkerson's front stoop the day before the murder. We left the property when he went to chase after the poor thing."

Candace looked at me. "You *forgot* that a cat got loose? *You?*"

"I-I'm sorry. Finding the body today is all I was thinking about and—"

"Understandable," Lydia said. "But we're not here about an escaped cat. We're here because this one"—she nodded at Candace—"seems to think I need to collect more evidence—not that I don't already need a frickin' Mack truck to carry what I've already got to the forensic unit."

"More evidence? From me? But Candace searched my house and—"

"Tell her, Candy," Lydia said. "This is your idea. I'm along for the ride 'cause I'm too damn tired to argue with you anymore."

Candace leaned toward me, hands clasped between her knees. "You were victimized by Mr. Wilkerson. From what Shawn says, he was, too."

I felt my tense shoulders relax a little. Shawn hadn't stonewalled them. He'd talked about how he suspected Wilkerson of breaking into the Sanctuary. "Thank God you believe him."

"I wouldn't go *that* far," Lydia said, her cynicism evident.

"Shawn wouldn't hurt anyone," I said. "He simply had a history with that man and—"

"No need to sign up for his defense team, Ms. Hart." Lydia blinked and finally realized she was losing a cosmetic appliance. She pulled off the dangling eyelash and stared at it. "I am through with these stupid things. Think I'll ask the cosmetic surgeon about an eyelash transplant next time I go in."

I couldn't hold back a smile, but Candace wasn't paying attention. She had her own agenda. "I'd like to take hair samples from all your cats," she said. "Some clear tape will do the trick. And that little one on your lap? I'll need that one's, too."

"Because the murder had something do with the cats?" I said. Thank God I wasn't the only one who thought the cats were important to solving the crime.

"We know Wilkerson took Syrah, and we know he came

back here to steal another one. Makes sense he may have angered the wrong person by doing the same thing to them," Candace said.

"But there must be a million cat hairs in his house," I said. "How could you ever sort through them?"

"That's what I told her." Lydia sighed again.

Candace stiffened. "Just because there's a lot of evidence doesn't mean you ignore it."

"And we are *not* ignoring it," Lydia said. "Do you mind, Ms. Hart?"

"Not at all. Let me hold them while you do this, though," I said.

The process was quick, but not without hissing and scratching involved. This was not the cats' idea; therefore it was an unacceptable intrusion. Candace put each piece of hair-laden tape in an evidence envelope and identified the sample with a short description of the cat it belonged to as well as the date and time.

"Wilkerson didn't take my other two cats, so why do you need samples from them?" I asked.

"And that reminds me. Why didn't he take all three the first time he broke in?" Lydia asked.

"Merlot and Chablis are pretty darn smart, Ms. Monk," I said. "Once they realized Mr. Wilkerson was up to no good, I'm sure they hid."

"Ah," she said, nodding wearily.

"Why do you need more samples, Candace?" I asked.

"See, I collected cat hairs from Wilkerson's clothing, and since he'd been in your house immediately before he was murdered, he probably had transfer on him," Candace said.

"Transfer?" I said.

"Trace evidence transferred from your animals to his clothing," Lydia said impatiently. "Do you have everything you need?"

Candace went on, "See, I need to exclude your cats' hairs and focus on the ones I might not be able to connect to your three or to any of the other cats we found in the house."

"You mean a cat might have been taken from the Pink House before I got there?" I said. "And you could find that out by looking at cat hair? That's amazing."

Candace's eyes were bright. "See, it's all about the evidence. Stuff you can examine and learn from and—"

"Yeah, yeah, yeah," Lydia interrupted. "Can we please get out of here?"

"What about cat nose prints?" I asked. "Did you find any of those?"

"What are you talking about?" Candace said.

"A cat's nose print is like a human fingerprint. One of a kind. If there's a nose print that doesn't belong to any of the cats that were in the house, then—"

"I imagine that a lot of cats passed through Mr. Wilkerson's hands," Candace said. "And just like human prints, we would have no idea when this unique nose print was left. It's also not like we have a database of cat nose prints to match up with what we find. Cat hair is a different story."

"Oh," I said, feeling deflated. "Just trying to help."

Candace said, "But that is really cool—the nose prints, I mean. Where did you learn about that, anyway?"

"There was a vendor at a cat show once who was selling pendants she made with a cat or a dog's nose print on them," I said. "In case the pet got lost or stolen. She told me all about nose prints."

"Trouble is, how often would we need to use something like a nose print?" Candace said. "Never had a case on *Forensics Files* that used cat nose prints. And I swear I've seen every episode twice. Cat and dog hair, however, can be very useful in solving some crimes. I read a research article not long ago about the DNA of cat hair and how cat hairs have led to suspects who were eventually convicted. The hair evidence was even presented in court. It had been left on both the corpse and the murderer."

Lydia sighed heavily. "Listen, I'll check with the FBI—

that being the Feline Bureau of Information—about all this cat hair and nose print stuff—maybe in my next life. But right now I have got to get home and get my beauty rest."

That got a laugh from all of us, and they left not long after. I returned to the living room and closed the blinds to shut out the night.

That eerie moon still hung low in the sky. It went well with that word *corpse*. Too well.

Twelve

Since Merlot seemed upset about the Persian invasion, I gave him a plum spot close to me when I went to bed. He was gone when I awoke the next morning—probably busy cornering my little invader and making sure she didn't get her fair share of food or a chance at the litter box. While I showered, I thought about how Shawn and I had gone on that mission to find my cat just days ago. He'd helped me, and now I felt like I'd betrayed him. We had to talk.

An hour later, I drove to the Sanctuary, but it was Allison, not Shawn, who came outside to greet me. Her dark hair was pulled back in a messy ponytail and she gripped a coffee mug with both hands. She looked as tired as I felt.

"Long night?" I asked as we stood in the packed dirt driveway.

"Shawn didn't sleep and neither did I," she said. "He's so upset, Jillian."

"I had to tell the police what I knew, but that doesn't mean I believe he had anything to do with that man's death."

"He doesn't quite see it that way," she said. "He thinks you pointed the finger at him to take the spotlight off yourself."

"But that's wrong. Can I talk to him?"

Allison glanced back at the Sanctuary. "He saw you drive up and he doesn't want to talk to you. Did you know they took his fingerprints? And that the police have been all over the Sanctuary and our house? This whole thing is humiliating to both of us."

"If it means anything, they searched my house, too."

"Can't say that helps. Give him time to get his head straight. As for me, I think you're a sweet person and maybe one day we can be friends."

Her words stung. "One day? But not now?"

"I have to support Shawn, and he's not feeling friendly right now."

"We're on the same side, Allison. Please ask him to listen to me for a few minutes. Mr. Wilkerson stole cats and Shawn was certain he broke into your shelter. He could shed light on the thefts as a possible motive. The cat thefts are important, at least to me. I need to understand why Mr. Wilkerson was doing what he was doing."

She smiled down into her coffee—which had to be as cold as the fall air. "Don't you think coming up with motives and suspects is the police's responsibility?" But then she looked past me. "Someone's coming."

I turned in time to see a Mercy Police squad car pull in and halt behind my van.

"Great," Allison said under her breath.

Chief Baca and Morris Ebeling got out of the car.

"Well, if it isn't the cat lady herself," Morris said. "Fancy finding you here."

Wearing a grave expression, Baca said, "Ms. Hart, Ms. Cuddahee."

Oh, this is not good.

"Your husband here, Ms. Cuddahee?" Morris said.

Shawn emerged from the shelter. "I'm here. You forget something last time you messed up the place?"

Morris looked at Baca and the chief nodded a silent affirmation.

"You're coming with us for a more formal interview." Morris walked toward Shawn.

"Is that cop lingo for you're arresting me?" Shawn's fair skin reddened.

Baca said, "Not arresting you yet. We had to borrow video equipment from the county to record your statement—and discuss a few other matters."

"What does all this mean, Mike?" Allison said. "He didn't do anything wrong."

"We need his statement again, that's all," Baca said.

Morris tried to take Shawn by the elbow, but he pulled away. "I know how to walk without help." He marched to the squad car with Morris on his heels.

I hoped I was wrong, but this sure looked like an arrest.

Baca turned to Allison. "We'll get this straightened out and he'll be home in no time." He started toward the car, but then stopped and looked at me. "Hope you're here simply as a friend, Ms. Hart."

What the heck did that mean? But he was apparently delivering a warning, not looking for an answer, because he walked away.

Allison didn't take her eyes off the car until it was out of sight. Then, tears in her eyes, she said, "See what you've done?" and hurried back toward the Sanctuary.

I stared at her as she retreated. Nothing I could have said would have made a difference. Not now.

I wouldn't find answers to what had just transpired by going home and hiding—which would have been the comfortable and cowardly thing to do. Instead, I drove into town and went straight to Belle's Beans. One thing I'd learned about Mercy in the last few days was that people spread the word about anything and everything. Someone surely knew why Shawn had been taken in for questioning again, and the only way I could find answers was by planting myself in the center of town and hoping someone would share the latest gossip.

I walked inside, but even the wonderful smells—coffee and butter-rich pastries—couldn't obliterate the guilt I felt about what had happened at the Sanctuary. How could someone like me, who at one time had every detail of her life carefully planned out, have a year like this? Everything seemed so . . . so out of control.

"You're lookin' a might ragged," the Belle of the Day behind the counter said. Her cornrowed hair sections were tipped with vibrant colored beads that clicked together with every movement.

I ordered the biggest latte they offered, and as I handed over the money she added, "Course you been through the wringer and back." This stranger probably knew more than I did about the current events in my life.

"What's your real name?" I said, managing a smile.

She grinned. "You've become a real Mercyite. You know the secret. My name is Shondra. Now let me fix your coffee. We're usin' Sumatra beans today. Sumatra is in Africa. Didn't know until I started working here how good African beans are. These are nice and smoky."

I waited for my coffee, wishing the original, very talkative Belle was here, but she wasn't sitting and reading like she had been the other day. Maybe I'd have to head for the tea shop down the street and have chicken salad for lunch, or buy flowers at the little florist place in the other direction. I could maybe strike up a conversation in one of those places.

Shondra handed over my coffee and I thought about chatting *her* up, but Tom Stewart arrived and boomed, "Hey, Shondra, I thought this was your day off." Then he spied me. "That is one big coffee. You planning an all-nighter?"

Boy, was I glad to see him. "Maybe. You want to join me?"

I took my drink to a corner table. Tom might know why Shawn had been taken in for another interview. While I waited for him, I checked my home video feed, and what I saw on my cell phone screen made me grin. Little Dove had wormed her way into Merlot's heart, at least while he thought I wasn't looking. They were curled up together on the couch. Gosh, she was a sweetheart, and Merlot was such a big softie.

"Everything working okay?" He took the stool across from me.

I closed my phone. "Yes, the security cameras work great. And I guess the threat to my cats is gone now anyway—though not in a way I would ever have wished for."

"Wilkerson died a pretty ugly death; that's for sure. He pissed someone off royal," Tom said.

I sipped my coffee. Shondra was right. Delicious stuff.

"Back in my law enforcement days—"

"You were a cop?" I said, surprised. But then, it made sense—and actually explained a lot of what I had considered odd behavior before. For instance, how he had reacted to me when he'd discovered me at Wilkerson's house.

"Police officer. For ten years. And back then I would have honed in on you as a suspect. That cat means the world to you and Flake stole him. The knife holder was right by that apple he'd just cut up and—"

"I never even noticed the knife holder, and you surely know the man was dead when I got there. And the police do, too, right?"

He held up both hands. "I am not privy to their thoughts on you as a suspect. What I'm trying to say is that I don't suspect you, even though my acting like a jackass yesterday may have left you uncertain about that."

"You did kind of scare me a bit. But that's behind us."

He smiled at me. "I like a forgiving woman. I'm glad you decided to try Belle's Beans."

"Why?" I said.

"Because I found you here today. I was thinking last night how rough you've had it in the past year and how it's not getting much better. But you seem to have handled what life's thrown at you with mettle."

"You must have me confused with Miss Upstate John Deere or Candace. I am not the least bit brave."

He laughed. "Winnebago. Miss Upstate Winnebago. She's something, huh?"

"I kinda like Lydia," I said.

"Because she let you off the hook yesterday?" he said. "Don't be fooled by that."

"She considers me a suspect?"

"Can we not go there? I don't know much of anything except not to trust Lydia. She's a nutcase. So let's talk about something else. I heard you took in one of Wilkerson's cats."

"No secrets in Mercy," I said. "But what's this about Lydia?"

"You do not want to know. Just let me say she'll show her true colors soon enough. I also heard Shawn's got himself in trouble."

"What exactly have you heard?" I said.

"He's down the street at the police station this minute trying to dig himself out of a hole."

"I know that much. I was at the Sanctuary when they took him in."

"Whoa. Really?"

"You think they'll arrest him?" I said.

"You're worried, huh?" he said. "Because you two are friends, I take it?"

"He's a good guy," I answered. "Why is he being interrogated again?"

"It's about his fingerprints, I hear. Fingerprints found in the wrong place."

"No way," I said, horrified. "Shawn's fingerprints were on the knife?"

Tom's ears reddened. "I didn't say that. I heard his fingerprints were found somewhere other than the places you'd expect—not just upstairs where the cats had been kept."

"Then they might not have been in *all* the wrong places." A morsel of relief eased the knot in my gut. "That makes me feel better, because I helped get Shawn into this mess."

"Hey, Jillian, you didn't make him do anything. You told the police the truth. That's what you're supposed to do. And maybe this is news to you, but most people in town know he can get into trouble all by himself."

"What does that mean?" I said.

"He has strong opinions about his animals," Tom said. "Mostly the way the county quickly carts off dogs and cats to county or state facilities rather than checking with Shawn to see if he has room to take them at the Sanctuary."

"That sounds like a passionate man who wants to take care of a problem," I said. "Gosh, I wish we hadn't gone to the Pink House the day before."

"The day before?" His blue eyes were wide with surprise.

I took a hefty swig of much-needed coffee before I explained about the visit Shawn and I made to Wilkerson's house and that I felt I'd gotten him in trouble by telling the police about it.

"You shouldn't be too worried about a small disagreement at Wilkerson's front door. I'm betting that's not the first time around for Shawn." Tom removed his cup lid so he could drink the dregs of his coffee.

"Still, it doesn't look good for him. He and Allison told me they refused to adopt cats out to Wilkerson," I said.

"I know," he said. "Shawn mentioned Wilkerson when I installed their security system. He said he suspected him of breaking in. But Shawn had a bad rep with the county. Guess he cussed out more than one person when he complained, and he figured Morris Ebeling didn't bother to do much investigating after the Sanctuary break-in."

"But that's so wrong," I said. "Animals were taken and—"

"This is small-town America, Jillian. You make friends and they're yours for life. You make enemies and the same thing is true."

"That doesn't make it right for the police to ignore—"

"Wait. I'm not saying they ignored Shawn's complaint. I don't have all the details. I was hoping to reassure you that the fact that he had a beef with Wilkerson isn't fresh news."

"I still want to help Shawn. He didn't kill that man."

"Help him? Then I hope you have information on

other possible suspects, because the cats sure didn't stick a knife in the man. Unless you're talking about yourself as a suspect—which doesn't make sense to me."

"I got the feeling Baca thought I was a suspect yesterday, but Lydia Monk was so nice and seemed to understand I wouldn't have had time to get to the house, kill the man, change my clothes and—"

"Hold on. Remember what I said about her? Do *not* trust that woman," he said.

"But she wants to find the truth, right? That's her job," I said.

"This has more to do with her personality than how she does her job. You should know that even though I don't suspect you, if I were still a cop, I couldn't rule you out simply by looking at you."

"She's trying to be the good cop when she talks to me?" I said.

"That would imply there's a bad cop. Are you thinking of Chief Baca? I'm sure she wants him to appear that way, believe me," he said. "In my opinion, this shows the coroner system is flawed. Mike Baca is better equipped to handle this case."

"I don't pretend to understand any of it, so I believe you. Now, back to Shawn. Even if he does have a temper, there's this wonderful compassionate side to him. He seems—"

"Yeah, yeah, so you like the guy. But surely you saw that he's happily married?"

"It's not like that." I was surprised at Tom's reaction—that I might be interested in Shawn as more than a friend. And though I felt a little guilty because John came immediately to mind, I realized the very good-looking Tom Stewart was acting, well, *jealous*. And it made me feel something I hadn't expected to feel again. *Attractive*.

"Then what is it like between you two?" Tom cocked his head.

I paused after that question. "I met him the other day and was impressed with the Sanctuary. I had already come to think of him as a friend. Like you've become. And that means I have to do something to help him. And besides, you see a person dead by such violent means and you ... you ... well, that makes it even more important to make sure justice is done. Especially since I'm certain Baca is wrong about Shawn."

"How can you be so sure about Shawn's innocence? Are you relying on instinct?" he said.

"Yes—maybe that's it. Though I do have a partial left brain," I said with a laugh. "You need a few math skills for making quilts. Angles, numbers, precision—all come into play."

He laughed. "I know nothing about making quilts. But if you want to teach me, that's great. Just don't tell anyone. Especially any guys."

My turn to smile. "There are plenty of wonderful male quilters. But as for this instinct thing, maybe I should pay attention to what my gut is telling me."

"Instinct I understand." He was nodding. "Cops rely on it all the time."

"You know how to run an investigation, so could you give me some pointers?"

"Huh? Why would you want to learn how to— Uh-oh." He was staring over my left shoulder and I turned to see why.

Lydia Monk and Candace had come inside the café. I heard Lydia say, "Get us two coffees to go, Candy. Plenty of sugar for me."

Candace put the order in with Shondra while Lydia walked over to us. She wore a tight denim skirt, a hot pink sweater that plunged nearly to her navel and high black boots with stiletto heels.

"I knew you'd be here, Tom, but Ms. Hart's presence is a surprise," Lydia said. "You two look plenty cozy in this corner. Are you talking about the murder? Or something more personal?"

"Everyone's talking about the murder," Tom said. He

leaned away from Lydia, reminding me of someone dealing with a rattlesnake—paying close attention yet keeping his distance.

She said, "What better person to discuss this hot topic with than Mercy's newest beauty? You haven't wasted any time getting close to her, have you?"

"What do you want, Lydia?" Tom said.

"We need to talk," she said.

"Not you and me in private," he said. "You know how I feel about that."

"I *will* talk to you, and we won't be as cozy as the two of you are right now. We'll do the interview at the Mercy police station. Meet you there." She started to walk away, but stopped and said, "Might as well join your new boyfriend, Ms. Hart. I'd like a word with you, too."

She may have liked me yesterday, but things certainly seemed to have changed. I was beginning to understand Tom's warning.

The Mercy police station, as well as the jail, was attached to the old city hall and court building in the center of town. We could have walked the two blocks, but both Tom and I took our vehicles. I checked my cat-cam before I started the engine. The clowder was sleeping the day away and I wished I was, too. I'd been on Lydia's good side prior to her seeing me at Belle's Beans. What was with her, anyway? I'd glanced Candace's way when Lydia stomped out, but all she offered was a shrug that said, "You got me."

Tom was waiting outside on the steps leading up to the old brick building when I pulled into one of the angled parking spots. As we started up the stairs, I said, "Okay, I've got to know. What's the deal with you and Lydia?"

"She seems to think we're destined to be together," he said. "How she decided that, I have no idea."

"She was so nice to me yesterday, I wasn't prepared for her to be so—so—"

"Venomous? I sure hope you're prepared now. My suggestion for when you talk to her is to say as little as possible. Thanks to being seen with me, you've landed on that woman's bad side, and it's not the nicest spot on earth. I live there. I know."

"I've told the police everything. What could she want from me now?" I said.

"She hasn't questioned me, so my guess is she brings me in, then checks with you to corroborate my story about meeting you at Wilkerson's place. I'm guessing she'll want to know why you called me. Again, don't say much. She'll think you have a personal interest in me aside from any murder investigation."

"We're friends and I asked you for help," I said. "What could she possibly read into that?"

"Does the word *stalker* mean anything to you? Some of her questions won't have anything to do with the case. She has this stupid . . . crazy . . ."

"Obsession with you?" I finished.

We reached the top step and stopped, and he said, "If she's getting all worked up about what she *thinks* might be cooking between you and me—which of course is nothing—you might land at the top of the suspect list again."

"That's ridiculous. She believed me yesterday, so—"

He shook his head, smiling. "What makes you think she believed you?"

"She seemed so nice and—"

"And she can be," he said. "No one knows that better than I do. Consider my advice and say as little as possible. We have a constitutional right to say whatever we want, but don't forget we have a right to keep quiet, too. Now let's get this over with."

As we walked, I felt this odd sense of relief that Tom had no interest in Lydia—a woman so opposite from me. And this thought was immediately followed by another dose of guilt. John hadn't even been gone a year and I was enjoying the company of an attractive man—and wanted to be attractive to him. But I pushed these thoughts aside as we entered the building.

I'd never ventured inside the courthouse complex before and was stunned by the old building's magnificence. The dark marble floor gleamed, and the curving wall on the opposite side of the lobby showcased a giant painting of a trial that looked to have occurred in the early twentieth century, judging from the clothing worn by the men pictured. All of them white men. But the mural was beautifully painted.

Tom took my elbow and led me to the left. By the time we'd walked a good distance down a drafty hallway, the splendor of the old days had been replaced by the grimy, smelly present. I caught the odor of vomit tinged with stale whiskey, and my stomach rebelled against the strong coffee I'd finished in too much of a hurry.

Molded plastic chairs lined the corridor. A woman was lying asleep across two of them, one tattooed arm slung over her eyes. We passed her and came to a scarred door with an old-fashioned frosted window. MERCY POLICE was stenciled on the window in green paint. Curse words had been carved into the wood in a few places—they looked fresh—and I wondered how many times a week the door had to be sanded.

Tom turned the knob and allowed me to enter first, a gentlemanly gesture I wished he'd forgone this one time. I was nervous. I wanted more than ever to go home and cuddle up with the cats in my secure, sweet-smelling home.

And when I saw Shawn standing in the center of the small reception area nearly eye to eye with Lydia, I wanted to run back out that door. His face was florid with anger, and he was stabbing his finger in Lydia's direction to emphasize each repetition of "I did not kill that man." After four times he added, "And Baca's an ass if he thinks different."

That was when he turned to leave and saw me. He flashed an angry glance my way as he stormed past Tom and me.

"Ah, police business," Tom said. "Gives you the warm fuzzies every time."

"Shut up and get in Baca's office." Lydia pointed a bloodred fingernail at me. "You? Sit out here with your girlfriend."

I hadn't had a chance to notice the huge oak desk to my left or the fact that Candace was sitting behind it. A computer monitor held her attention until the door identified on a brass plate as the OFFICE OF POLICE CHIEF MICHAEL BACA slammed shut.

"You look a lot more upset than I've ever seen you. What's going on?" I asked her.

"Lydia's got the hots for Tom Stewart, and when she saw the two of you together she flipped out, started dissing you the minute we walked out of Belle's Beans. I stuck up for you, and that was apparently a huge mistake. First thing she did when we got here was get the chief to kick me off the case because I'm too friendly with you to be objective."

"And he agreed? But that's wrong. You're such a good officer and—"

She held up her hand. "Don't say stuff like that right now because I might start crying—and girl cops aren't supposed to cry. This was my shot at a big case and now—" She took a deep breath. "I'm thinking the chief only agreed to kick me to the curb because he wanted to calm Lydia down."

"I am so sorry," I said. "Somehow I feel like this is my fault and—"

"Nope. It's Lydia and the chief's fault. What I don't get is how *she* can work with the chief after they had a damn affair while I get pushed aside because of a friendship."

"Good question," I said. "They're not together, right? He has some other girlfriend, if I remember right."

"He's moved on, true. What he saw in Lydia I'll never know. Maybe he went nuts after his wife ran off and he turned to Lydia for comfort. But they were the oddest pair. The chief is Mr. Conservative and Lydia's gussied up most of the time." Candace took another deep breath. "Sorry. I shouldn't be saying any of this—at least not while I'm on the job. The two of them have just made me so darn mad."

"Okay, let's change the subject. I see Shawn didn't end up in jail. That's good."

"Not enough evidence to hold him," Candace said. "But tell me again what dumb notion sent you to the Sanctuary this morning? Because you should keep your distance from him."

"He didn't kill anyone, Candace," I said.

"And I have heard him tell God and everyone that same thing about a hundred times today and yesterday. Police work isn't about 'you say it enough times and it's true.' "

"Got it. Now, why am *I* here?" I said.

"Probably because you were sitting with the love of Lydia's life and she didn't like it. I can't think of any other reason."

"Did Tom lead her on and then dump her or something?" I said.

"*Him?* No way. He's got better taste. Maybe something he said or did convinced Lydia he was interested, though. Something no one knows about."

The phone rang and she picked up the receiver. "Mercy Police."

While she took the call, I stood and wandered toward the chief's office, hoping to catch some of the conversation. The door opened without warning and I started.

It was Chief Baca. "Join us, please, Ms. Hart. Seems you were planning on that anyway, in a fashion."

I felt like a kid caught stealing a cookie. He held the door open and I sidled past him into the office.

Much nicer digs than the hall or reception area. The chairs were padded, the desk mahogany and the wall color a soothing pale green. But the air was thick with tension between a seemingly angry Lydia and what looked like a less-than-interested Tom.

"Thank you for coming, Ms. Hart." Baca settled into his leather high-backed swivel chair.

"Anything I can do to help," I said.

"Tell us about yesterday. Before you arrived at the Wilkerson house. You went there because you saw Mr. Wilkerson on video surveillance inside your home, correct?"

"Yes. I was certain he'd stolen my cat and—"

"This decision to go to his house without contacting the authorities—tell me more."

"Am I in trouble for that? Because there was that fire and I saw my cat run into the house and Mr. Wilkerson's door was open and—"

"You are not in trouble," he said. "This is an informal interview, and I'm not even taking notes. We just want to figure this whole mess out."

That brought the first sound from Lydia since I'd sat down—a noise reminiscent of Chablis hacking up a hairball. Lydia was apparently disgusted, but with him? With me? I had no idea.

Baca shot her a glance as if to tell her to quit with the attitude. "Go on, Ms. Hart."

"I don't need a lawyer or anything?" I said.

"We certainly can delay all this until you find one," he said. "But I sense you don't have anything to hide, right?"

I wanted to check Tom's expression, see if I could read his eyes and if that would tell me what I should do. But I could tell that would certainly not help him, with Lydia fuming close enough to catch his clothes on fire, so I decided I should keep answering the questions—though briefly, as Tom had suggested.

"I've been talking with Mr. Stewart, and he tells me you asked for his assistance at the Wilkerson place? Why was that?" Baca asked.

"Yeah, I'd like to know the answer to that one, too, seeing as how Shawn Cuddahee seems to be your go-to guy," Lydia said.

Baca started to speak but was interrupted by an obviously pissed-off Tom, who said, "Leave her alone, Lydia."

Chief Baca slammed a fist on his desk and I nearly

jumped a foot in the air. His voice, in contrast, was soft and controlled when he said, "Shut up, both of you. Deputy Coroner Monk, I appreciate your assistance and your need for information, but this is exactly why you will *not* be working this case except in a secondary capacity."

"What?" She rose halfway off her chair. "That's not the way this works."

"I've spoken with Coroner Beecham, and he has decided that I will be running this investigation."

She stood. "Why? Because I dumped you? Or because you can make a name for yourself if you solve this? Maybe run for county office down the road?"

Baca flushed. "Prior relationships have nothing to do with the decision. The coroner believes that the Mercy police have the resources to handle this case. We know the town better, and besides, you have a lot on your plate. You did your part by coming out and coordinating the evidence collection yesterday, and we're grateful for—"

"Save it, Baca," she said. Chin high, breasts leading the way, she left the office, and I was thankful for no slamming of doors. I felt rattled enough.

Baca looked at me. "Do I need to repeat the question?"

"Yes, please," I said.

"Did Mr. Stewart know why you needed his assistance at the Pink House yesterday morning?"

I hesitated, trying to think back to that brief conversation. "I'm sure I told him, but everything happened so fast and—" I glanced at Tom. "Did I tell you?"

He was looking down, shaking his head, his hand to his forehead.

Wrong answer, Jillian. First Shawn, then Candace and now Tom. Who else could I get in trouble?

Thirteen

"Please think real hard, Ms. Hart," Baca said, all his South Carolina charm dripping into every word. "Why did you call Mr. Stewart for help?"

What was I missing here? He seemed to be looking for a specific answer, probably something I knew nothing about, or at least I didn't think I did. I looked over at Tom again, but he still had his head down. "I called Tom because I know very few people in town, and since the police had responded to that fire, I didn't want to bother them."

"But Mr. Cuddahee helped you the day before. Like Ms. Monk said, why not call him?" Baca said.

Perhaps I'd been so disturbed by Shawn's behavior with Wilkerson the day before, I'd never even thought of phoning him instead of Tom. But mentioning that might hurt Shawn even more as far as suspect status. I had to say something, though. "I guess Tom came to mind because he'd put in my security system Saturday night. He'd helped me."

"And Mr. Stewart could be of more assistance than a man like Mr. Cuddahee, who we all know tends to be confrontational?"

"That wasn't my first thought when I called Tom."

"Sounds like you did think about it, though," Baca said. "Mind if I look at your cell phone? Confirm this call was made?"

"You think I'd lie?" I was surprised how much his words upset me.

"I have to confirm the call, that's all," he said.

Tom finally spoke. "Take mine. Like I told you, the call was short and sweet." He shoved his phone across the desk.

Baca pressed buttons on the phone and apparently found what he wanted because he read off my cell number, then said, "That yours?"

I nodded.

He pressed another button, and I heard my muffled ringtone coming from my jeans pocket. It stopped when Baca closed Tom's phone.

"Thanks," Baca said, handing the cell back to Tom.

Despite Tom's warning to say as little as possible, I felt the need to explain further. The police do seem to have a way of making you feel guilty even when you're not. "I do remember the conversation better now. Tom said he knew where Flake Wilkerson lived when I asked if he needed directions. He agreed to meet me there, and that was about it."

"He said he knew where he lived?" Though he was speaking to me, Baca was looking at Tom.

Uh-oh. What had I done now? I quickly added, "I also said something about Tom meeting me in five minutes. I'll admit I was upset with Mr. Wilkerson for breaking into my house and I was sure he had stolen my cat. I'm certain that even if Tom hadn't agreed to help me with that problem, I would have gone to the Pink House no matter what."

"Really?" Baca settled back, hands intertwined behind his neck, and said, "You were that angry?"

"Angry?" I said. "No. That's the wrong—"

"I don't think you should say anything else," Tom said.

"You got a law degree, too, Mr. Stewart?" Baca said.

"Would you quit with the cop crap? I'm Tom and you're Mike. We're friends, remember?"

"The *cop crap*? Is that what murder was to you when you were on the force?" Baca said.

"That's not what I'm talking about and you know it," Tom said.

I stood, tired of all these complicated Mercy relationships coming into play. "You know what?" I said. "No matter what Flake Wilkerson did, I would never kill him. That's not the kind of person I am. Now, I'm leaving." I walked out of the office, my heart beating so fast I had trouble breathing. Could you actually walk away from the police without ending up in handcuffs?

Seemed I could, because no one called my name and told me to stop, and no one followed me. Candace might have, if she'd been in the waiting area—but a new person sat behind the desk, a young man who could have passed for twelve. Since he was wearing a Mercy Police uniform, he was probably closer to eighteen or nineteen.

I hurried down the hall and out of the building, making a beeline for my minivan. The sun was desperately attempting to break through the cloud cover. A warm change was imminent—the humidity told me as much. Yes, in many ways this was a different world than it had been a few days ago. But it would not be a world where I hid in my sewing room trying to pretend none of this had happened. I had to find out why Flake Wilkerson stole my cat and what, if anything, that had to do with his death.

On the drive home I considered how I could accomplish those two things. I wasn't a police officer. I didn't know anything about being a detective. Yet I was smack in the middle of a mystery where people were thinking the worst of me and keeping secrets. People like Mike Baca, who was only doing his job, but it still hurt my feelings. And people like Tom. Had he been protecting me when he offered his cell phone? Was he afraid there might be something incriminating on mine? I had no idea.

When I made the last turn for home, I saw a squad car in my driveway. Apparently I hadn't made a clean escape after all. When I pulled in behind the car, Candace got out and walked toward me. Maybe they needed a female officer to put me in jail and that was why I hadn't been stopped when I left.

Oh God, I'm going to jail.

"What happened in there with you and the chief?" Candace's eyes were dancing with interest.

"You're not here to arrest me?" I said.

"What?" came her confused reply. "Remember? I'm off this case. The only thing that makes the taste in my mouth a little less bitter is that Lydia's been kicked off, too. She made sure I knew as much, and for some reason she thinks it's all your fault."

"But that's crazy," I said.

"And you expected . . . what, exactly?"

I shrugged. "I have so much to learn about this town."

Candace glanced toward my house. "It's my lunch break, so can we talk inside? I want to know every detail of what went on in that office."

I smiled and waved for her to follow me. Once inside, I fixed us tall sweet teas, and then Candace and I settled in the living room. Dove, who I'd decided was the inspiration for the song "We Are the World" because she seemed to love everyone, jumped into Candace's lap. Merlot sat close to me on the couch, and the other two sniffed and rubbed on Candace before they went off to find a dark, quiet spot to sleep. They'd been stressed in the last few days and needed to catch up on their z's.

I related my rather perplexing visit with the chief and Tom and summed up by saying, "I think I'm still a suspect. But there's an issue between Tom and Mike, one they sure didn't share with me."

"Interesting," Candace said. "Tom stays pretty busy between the security setups and his PI work. Maybe he and Wilkerson had a history."

"That might explain things," I said. "I can't help but feel that my calling Tom yesterday got him in trouble, too."

"You were smart enough to know you needed help at the Pink House. You did the right thing. The only mistake you made was a lack of patience. You should have waited for Tom to get there."

"I couldn't wait. Not when I saw Syrah in the driveway," I said.

"I understand, but I don't think the chief does. He doesn't trust you, Lydia's pissed off, and he and Tom aren't on good terms. I mean, what a mess. I have a mind to solve this case myself and show those boys how to get answers without antagonizing the entire town at the same time."

"Lydia was like a different person from the minute she saw me with Tom," I said.

Candace laughed. "She was bouncing mad when she stormed outta Baca's office. And we both know what was bouncing the most."

"I'd like to clear my name and Shawn's, too. Can you and I work on that?" I said.

"As long as they don't make me the paperwork princess, I would love to. But only as your friend—not while I'm on the clock. Got to do what I can to keep from getting fired—at least until I can save enough to go back to school and get a job in forensics. This small-town stuff is wearing me out."

She had to leave then but told me her shift was over at three and she'd be back to brainstorm on how we should proceed. At the back door she gave me a big hug and said, "I do so like you, girlfriend. You and me are gonna get to the bottom of this."

I busied myself with my quilt orders for the next several hours and then went to the computer to send e-mails to a few customers. Several of the Syrah flyers that hadn't printed well were in the wastebasket near my desk, and I thought about how I'd put them around town before knowing they'd be gone within hours thanks to the sign ordinance.

That got me wondering who removed signs for the city. I recalled Belle mentioning that she'd wanted to put up signs when her cat had disappeared, too. How many other people had done the same when their pet went missing? Could this "sign remover" know about any missing cats? Like the three cats Shawn took from Wilkerson's place after the murder? This might not lead anywhere, but I would run it by Candace when she came back later today. Maybe it would help us find other people who had reason to be upset with Wilkerson for stealing their cats.

My cell phone rang and I hurried to the kitchen, where I'd left it. Syrah found this entertaining and chased me. When I reached the phone, he leaped onto the counter and sat down, ready to listen.

"You okay?" Tom said when I answered.

"Fine. I take it this isn't your one phone call from jail," I said.

"Nope," he said. "Looks like both of us lucked out today. I can't tell you what Mike was referring to in that odd interview because I don't know. Maybe he thinks you and I conspired to commit murder together."

"Yeah, right. Having never been interviewed by even one police officer before all this, I couldn't tell you if it was odd or not."

"You want to get a bite tonight?" Tom blurted out.

The ensuing silence was deafening. I was completely taken aback. Was Tom asking me out? If he was, I had no idea what to say. He was attractive and smart, and I liked him, but the only man I could really think about, even now, was John.

After the silence had become awkwardly long, Tom said, "I get it. It's okay."

"I-I'm not sure," I stammered. "Are you asking me out on a date?"

"I guess I am," he said.

Before I could think through my response, I said, "I don't know, Tom. The coffee was great this morning, but I don't think I'm ready for dinner."

"Sure. I didn't mean to push you or anything. Take care." He disconnected abruptly and I found myself holding the dead receiver.

And then, suddenly, my feelings surprised me, and I realized I was sorry I hadn't taken him up on his offer.

Fourteen

Candace arrived at four p.m., dressed in blue jeans and an Atlanta Braves T-shirt. Her blond hair rested on her shoulders, the first time she'd worn it like that since we'd met. Without the police uniform she was one hot chick, and if fireman extraordinaire Billy Cranor didn't notice, he was an idiot.

I mentioned my idea about the guy who removed the signs. Candace knew who that was and thought talking to him was a good idea. We agreed to do so right away.

After I engaged the security system, we left through the back door and she said, "Ed Duffy is the guy's name. He's hired by the city for odd jobs—removing graffiti, cleaning up after the Little League and Fourth of July parades, stuff like that. Taking down the signs for garage sales and lost pets keeps him pretty busy."

We sped through town in her small SUV, a beat-up RAV4, and she blasted "Sweet Home Alabama" on the stereo all the way to our destination. Classic rock is great but not played loud enough that Martians can hear the music. My ears and brain were immensely grateful when we arrived at Ed's Swap Shop. The temperature had risen probably twenty degrees over the course of the day, and I shed my sweater before I got out of the Toyota.

The "shop" was actually a small one-story house desperately in need of fresh paint. The gutters sagged, and a broken window had been repaired with duct tape. Reminded me of the problem that had led me here today. That stupid broken window.

Once we passed through a rusty front gate, I realized the house was in better shape than anything else on the property. The yard overflowed with tires, lawn mowers, cement birdbaths, old bed springs and so much other decrepit stuff that we had to zigzag as if we were walking through a minefield to get to the weather-beaten front door.

Candace was far more adept at zigzagging than I was; I nearly fell twice. I decided she must do obstacle courses in her spare time. Either that or she'd made this trip many times before. She didn't bother to knock but called out, "Ed Duffy, where you at?" as we went inside.

"That you, Candy?" A man with shaggy gray hair and a full beard that reached his shirt collar stood squinting at us from behind a long glass display case. He wore overalls and a welcoming smile.

Witness Protection Program? I thought.

Candace said, "How you doing?"

"Fine, now that you're here. But who's the pretty lady with you?"

We had to meander through Ed's "merchandise" to reach him—magazines and newspapers piled as high as the ceiling, baskets filled with crocheted or embroidered linens, toys and ancient end tables and so much more.

"This here is a newcomer to Mercy," Candace said. "Jillian Hart."

"Oh," he said, still smiling, "you're that lady who killed off Flake. 'Bout time someone did what needed doing."

I felt my eyes widen. Thank goodness for Candace, who quickly said, "She did no such thing. And don't you be spreading that around town, neither."

I'd noticed her lapse into what I now understood as the "native language." If I wanted to learn how to converse in the "upstate" voice and perhaps set people at ease, I needed to pay attention to the dialect.

He lowered his gaze. "I meant no harm. Some things

need doin' is all." He looked at Candace. "You understand, don't you?"

"I sure enough do," she said. "No harm, right, Jillian?"

I smiled at Ed. "No offense taken."

Ed's features relaxed, and I realized that with all the sun damage to what little of his face I could see, he could have been fifty years old or a hundred.

"What can I do you two ladies?" he said. "I'm hoping you came to shop."

"In a way," Candace said. "Jillian, you want to explain about the signs?"

"Sure." I was surprised she handed this over to me. But then, I was the one who put up the signs in the first place. "I understand you take down signs people put up—for instance, in my case, I lost my cat and I stuck up flyers around town."

"Oh yeah, that's my job. Keeps me busy, too. And that's why you won't hear me complaining to the town council about that kinda stuff." He grinned, and it was such an infectious, happy smile I found myself letting go a little inside. Funny how you never know how wound up you are until you begin to let go.

"Do you remember taking down my flyers last Friday? They had a picture of my lost amber cat along with my name and phone number," I said.

He hooked his thumbs in his overalls, his eyes narrowed in concentration. "A lost cat, you say?"

"That's right," I said.

"Can't say as I do recall. See, I just go about my business, rip 'em down and toss 'em out," he said.

"Don't you be lying, Ed Duffy," a female voice said from behind us.

Candace and I turned. A woman who seemed to be about sixty years old stood in the doorway, her patent leather purse on one arm, her free hand on her hip. She was in full winter gear—gray wool coat, tall boots and black gloves. Her short dark hair was pulled away from her face and held in place by rhinestone-studded bobby pins.

Candace said, "Hi, Karen. Long time, no see. Karen, this is my friend Jillian." She turned to look at me. "Karen is Ed's closest, um, *friend*."

She nodded. "What Candy means is that we usually spend the night together. I assume this is our widow, Ms. Hart, the one we have all heard so much about?"

"That's me. Nice to meet you, Karen," I said.

She eyed me with an inscrutable stare that made my stomach tighten up again. Finally she said, "You are not at all what I pictured. Why, you're immensely attractive. I suppose I was expecting the devil incarnate after I heard about the murder." The smile she offered came more from her deep blue eyes than from her lips.

Is this what people in town think of me?

Candace came to my defense again. "She didn't kill anyone."

"I'm sure you are correct. She doesn't look the least bit evil." Now Karen smiled.

Ed said, "Sweet Pea, what brings you back?"

"Forgot my hat," she said. "You two ladies can surely understand why a woman might forget something in this place. I would be more accurate saying I lost my hat and I am hoping it's not been crushed under a pile of junk."

Ed whipped out a black cloche from beneath the counter. "Would this be what you're looking for, Sweet Pea?"

"You know it would. But you're not getting rid of me that easily. I seem to have arrived at precisely the correct moment." She looked at me. "God works in mysterious ways, and though I believed I came about a hat, it would seem I have arrived to keep an otherwise kind and honest man from presenting a falsehood to, of all people, a policeperson."

Candace focused on Ed. "And what falsehood would that be?"

"Why, I have no idea what Miss Karen is talking about." But his cheeks were flushed.

"Edwin Duffy, you tell the truth or I will be forced to do it for you," Karen said.

He hung his head. "Okay, okay," he said, hands held up in surrender. "I don't toss the flyers."

"There's more," Karen said. "God is offering you an opportunity to be forthright and you should honor His bidding."

"What *are* you talking about?" Ed said.

Karen gave him a stern look. "You know I am perfectly aware of this affliction of yours, Ed. What exactly *do* you 'toss'?"

He took his time answering, but at last, in barely a whisper, he said, "Nothing."

"Oh my," she cried. "I am so proud of you for speaking the truth out loud. So very proud." And with that, she practically leaped over tables and toys and came around the counter. She hugged him for what seemed a very long time while Candace and I stood and watched. I didn't know about Candace, but I was baffled.

After several kisses, which marked Ed's mouth with Karen's bright red lipstick, he turned to us. "I have the flyers. Just haven't had time to sort through and file them."

Karen offered a dismissive laugh and addressed us. "That filing system is a trunk in the back room. And when the trunk gets full, the flyers and whatever else he's gathered from people's lawns or out of ditches or what's meant for the garbage collector is transferred to a cardboard box and dated."

Ed squared his shoulders. "It is my belief that what is offered to me on the streets of Mercy is valuable, even though the city wants to throw it all out. See, you two have come searchin' for something, and I believe that's proof that I have collected an important piece of—well, I don't know, but it's something."

I cocked my head. "You know what, Ed? You might just be right."

Karen rolled her eyes. "Please do not encourage the man."

"That's not our intent," Candace said.

"Oh, sweetheart, I know that. It's just that Ed and I have been working on his problem with him collecting stuff, mostly because we need to downsize. I read all about this downsizing idea in the money magazines. When you're ready to retire, that's one of the first steps."

"Could we have a look at all the papers you've collected over the last few months?" I said.

"It's only a bunch of paper," Karen said.

"But what Ed's collected might provide a clue as to who killed Flake Wilkerson," Candace said. "Might tell us other people who've lost cats in the last few months. See, a few kitties were found in the house, and maybe somebody is sorely missing them."

"Missing them enough to kill the man?" Karen asked.

"I'm not saying that for sure," Candace explained. "But it's a place to start."

Ed turned on his amazing smile. "In that case, have at it, ladies."

The two of them led us to a hallway to the right—no easy task with a treadmill and a slew of old computer monitors in the way. We had been standing in what must have been the living room of the old house, and now we passed a kitchen on our right—at least I thought I saw a refrigerator and a stove. But this had apparently become the kitchen item collection spot. Blenders, microwaves, tables, even sheets of Formica filled the space.

To the left, however, was a tidy and usable bathroom, and up ahead a bedroom that was neat and habitable.

Karen was quick to point out that this was her doing. "The man has to have facilities and a place to lay his head when he needs a nap. You two will find later on in life that naps are quite the necessity. Ed does take his meals with me, though. That kitchen here is too much for me to deal with. And that reminds me, I need to get home and fix his supper. Ed's metabolism keeps him thin as a bed slat. He needs his meals."

She told us good-bye and left.

We'd reached the end of the hall, and Ed was dragging around an old steamer trunk stacked with file boxes. Candace hurried in to help him, and together they pushed it into the hallway, where there was actually space for us to open it.

"What time period are we looking at with these particular contents?" I asked.

Ed squinted into the room at the file boxes. "Looks like last time I filed was the end of March."

"Seven months' worth of paper?" Candace said, sounding overwhelmed already.

"Trees died and men and women labored to make this paper, Candy. Destroying it just don't seem right."

An eco-friendly hoarder. In his peculiar and obstinate way, he made sense.

He said, "You two go ahead and look for what you want. Use my bedroom if you're too cramped. Meanwhile I got all of Helen Harper's costume jewelry from her daughter. She swapped it out for a new toaster oven. Did you know Helen passed two weeks ago, Candy?"

"I did. Attended the visitation. She was a nice lady."

"She was indeed. Now, get busy. You don't want to miss your supper 'cause you're stuck here."

He went back to the front and we both sat cross-legged by the trunk. Candace released all three brass latches and lifted the lid. Papers were crammed to the brim and some fell out and scattered around us.

"Guess we should separate any lost-cat flyers from the rest," I said.

"Exactly." Candace reached in with two hands and grabbed as much as she could hold, then handed the mass of papers to me. She repeated the process, putting a pile on her lap.

The sorting took almost ninety minutes with neither of us taking time to look closely at what we had. I did notice several of my own flyers, but far fewer than I expected. Perhaps someone else was out collecting paper, too. Finally we had what we needed—information on plenty of lost cats. Candace and I then "refiled" the rest of Ed's finds, which included not only garage sale signs but Frisbees, tennis balls and even a dog leash.

We decided to take all the cat flyers to my house so we could examine them, take down names and numbers and perhaps get a feel for what had been happening to Mercy cats in the last several months. But first we needed to eat. So after thanking Ed and saying our good-byes, we went back to the car.

Candace said she didn't want to go to the Little Pig, even though she was craving slaw dogs—a regional favorite I had yet to try. Seemed any cops on duty usually went there on their break.

"Let's eat at McMurtry's Pub," she said, her RAV4 peeling around a corner and onto Main Street.

I held on for dear life and vowed to drive if we ever went out on another search-and-find mission.

She said, "The Pub is a touristy spot with a weird menu, but they have their own special recipe for sweet tea that beats about anything I've ever tasted."

Turned out the weird menu was typical pub fare, bangers and mash, fish and chips, that kind of thing. But there were also the hamburgers typical for the area, "a-plenty burgers," where the fries and onion rings were mounded so high they fell off the plate. The sweet tea sure did have something extra—but the waitress wasn't about to give up the secret, even though I asked more than once.

As we shared a trifle for dessert, Candace said, "That cat I took in is so hilarious. Cries like a baby."

I took out my phone. "That reminds me, I haven't checked on my crew in hours." Once I was connected to the cat-cam, I saw I had nothing to worry about. They were all asleep in the living room.

"My mom's keeping Boy today—that's what I call him, Boy. Didn't want to leave him alone on the very first day he's free from the likes of a mean old man like Flake Wilkerson. Those cats may have something to do with him being murdered, but I can't help thinking what if it's something else? I know the chief is looking into other things."

"What would those other things be?" I said.

"Well, there's the missing computer. I can tell you about that because you heard it was missing the day we found the body. It's a safe assumption something on the hard drive connects the killer to Wilkerson, especially since we saw no evidence of robbery. The man had several thousand dollars in a bedroom drawer."

"Wasn't the computer keyboard gone, too?" I said. "Why take—oh, I get it. Fingerprints."

She pointed her spoon at me. "That's right. Wiping down a keyboard would be tough, especially if you were in a hurry. Then there's his daughter. I can also tell you about her because when we notified her about Mr. Wilkerson, she said she was coming in from Columbia tomorrow to make the arrangements. That's probably common knowledge in this town already. Chief Baca had me make the phone call to her, and I have to say, she didn't sound all that upset that he was dead. If something like that happened to my daddy, I'd be hysterical. We need to know what she was up to around the time of the murder."

"Columbia's not that far away, right?" I scraped the edge of the trifle dish to get every morsel of whipped cream.

"No. She coulda come into town, killed off Flake and been back home by nightfall—if she had a reason to knock him off. Could be there's money involved. I haven't heard anything about the vic's finances yet."

"Bet Baca hasn't shared anything about her possible motive or alibi with you, huh?"

"No," she said, her expression morose. Candace eyed the empty trifle dish, cleaned inside the bowl with her index finger and licked away the last of our dessert.

"What's the daughter's name? Maybe I could go over there and offer my condolences. I do feel terrible about my part in all this, and she might tell me something we don't know about Mr. Wilkerson. Like why he was collecting cats."

"That's an idea. Her name is Daphne, and she didn't sound all that friendly. Maybe I'll go with you."

"Good, because the last time I went to that house—well, you know what I found."

Candace said, "And don't be mentioning this to anyone. I'm off the case and might get myself in some boiling-hot water if the chief finds out."

Back at my house a short time later, we switched from sweet tea to white wine, which helped Candace and me deal with the tedious task of writing down names and numbers off about fifty stained, wrinkled and mildewed flyers. Who knew so many cats would get themselves lost—but the pile we had went back more than six months.

We'd laid them out on my dining room table, to the joy of all four cats. At one point Merlot even stretched out on the paper-covered space between Candace and me. Cats always have to be in your business.

The tedium was interrupted when I came to a particular cat picture. I tapped the faded photo, the one a person named Dale Bartlett had added to his or her plea for help finding the lost cat Beatrice. "That's the Tonkinese we found at Wilkerson's house."

Candace was looking a little blurry-eyed anyway, and now confusion clouded her features even more. "Tonka-what? I thought we were talking about cats, not little trucks."

"Tonkinese is a cat breed," I said.

"Oh. Gotcha."

"I think that cat is with Shawn. Now that we have the owner's phone number, we can reunite them. I wonder if we'll find a flyer for the tuxedo, too," I said.

"Trucks and tuxedos? One of us has had too much wine. What in heck are you talking about?"

"Sorry. Tuxedo cats are black and white—marked, sort of like penguins. Remember, I told you about the cat that escaped the day before the murder?"

"The cat that ran off into the woods?" she said.

"Yes. The one Shawn picked up by the side of the road after we left."

"Save that for sure, because every cat is a possible lead."

"I'm not sure I even told Baca about Shawn picking up the tuxedo. Guess I'll do that tomorrow," I said.

"I never got the chance to tell him, but it is in my report," she said. "Maybe he'll begin to understand the importance of the cats if you mention it. I got the feeling he couldn't care less. Make sure you tell him you forgot and that's why you failed to mention that penguin cat."

"Tuxedo."

"Whatever. And now that I'm considering this full-disclosure idea, I definitely have to give the chief our lost-cat list tomorrow, even though he'll probably laugh me out of his office and order me back to answering phones."

"Can I copy it first?" I still had to find out about these missing cats, with or without Baca's help.

"It's your list, not mine, so of course." She paused and her expression grew worried. "But maybe there will be no laughing, Jillian. Maybe I'll be suspended for not following orders. Maybe you should keep the list to yourself."

"No. Tell him what we've done. Honesty is on our side. Let's keep it that way."

She offered a small smile. "That's exactly what my mom would say. And my mom is always right."

Fifteen

The next day I decided to tell Baca about the tuxedo cat right away. So I headed over to the police station bright and early. The visit to the chief started out pretty well. I didn't see Candace answering phones, thank God, and I waited less than a minute for Baca to wave me into his office.

I took a seat in the same chair as yesterday, his big, shiny desk between us. To my chagrin, my hands trembled. I clutched them in my lap to hide my nerves. I hadn't left here the last time in a very pleasant manner, and for some reason that made me nervous.

Before he could even ask me why I was here, I blurted, "I forgot to tell you something yesterday. I'm sorry."

His expression didn't change. He just calmly said, "And what would that be, Ms. Hart?"

"Could you call me Jillian? I'd feel a lot more comfortable if you did."

"Sure, Jillian. Now, what exactly is bothering you this morning?"

I explained about the tuxedo cat, and Baca simply smiled politely. For some reason I found this maddening.

"Say something," I said, my frustration fairly obvious.

He laughed. "How's this? I appreciate you returning after how things went down yesterday, but we already know about the black-and-white cat and have found the owner."

"Oh, did—"

Baca went on, "Shawn Cuddahee gave us all the details of your visit to Mr. Wilkerson the day before the murder. That black-and-white cat had an implanted microchip. When Shawn figured that out, he felt obliged to tell us so we could ask the local vet for help. The doc scanned the chip, and the cat is already back home."

I breathed a sigh of relief. "That's great. Did he check all the cats Mr. Wilkerson had for those microchips?"

Baca said, "Yup. That was the only one. Candy provided us with the list you two compiled from those flyers. Nice work, I'll admit. Lydia wanted Candy off the case, but I see that's not stopping her. As for you, what you've been doing is a little far afield from making quilts—that is what you do?"

His Southern charm was really cloying to me now. "Yes. For charity *and* for cats."

"Like the ones we found in Flake Wilkerson's house? Come up with any leads on how he got ahold of those?" he asked.

He was keeping up the "I'm so sweet I'd rot your teeth" act, but I got the distinct feeling the man still suspected me of something nefarious. Aside from Candace, the whole police force probably did.

"I didn't find anything in my files," I said. "But I put a business card on the vet's bulletin board months ago, and Mr. Wilkerson could have gotten my address on a visit there. Maybe he drove by and saw my cats in the window, then chose my house for a break-in."

"And stole the quilts along with the cat?" he said.

"No. He must have had them for some time. I'm certain of this because of the fabric and the patterns. I sold out of those particular quilts months ago."

"I don't understand," he said.

"When I buy fabric, I tend to use it in several quilts until all the yardage is gone. And I also choose a certain pattern—say a rail fence or an Irish chain—for a batch of cat quilts. I recognized the quilts I saw at the house as some that I made maybe seven or eight months ago."

"You didn't decide to go to the Pink House because you remembered selling those quilts to Mr. Wilkerson and for some reason wanted them back?"

"Of course not. I didn't even know he had them until the day of the murder—when I went upstairs and saw them. I went there the morning of the murder to get Syrah, not to recover quilts I didn't know Mr. Wilkerson had."

"Had to ask," he said. "Moving on, your coming here and your working with Candy on that list tells me this investigation has grabbed your interest. It would grab mine, too, if I walked into a house—even if uninvited—and found a corpse."

"I'm interested solely because of the cats. There has to be a connection to them and Mr. Wilkerson's death, right?"

"Only if his activities concerning the animals angered Shawn Cuddahee enough to make him murder the man."

"Shawn wouldn't do that. He couldn't. It must have been someone else," I said. "Maybe someone whose cat Mr. Wilkerson took."

"Big maybe. Doesn't feel right to me—killing someone over a cat. I'm considering other motives," he said. "And now I'm hoping you've thought about the danger you put yourself in as much as you've thought about the rest of this case."

"Wait a minute. You don't believe the cats had anything to do with the murder?"

"There could be a connection, but it's not exactly a motive I'd put at the top of my list," he said.

"Aren't you even going to question the person who owns the tuxedo cat, just to see how angry he was that Flake took his baby? And what about the business card idea and the list of people who put up flyers about lost cats? Why not ask them if they used the same vet? That veterinary hospital might be where Flake went to hunt for his prey."

"Prey?" he said.

"Cats to steal. The man was a mean cat thief." I felt warmth on my cheeks. Now I'd spoken ill of the dead. I hadn't meant to do that.

"Okay, I'll give you this much. If cat theft was the motive, we'll find out. But right now, it seems far-fetched. I'm not inclined to believe someone stuck a knife in Mr. Wilkerson's abdomen because he nabbed a pet. I'm not ruling it out, but I believe there's more to it than that. I'm betting on the money."

"The *money*? I get it," I said, excited now. "Mr. Wilkerson was selling those cats, wasn't he? I knew it."

"Not what I was thinking," he said quickly. He seemed flustered by letting this money angle slip. I kinda liked him better flustered, rather than all uptight and oh-so-professional.

Baca pulled a sheet of paper toward him. "Let me confirm a few things."

"But I've given a statement and—"

"This isn't about the other day." He glanced down at the paper. "According to what I've learned, you and your husband moved here less than a year ago, he died unexpectedly—a retired financial adviser, I see—and you started up this cat quilt business."

"You've got that wrong," I said. Why did he have to bring up John? He had nothing to do with this.

"What have I got wrong?" Baca said.

"I started the business *before* John's death. We both loved cats, and since I'd been quilting for years and was stuck in a boring job, John encouraged me to combine the two. And I'm so glad I did."

"I got the sequence of events incorrect. Sorry."

"But what does my husband or our past have to do with anything?" I said.

"You're new in town, so I had to do a background check. You've got no secrets that I could find. And I would think that the community is glad someone like you—who seems to be a kind and caring person, by the way—chose to move here."

Maybe he did like me, but having the police nose around in my business was unsettling, to say the least. That was what

I got for walking into a house uninvited and finding a dead man. But still, I felt even more heat on my cheeks. It was like someone had broken into my house all over again—this time my metaphorical house.

"I can tell you're upset," he said. "Please understand I'm only doing the police work the citizens of Mercy pay me to do."

"I know. It's just not much fun to be, well, *investigated*."

"There's more, but it's good news again. I found no evidence on your cell phone bill that you spoke with Mr. Wilkerson at any time. Plus, no money seemed to have changed hands between the two of you—aside from him buying those quilts, of course. And we don't have any evidence of that. My guess is he stole them when he stole your cat and you just don't remember you had them lying around."

"That's not something I would forget, Chief. He got them some other way."

"If you remember who you sold the quilts to, let me know." He sounded like he was done with me.

"I promise you'll be the first to know if I recover from my Alzheimer's anytime soon," I said.

He smiled at my lame joke. "Don't believe I'm dismissing them. It's just that those quilts could be one mystery we never solve, and it's probably not important, just an odd connection between you and Mr. Wilkerson. You'll be relieved to know we do not consider you a suspect in this murder." He stood. "Thanks for coming in, Ms.—sorry—Jillian."

I rose and took the flyer from my pocket, the one of the Tonkinese. "This is one of the cats Shawn has. You may want to call the owner so he can get his cat back. He's someone who might have been angry with Mr. Wilkerson."

He glanced at the paper. "Is this one of the people you were so anxious to have me call? As soon as the story broke, this man called us. Seems his cat had just disappeared and he wondered if it was in the Pink House. He's already picked up his cat from the Sanctuary. And before you ask, this man has a solid alibi."

"Another reason to believe this isn't about the cats?" I said.

"If it makes you feel better, I'll try to be clear: I'm not crossing stolen cats off the list of possible motives. There could be very angry owners out there, but right now we have what, the five cats found in the house? I know you have more names from the flyers you went through, but we don't have any connection between all those cats and the victim. If more evidence accumulates, I'll—"

"I get it," I said. "But perhaps this is about a cat not found in the house—maybe it's about one that *was* there and was taken away when the killer left."

Baca squinted at me, considering this. "I'll keep that idea in mind."

"You think that's implausible, I know, but if that's the case, you won't mind if I try to reunite a few owners with the pets that Wilkerson might have stolen. After all, I have the same list of possibilities that Candace gave you this morning."

His eyes darkened. Made him look all brooding in a Gothic novel sort of way. "Please don't get in my way. A brutal crime was committed, Jillian. That should scare you. I know it scares me."

"After what I've been through this past year, I'm done being scared about what life throws at me. I'll try hard not to get in your way, but I won't be sitting around, either. Cat people may have lost their friends because of this man."

He sighed. "I can't stop you—unless you interfere in my investigation. Then we call it obstruction of justice."

"I call it *finding* justice—for those cats and their owners. They were victims, too." *And*, I thought, *if I follow the cats while you're following the money, one of us might find a killer.*

He looked down and shook his head. "You and Shawn. What a pair."

Minutes later, I left the court building and headed straight for Shawn and Allison's Sanctuary. While I drove, I thought about a police officer's job and the need to prioritize. I got that. But I'd prioritized, too, and those cats were at the top of *my* list. I knew that Shawn's fingerprints were found somewhere at the scene—somewhere they shouldn't have been. Baca would never tell me about that, nor would Candace, but if I could make amends with Shawn—which I so wanted to do no matter what—maybe he'd tell me.

I made my way up the dirt driveway to the Sanctuary, the strangling kudzu vines on either side of me a healthy green and gripping onto trees and shrubs as if we hadn't had a cold snap at all. No, that stuff would seize and control every plant until a hard freeze. I could only hope Shawn wouldn't hang on to his anger that tightly.

This time Shawn rather than Allison came out to meet me. His stiff posture and unsmiling face indicated he was still very unhappy with me. I drew a deep breath and left the van.

"I sure hope you'll talk to me, Shawn. I know you didn't kill anyone. I know you could never do that."

"You threw me under the bus." His freckled fists were on his hips, his legs spread as if to stop me from going any farther.

"It wasn't like that," I said. "Should I have omitted that you had an argument with Mr. Wilkerson when they questioned me?"

"You told them that to save your own ass."

"Shawn. Look at me." I made the back-and-forth two-finger gesture for "look me straight in the eye."

He did so, though grudgingly.

I said, "They would have found out anyway. I wasn't the only person who knew you had a history with the man."

He hesitated, then said, "You did what you had to do. I get that."

"No, you don't. You're still angry, and that hurts. Please try to understand? I value your friendship—and Allison's, too. And the work you do here is so important. I respect you."

"They locked me up like a criminal on some frickin' material witness excuse. Do you have any idea what that's like?"

"It must have been awful," I said.

"Two hours might as well have been two months. I do have a temper, but I'm an honest, God-fearing man, not a killer."

I said, "I know that. Can we talk? My interest is the cats, as I'm sure yours is, too. We're on the same page, Shawn."

He still seemed uncertain, but when his shoulders slumped and his hands fell to his sides, I knew this silly standoff was over.

He waved and said, "Come on, then."

Snug, the African grey parrot, greeted me with a "Hey there" when I entered the office, and Allison must have heard us arrive because she came in from the cat area. She looked back and forth between Shawn and me as if to ask, "Is everything okay?"

"We're good," Shawn replied to her silent question.

"I am so glad." She reached out her hands and came over to me. Her hug felt as friendly and warm as the first time we'd met.

We sat around the scarred desk—so unlike Mike Baca's—the canaries singing and the spider hiding somewhere in his tank, thank goodness. I summarized my two visits with the chief, told Shawn about the flyers and the list of lost or possibly stolen cats and finished up by saying, "He claims they don't consider Mr. Wilkerson's cat thievery a solid motive. But you and I know different, don't we?"

"Damn straight we do," Shawn said. "He's never seen the desperation that I've witnessed when folks come in here looking for their lost friends. Does the man not realize someone would do murder to get their best buddy back? If not, he doesn't know squat."

"He didn't say it was impossible. He's just focusing on other things."

"Like me. Only because I looked in Wilkerson's windows. That's why they arrested me. Said there was evidence of trespassing."

"I heard they found your fingerprints. You're saying they were on the windows outside?" I said.

"Yeah. After I picked up the tuxedo, I went back to see what other cats Wilkerson might have been hiding away. Didn't see any, though. I left before Wilkerson spotted me."

Allison stood abruptly. "I think we could all use some coffee. How's about it, Shawn?"

"Yeah. Coffee." But he was looking at me, not her.

She busied herself at an ancient Mr. Coffee machine sitting on a long table near the only window.

"How'd you know about the fingerprints?" he said.

"You understand better than I do that there are no secrets in Mercy. And I got a new lesson in exactly that when I visited Baca today. They did a background check on me. Can you believe that?"

"At least they didn't arrest you. Anyway, what's this you said about a list of other people who lost cats?"

"I was hoping you could look at the flyers Candace and I collected that have pictures on them. See if you recognize any of those cats. Maybe they came through here at some point and Mr. Wilkerson somehow got hold of them."

"I guess I could do that. By the way, the Tonkinese's owner called the police when the story broke, and the tuxedo had a chip. He belongs to a rich dude named Chase Cook. What mama would ever name a son Chase is what I want to know. Fits him, though. But he loves that cat and that's all that matters."

"That makes me smile," I said.

"The pretty Tonkinese went this morning, and the Cook guy came last night. He was thrilled to be reunited with his Roscoe."

"If he loved Roscoe that much, I wonder what he did to find him. We didn't come across any flyers for missing tuxedos. Maybe I should ask the man about his cat's disappearance. Can you give me his address?"

Allison set a mug of coffee in front of her husband. "Don't you be thinking about going along with her." She looked at me. "No offense, Jillian, but we all know what happened the last time you two went visiting. Now, what do you like in your coffee?"

Sixteen

Chase Cook, it turned out, lived in a house on Mercy Lake, too, though maybe a mile from me. As I parked in his drive, I couldn't help but wonder if other cats from this area had been targeted by Flake Wilkerson. Apparently the man liked mine so much he came back to steal another one. That could mean he'd been watching me and I'd never had a clue. Goose bumps rose on my arms at the thought.

Mr. Wilkerson made his move while I was out of town, so he probably knew I'd be gone. Rolling a suitcase out to your car is a big clue that you're taking a trip. Had he been hiding outside that morning, waiting for his chance? The thought of him spying on me creeped me out. I gathered myself with a deep breath and pressed the doorbell.

The man who answered looked close to my age. He had short bleached-blond hair volumized with enough product to stock a Walgreens shelf. His smile was brightened by the whitest teeth I'd ever seen—I mean, they might glow in the dark. But he *was* smiling after I introduced myself and mentioned that both of our cats had ended up in the Pink House.

"I heard all about it from Shawn when I picked up Roscoe. You, my dear," he said, "are a fellow victim of that awful Flake Wilkerson's vile obsession. We are comrades."

Okay, I thought. *Vile* is a good word. And maybe it *was* an obsession for Wilkerson—sort of like Lydia had for Tom.

Chase Cook invited me in and led me through the foyer

to a living room with floor-to-ceiling windows overlooking the lake and elegant modern furniture. The room was decorated in blacks and whites with an occasional splash of red.

"I am so proud that Roscoe made a heroic run for his life," he said. "And I'm glad I can thank you in person. If you two hadn't gone to Flake's door—well, Roscoe might have been sent away before the man was murdered."

"Sent away?" I asked.

"He was doing *something* with his cat collection, wasn't he? Don't you think that was the reason he was taking other people's pets? To sell them off?"

"I had the same thought—either that or he was holding the cats for ransom," I said. "But the chief and I don't agree on that."

"Then he needs to get real, because it seems obvious. Have a seat. Can I get you a sparkling water? An orange juice?" Chase said.

I opted for the water and he left the room. Getting money for the cats Wilkerson stole seemed plausible to me and to this man, so why not to Baca? There had to be a plan for those animals. Or was Mr. Wilkerson simply a weirdo intent on causing other people misery?

Roscoe came bounding into the room, and all thoughts of motive and money disappeared. He was shiny and bright-eyed, and I wondered if Chase chose a black-and-white cat to match his black-and-white house. I said, "There you are, handsome," and bent to greet him.

He meandered up to the leather sofa where I'd taken a seat and rubbed against my legs, then looked up at me with golden eyes. I put my fingers down, and he rubbed his head against them and began to purr.

Chase returned with a tray and put it on the black laminate coffee table in front of me. On the tray sat an expensive-looking etched goblet, a small dish of sliced lemon and a chilled bottle of San Pellegrino. Chase poured my glass half full.

Roscoe began weaving between his owner's legs, immediately leaving black hairs all over the well-creased, impeccably clean chinos.

"He's a beautiful cat. So healthy-looking," I said.

Chase settled across from me on a white leather and chrome chair. Roscoe leaped into his lap. "He does have a luxurious coat, doesn't he? Toby and I have been lost without him. Toby is my partner—and don't worry; it's no secret that we're gay. Everyone knows. Many men keep their distance like they might catch our *affliction*, but women like yourself are warm and friendly."

"Not a problem for me," I said.

"What brings you here, Jillian? I love your name, by the way. It suits your gorgeous spicy hair, and I'll bet there's some freckles hiding under your makeup."

"There are. As to why I'm here, I have a question about Roscoe—actually about what you did when you discovered you'd lost him."

"What a day that was. Toby was working a long job— he's a contractor—built this absolutely stupendous home we share, by the way—and I was frantic. I'd come back from a meeting with one of my clients in Manhattan and found our boy gone. I couldn't reach Toby because he's always on the phone calling someone for wood or tile or sinks or whatever."

Here was someone else who'd left home and returned to find a cat missing. Was this simply a coincidence? "You thought Roscoe was with Toby?" I asked.

"Oh no. That would have been ridiculous, wouldn't it?" He stroked a contented Roscoe. "No, I thought our poor baby was sick or, God forbid, had died while I was gone. We used to spoil him with all the wrong food, and he ended up with a kidney stone, so I had reason to worry. Now he's thriving on a special diet."

"Did you call the vet to see if Roscoe was there?" I asked.

"Yes, and when he wasn't I considered calling the police.

But Toby brought me to my senses when he came home that evening. He said, 'Do you think Morris Ebeling would come over to the queer house'—that's what Morris calls it—'to investigate a lost cat?' I had to agree. We do try to limit the humiliation that Mercy sometimes offers up. This is a breathtaking place to live and we aren't about to leave, so we pick our battles."

"There was no sign anyone broke in?"

"No. Since we were once a victim of hateful vandalism—very unkind words spray-painted on our home—this place is practically a fortress now."

"Tom Stewart put in a security system for me after the first break-in, but that didn't stop Wilkerson from doing it again," I said.

"Tom installed our system as well." He flashed his sparkling smile. "Flake must have wanted your other cats in the worst way to come a second time, which means they're very special. Do you have pictures?"

For the next few minutes, Chase oohed and aahed over the photos of my trio, ones I'd taken with my cell phone. And he was so tickled when I showed him the live feed that he vowed to have Tom set up one for him as well. It was nice to talk to someone who loved his cat as much as I loved mine.

But I was getting off track, so I closed my phone and said, "How do you think Roscoe ended up with Mr. Wilkerson if there was no break-in?"

"I'll tell you what I never would say to Toby," Chase said. "I think he left the door ajar, maybe when he was taking out the trash. He has so many things going on at once, he tends to get distracted."

"I see. And what did you do to find Roscoe?"

"I put up flyers, but of course Ed took care of them in short order. Do you know Ed?"

"I do, as a matter of fact," I said.

"I thought the flyers were worth a try. Ed sometimes lets

lost-pet signs stay up for a day—or at least that's what he tells me. Nice man, very interesting person."

Interesting was an understatement. "Did you put a picture of Roscoe on your flyers?" I asked.

"I'm a graphic designer," he said. "What do you think?" He reached under the coffee table and picked up a laptop computer. Soon I was looking at the flyer he'd created, and boy, did it put mine to shame. Professional job, that was for sure.

I sipped my water, then said, "This is a beautiful photograph. When did Roscoe disappear?" I asked.

"A month ago." He glanced at what appeared to be a TAG Heuer watch. "Actually to the day."

"How many flyers?" I asked.

He offered a puzzled expression. "Just curious, but why is this important?"

"The police don't seem particularly interested in the fact that five cats were found in that house, cats that didn't all get lost like yours. The police might not care, but I do. I mean, what if there are other cats that he took, ones already sold?"

"You are passionate about this, aren't you? Why this cause?" he said.

"Maybe because my husband and I worked in the animal shelters after Katrina. I saw people reunited with their animals, and I realized how important those pets were, as if they were family members, really. And when I lost Syrah, I understood even better."

"Is your husband helping you with this . . . investigation?" Chase asked.

"No. He died ten months ago."

"I am so sorry. But you're doing what you and your husband would have done together—doing what your heart commands."

I didn't say anything for a few seconds because not only did he understand me, but he had helped me understand myself. "You speak your mind. I like that about you," I said.

"I can be quite likable," Chase said. "As long as you don't get between me and my cat."

I smiled. "Same here. Now, we were talking about Ed. I've been to the Swap Shop and I know he collected the lost-cat flyers he tore down. But I didn't see any for Roscoe."

"Really? Ed keeps such things?"

"He has a little hoarding problem," I said.

"*Little? Humongous* is a better word for it. But I have found some absolute gems in his place. I collect vinyl records. Jazz, mostly."

"I'm wondering why flyers like yours, done by a professional, didn't end up in Ed's collection. Could they have been destroyed by bad weather?"

"The weather was gorgeous—always is in September. I was so upset about losing my cat, I have to say I forgot about the signs. I accepted Toby's explanation that since Roscoe's such a friendly guy, a neighbor probably took him in. But no one came by or called to tell me that they'd found him."

Why were there no Roscoe flyers in my pile?

"What are you thinking, Jillian?"

"I'm wondering if Flake Wilkerson saw your flyers, took them down so no one else would know Roscoe was missing and went looking for him. Cats stay pretty close to home when they get out like Roscoe did. They have something like feline GPS, I've read. He was probably near your house, exploring the neighborhood, and Mr. Wilkerson found him before you did."

"And you'll take cat trivia for one thousand," Chase said with a laugh. "Very clever of you to think this through. That could be what happened, I suppose. Flake always struck me as capable of the most devious of behaviors, and cat stalking might be among them."

"You knew him?"

"Oh yes. Ran into him all the time at Belle's. But you know,

I haven't seen him there in some time." He stroked Roscoe lovingly. "And I won't be seeing him anymore, will I?"

He didn't smile, but I had the feeling he wanted to. I left Chase's house shortly afterward, even though he offered to prepare me a "lunch to die for." Not exactly the greatest choice of phrase, considering the murder.

I wanted to get to Belle's Beans in the worst way. If Chase had met Mr. Wilkerson there, other people must have, too. Learning about a dead man might help me figure out how the stolen cats might have led to his murder.

Plus, I thought as I drove into town, *this new piece of information Chase provided is interesting*. I mean, I had a stack of flyers—but how many *didn't* I have? Did Wilkerson take down flyers so he could stalk his prey in the Mercy neighborhoods? Improbable, but possible.

If I could get inside the Pink House again, maybe I could prove that Wilkerson was collecting lost flyers before Ed ever got to them. When I thought more about this, I decided holding cats for ransom would have been risky. I mean, if this had been going on for a long time, someone surely would have reported Mr. Wilkerson to the police. Trying to organize my thoughts was giving me a headache. Once I talked to Candace, perhaps I would be able to think more clearly, because gosh, I was confused. I needed schooling, a class in Detecting 101, not just a strong belief in my own theory.

I parked in a spot near the café and went inside. Since Belle's Beans offered wrapped deli sandwiches, I grabbed a ham and cheese from the cooler to go with my large latte. With the limited table space, I had to take a spot with someone else who'd stopped in for lunch.

All the customers except one were twosomes or threesomes, so I chose a woman reading a paperback and sipping on a large coffee. I asked if she'd mind if I joined her.

"Please do. I'm Marian Mae Temple, by the way." She smiled politely, and maybe I was paranoid, but I had the feeling she knew about my infamous recent past.

"I'm Jillian Hart and I'm guessing you've heard about me." I unwrapped the sandwich and lifted the bread for a peek. Wilted lettuce and way too much mayo. But I hadn't really come here to eat. I'd come here to find out what people thought of the murder victim.

Marian Mae blushed. "A little hard not to hear things." She was fortyish, with highlighted ash blond hair, perfect makeup and a French manicure. The word *classy* came to mind.

"Guess that will be my Mercy claim to fame for as long as I live here—I found a dead man." I tried to sound light and friendly. But inside I felt anxious, even before I'd had a sip of my high-octane coffee. Why did I ever think I could cozy up and get answers just like that? I felt like a weasel.

"This murder news will all pass sooner than you think," she said. "I understand you're a widow. Such a sad thing. I'd guess you're not much older than me."

I said, "I'm doing fine. I like it here and I'm trying to make a new, independent life for myself, but I won't say it's been easy."

"I parted ways with my husband through divorce, not death, but you do grieve even after an unpleasant split," she said.

"I suppose you do. And I am so concerned for Mr. Wilkerson's family and their tragedy. What an awful way to lose someone," I said.

"I'm sure," she replied.

I sensed her discomfort at once. Fearing that she would close down on me, I said, "Did you know him?"

"Everyone knew him," she answered.

"He came in here quite a bit, I hear," I said.

"That's true. Most of the town does." She took an interest in her lightened coffee by using the wooden stir stick to mix in more thoroughly what looked like cinnamon.

"He wasn't a friend or anything, though? I only ask because, well, I found him dead and I feel this odd connection to him. I'm interested to know what he was like,

besides unpleasant—which is about all I've heard, to tell
the truth."

"We were . . . acquaintances. He would come and sit with
me on occasion. He could be nice, and not to sound like I'm
flattering myself, but I got the feeling he wanted to be more
than friends. That, of course, was out of the question."

"Did he ever talk about his cats? Having been inside the
house, I know he had quite a few," I said.

"Like the one he stole from you?" she asked, one art-
fully penciled brow raised.

"Yes. His name is Syrah. He's an Abyssinian and I'm so
happy to have him home."

She smiled and this time I saw genuine warmth in her
features. "You've had a difficult time. The comfort of a beloved pet is truly remarkable, isn't it? I'm a cat person myself, so I understand."

Emotion swelled into my throat. Why did this happen
after a mere hint of kindness from a stranger? "Cats are
special in so many ways. But as for Mr. Wilkerson—what
else can you tell me about him?"

"Do you truly want to explore that man's character? In
my opinion, he was a dark, brooding, unhappy man."

"And you say this because . . . ?"

"We talked occasionally—like I'm doing with you right
now. He had a daughter, I think. But never once did he
bring up those cats. I was so surprised to read about them
in the newspaper."

"Because he didn't seem the type to have pets or—"

She rested a hand on my forearm. "Listen, I understand
your curiosity, but I'd prefer we talk about you. Aside from
this awful murder, do you like living in Mercy?"

"Yes. I never realized how soothing it would be to live
by the water. Sometimes I hear lapping against the dock or
rain splatting on the lake and it calms me almost at once."

We continued to make small talk for a few minutes, and
then Marian Mae said she had an appointment and left.

I lifted the bread and took another glance at the sandwich innards. The soggy ham and cheese looked no better than the first time, but I took a bite because I was hungry enough to try it. Not as bad as it looked. I ate slowly, hoping Belle would come in. She seemed the person most likely to offer up something about Flake Wilkerson, anything to help me understand what made the man tick.

Thanks to Chase, I realized I needed to keep my focus on learning why Mr. Wilkerson was obsessed with felines, especially since I couldn't picture him as a true cat lover. And yet he stole cats. Maybe the chief and I were on the same path after all—this was about cats and money. But there had to be more.

The familiar tinkle that sounded every time the door opened made me glance that way, and this time someone I recognized came in and walked up to the Belle of the Day taking orders.

Lydia wore tight black jeans and a cherry red tunic-style sweater. I couldn't see her shoes from where I sat, but she seemed especially tall today. Could the stilettos get any higher than what I'd seen her in before? Or was it the teased hair piled and wrapped like a turban? Had to be the hair.

She caught me staring and actually smiled. That was a surprise after the way she'd behaved yesterday. Once the Belle of the Day handed her a whipped-cream concoction, Lydia came over and sat down.

"Nice to see you under more acceptable circumstances, Jillian," she said.

I blinked. "What do you mean?"

"Tom's not with you—and that's excellent. If you keep reminding yourself that he belongs to me, we can be best buddies. All you have to do is keep your distance from him."

"He's just a friend," I said.

"I saw the way he looked at you. You're ruining my game and we can't have that, can we?" She played with the straw in her drink.

"No. Certainly not." From what I'd witnessed yesterday, I preferred not to get on her bad side and therefore wasn't about to argue with anything she said. This lady was a little wacko. I felt sorry for Tom. How long had he been dealing with this situation?

"Know what my important duties are for this case?" she said sarcastically. "I get to do things like supervise Candace."

"I'm not sure I understand," I said.

"Candace wanted to take samples of all the cat hairs she could find at the Pink House and Baca allowed it. He's backpedaling after he agreed to take her off the case, if you ask me. He does seem to like her, and you know what that leads to."

"What *does* that lead to?" I said.

"With him and me, it led to plenty. And now I'm shoved off the biggest case ever because I dumped him. Ego. It's all about ego with him."

"But that's not what he told me. He said—"

"You are so naive," Lydia cut in. "I should be running this show, but I've been kicked down to go-between."

"You're a go-between? Because you're working with Candace? I'm still not sure I understand."

"Besides watching Candace pull hair-laden pieces of tape off rugs and furniture—which is the forensic equivalent of watching paint dry, let me tell you—I was also instructed to arrange for the county forensics unit to return for a last run-through to make sure they didn't miss anything before the daughter gets into town. Between the unit folks and Candace, I did a lot of sitting around." She stuck out one leg. "Look at my pants. You ever seen so much cat hair in your life?"

I reached for my bag on the chair next to me and removed a mini pet hair roller. "Be my guest."

Lydia looked at it for a moment. "Isn't this the cutest thing ever? Purse size." She began rolling it on her pants.

"Did I hear you mention Flake Wilkerson's daughter?"

I'd already heard about her, but maybe Lydia's anger at her ex-boyfriend would keep her talking.

"Yup. She's expected this afternoon. Baca wanted all the tags, the fingerprint dust and the blood gone. Which was a job and a half, thank you very much. You see me wearing a badge that says CLEANUP CREW? *No* would be the answer. Anyhow, he thinks he's a hero or something, making the world all bright and beautiful for Daphne What's-Her-Name. Or maybe he's thinking about hitting on her since she'll probably be getting plenty of money."

There it was again. *The money.* Was that the money Baca had been referring to? I sipped my coffee and tried to sound nonchalant when I said, "Was Mr. Wilkerson well-off?"

Lydia tore off a hair-filled sticky sheet and used the pet roller again on her pants. "Not certain about that, but we did find one promising insurance policy the day of the murder, with the daughter as the beneficiary. As for anything more? Well, I'm not in charge, so I don't know if Mr. Wilkerson even had a will. All I know is the daughter's coming to town."

"She does have to make funeral arrangements—or someone does, right?" I said.

"Yeah, yeah, yeah. Guess I'm being cynical thinking she's coming to see how much cold hard cash she'll walk away with." She balled up the used roller tape. "But if I had a say, which I do not, I'd be finding out where that young woman was two days ago. I'd want her to account for every minute."

Lydia stood and looked down at her pants. "You are a savior. Good as new." She looked me straight in the eye and said, "Let me give you a piece of advice. I understand that you're not just being small-town curious with all your questions. Maybe you and Tom want to play detective to-gether. But getting involved in this hateful business might not be good for your health. Especially if you're tangled up with Tom. He's mine." She pointed a glittery finger at me. "Don't you forget it, neither."

She pushed in her stool, smiled and handed me back my

roller. Then she walked away, high heels clicking on the tile. She sipped on that milk shake disguised as coffee all the way out the door.

Whoa, I thought. *Did she just threaten me? Or was she simply talking about chasing after murderers?* Maybe Candace could help me understand, but it would have to wait until she was off her shift. Knowing I had enough quilt orders to keep me busy until later today, I put the roller back in my bag and was preparing to leave, but then the real Belle came in.

Maybe, I thought, *here is someone who truly knew Mr. Wilkerson and can portray him as more than the one-dimensional man everyone else makes him out to be*.

Belle spotted me at once and called, "Sit tight. I'll be right over to chat, pretty lady."

After the Belle of the Day prepared her coffee, as well as a repeat of my own latte, she joined me.

She set the coffee in front of me and smiled. "I could say, 'Look what the cat dragged in,' but I wouldn't want you to take my joke wrong. Hope a coffee on the house will cheer you up. You've had your share of sorry luck lately, haven't you?"

Not a white hair was out of place, but oh my God, would anyone ever tell her about the lipstick problem? She'd applied the stuff past her bottom lip by a good quarter inch.

"It's been an unsettling few days," I said. "But I do have my Syrah back. Not that I wanted anyone to die to make that happen."

"Of course you didn't. And I'll slap silly anyone who dares to say as much."

I smiled. I was sure she would.

She went on, saying, "We've had very few violent deaths in Mercy that I can remember, so tell me all about it. Was it just sickeningly awful?"

"That about sums it up," I said.

She rested her elbows on the table and her chin on her fists. "I want details."

This was how the grapevine worked. And if I wanted to be a part of it ... well, no one told me *not* to say anything about the murder. I related the events of that terrible day, making sure to stick to what I saw and heard firsthand. The only thing I said about Shawn was that he'd picked up the remaining cats. He didn't need me contributing to his reputation as a hothead, and that might happen if I shared details of the day before the murder.

When I'd finished, I said, "I understand Flake Wilkerson came here often."

"He did. Not that I was always present, mind you, but I heard. He was always arguing with the men and I heard tell he and Shawn Cuddahee almost came to blows one time. I woulda kicked the two of them down the street if I'd been here. Anyway, when I *was* here, Flake went out of his way to make conversation. He wasn't good at conversation, though. Not a Southern gentleman at all, our Flake."

I said, "But he tried to be nice to you?"

"Tried and failed," she said. "Your true spirit always comes through. And his spirit was troubled, maybe damaged by some long-ago injury. You never know what people are hiding."

I stirred my coffee for a second. "What did Mr. Wilkerson talk about?"

"The weather. Road construction. Gas prices. All the boring stuff old men bring up when they don't know what to say. I'm a widow and he knew as much. I had the feeling he wanted to inquire about me, ask me on a date. Do the young people still call them dates? Anyway, I am most certainly glad he didn't."

"I understand from Chase Cook that Mr. Wilkerson quit coming in here after Chase's cat, Roscoe, disappeared. Since we know Wilkerson had Roscoe, maybe that was no accident."

"Oh my. I had no idea Flake took Roscoe. That's despicable. Bless his heart, Chase was sick with worry when his cat disappeared."

"Roscoe's home now, safe and sound," I said.

She smiled broadly, making the lipstick mistake all the more prominent. "Wonderful news. But though Flake may have stopped coming in at the same time as Chase did, he still showed up and drank his large black coffees until the day before he died. You know, some folks should not drink coffee. Makes 'em downright spiteful."

"Coming here was part of Mr. Wilkerson's daily routine?" I asked.

She nodded. "Same as for lots of folks. Hope to see you here on a regular basis as well."

"I'm already a regular," I said with a laugh. "You have that bulletin board over there, and I recall you saying I could put up Syrah's picture. Did Flake ever take an interest in that board?"

Her eyes widened. "Oh my precious Jesus. What did that man do? Get information from my establishment and then steal cats he'd learned about?"

"I didn't mean to upset you, but yes, that's what I was thinking." A little lipstick problem didn't mean Belle wasn't a bright, perceptive woman.

"Oh my. Very troubling," she said.

"Please don't worry about information coming from the worst wannabe detective in the world," I said.

"You don't understand. When my cat disappeared, I put her picture up there." Her eyes brimmed with tears. "Do you think he took Java?"

"Oh my gosh. You lost a kitten, right?"

"Yes. She was only six months old." The color seeped from Belle's skin, leaving behind garish circles of coral blush on her cheekbones. "They didn't find any cat bodies in that wicked man's house, did they?"

"No. I promise. Not a one. What kind of cat was she?" I said.

"A brown Persian. Just like coffee. That's why I called her Java." A few tears trickled down her cheeks.

A brown Persian? Like the one at my house?

"Let me show you something," I said.

"Show me what?"

"I have what's called a cat-cam—a video feed connected to a camera at home. You can see my living room in real time." Too late I realized that if the cat Shawn gave me to care for wasn't Belle's, she would be so disappointed.

Belle got down from her stool and stared over my shoulder. She said, "Why am I looking at your home?"

"I want you to see something, but the one time I need them to be sleeping in the living room, they aren't there." I turned and looked at Belle. "Do you have time for a trip to my house?"

Seventeen

Good thing the drive to my house wasn't long. Belle and I had taken my car, and after I told her I might—and I emphasized the word *might*—have her kitten, she was absolutely giddy with excitement.

That meant she talked nonstop, saying things like, "He had my Java the whole time?" and "I was nothing but kind to that awful man." Finally she said, "Do your cats have 'special powers'?"

I was focused on pulling into the driveway, so it took a second for my brain to catch up. I decided I couldn't have heard right.

"Huh?" I said.

"Have your cats told you what it was like for Java in that man's house?"

My eyes widened. Though Belle seemed like a kind Southern grandmother, there was plenty I didn't know about her. Stress *will* reveal much about character.

"They rarely talk to me," I said with a small laugh. But I was thinking that little chocolate Persian better belong to Belle or the next thing I knew we'd be sitting down for a kitty séance.

Once we got inside, the official greeter was Merlot. Belle immediately knelt and extended a hand, but she was looking beyond him, waiting for her own cat to appear.

"Come on into the living room and—"

The Persian made her entrance into the foyer and Belle

clutched her chest, her skin the color of Elmer's Glue. I thought I might have to do CPR on the poor woman right here.

"My baby. Oh, my sweet baby. Where have you been?" she said.

Another cat mystery solved, I thought with a smile.

The fluffy little munchkin walked up to Belle and planted herself sideways against the woman's bony, aging knees, her back arched, her bushy tail in the air.

Belle carefully picked up the cat and rose. "You found her. How can I ever thank you?" There were tears of happiness streaming down her face.

"You're sure this is Java?"

"Of course." She pointed at the cat's face. "See the dark stripes between her nose and the light hair around her ears? This is my Java."

"Let's go into the living room, okay?" I said. "I need to call Candace, see if she can come over."

"Why?" Belle said, one arthritic hand stroking Java's cheek.

"Your kitten was found in a murdered man's house. The police need to know that there's another happy cat owner in town. All the cats in the house were originally considered to be evidence, and Candace keeps pounding into my head that we have to pay close attention to evidence. That means giving her a heads-up about Java."

"Oh. I understand. But she won't take her away from me, right?"

"Why would she? Two other cats—or three if you count mine—are already back with their owners. But the police still might want to talk to you." From what Lydia said, it sounded like Candace was at least peripherally involved in the investigation again, so I was glad I could phone her and not Baca.

I led Belle, who was clinging to Java for dear life, into my living room and she settled on the sofa—which seemed perfectly fine by Java. She was happy to be reunited with

Belle and vice versa. I walked around the counter and into the kitchen, slipped my phone from my jeans pocket and dialed Candace. "Hi," I said.

"Hi back. What's up?" she said.

"Do you have time to stop by my house?" I said. "The brown Persian belongs to Belle."

"*What?* How did you figure that out?"

"Talking in this town will get you everywhere," I said. "Can you come?"

"Maybe. Morris just went into Belle's Beans to get a slice of cake—cake is his best friend. I could tell him to eat it there, that I have an errand to run for my mom."

"Great." I closed the phone and went back to the living room. "Candace won't be long," I said. "In the meantime, why don't we have a glass of sweet tea? Unless you want more coffee, of course."

"All I want is to take darling Java home. I still have her little pink bed and all her toys. I guess God knew Java would come home and that's why He wouldn't let me touch her things."

Pretty soon my entire crew joined us, curious to meet yet another new person. There'd been plenty of traffic in this house lately—more than in the last ten months combined.

Five minutes later an elated Belle and a purring Java followed me as I went to let Candace in.

When she entered, Candace said, "Hi, Belle. What you got there?"

"Jillian found my kitten," Belle said. "Do you know if Flake had Java the whole time?"

"Um," Candace said, "we're not completely sure. But I'd like to talk to you about her disappearance, if that's okay?"

We all walked back into the living room, where Merlot chose to watch over Belle and Java. Maine coons are a lot like dogs in that way—always on the lookout when tension or excitement is in the air. My other two cats decided they needed their beauty rest more than visiting time and went off down the hall.

I offered sweet tea again, and this time Belle took me up on the offer. Candace followed me to the refrigerator. Since there were no walls separating us from Belle, Candace grabbed a magnetic notepad and pencil off the fridge door and scribbled, "You should have phoned me the minute you had a clue about this kitten."

I mouthed "sorry" and poured the tea.

Once we were all settled with our drinks, Candace quizzed Belle about the specifics of when and how Java had disappeared. She got the same information I did: an open door and the belief that the cat left on her own.

Belle said, "I must say that it is extremely disappointing to learn Java was stolen. I had never been anything but kind to Flake, and then he goes and takes my cat. What did he intend to do with her?"

"Don't know," Candace said. "That's what we're trying to figure out. I take it Wilkerson knew about Java?"

"Most certainly. You know I never met a stranger and I showed pictures to everyone I knew—even you."

"You did?" Candace said.

"Young people," Belle said, shaking her head. "You don't pay attention to anything but television and tabloids. You might have been the one to bring me here to reunite with Java if you'd been paying attention." Belle closed her eyes tightly, apparently fighting tears. "Seniors talk and no one listens. It's a sad thing."

"I'm sorry, Belle," Candace said. "You're absolutely right."

"And I'm sorry for running my mouth. Free coffee for both of you next time you come in, okay?"

"That's sweet," I said, "but I didn't do much. I was just looking for my cat and found Java, too."

"Very brave of you, young woman. Very brave. Chase has Roscoe thanks to you, and now I have Java."

"I have another question. It's something we're asking everyone we interview," Candace said. "Where were you last Sunday morning?"

"I don't even remember what I had for breakfast, much less what I was doing several days ago." But when Candace kept staring at her, she got more serious. "I guess I did some baking . . . always make cakes for the shop on Sundays. Other than that, I'd have to think on this to come up with specific times."

"Good," said Candace. "Think on it. Maybe you'll recall something someone said that might relate to the crime. You talk to plenty of folks, that's for sure. The more information we have, the better we can handle this investigation."

"You've never had to ask me these sort of questions, have you, Candy?" Belle said. "Must be hard for a sweet girl like you to be tough on the town folks."

Candace laughed. "Some folks make it darn easy to be tough—but you're right. I would never want to offend you."

"I am a sensitive sort, but I know you're a sweetheart," Belle said.

"Would you mind if I called Chief Baca to make sure it's okay if you take Java home? All the cats we found in the house are evidence."

"That's what Jillian said, but Java's a living, breathing animal, not a piece of property."

"I know. Don't get me wrong," Candace said. "Let me call and I'm sure he'll allow you to take Java home." She stood, took her cell phone from her police belt and beat a hasty retreat into the foyer and out of earshot.

Belle said, "I am trying my hardest to cooperate, but I want to take Java home right now."

"I'm sorry, Belle. Candace is doing her job." All of a sudden I'd been thrust into the role of "good cop." But it wasn't a stretch—I couldn't picture Belle sticking a knife in anything other than a piece of cheesecake.

"I suppose she's having trouble wearing her police hat and her friend hat at the same time," Belle said, turning her attention back to Java. "She looks beautiful—none the worse for wear. But how exactly did she end up with you?"

"Remember I told you that Shawn took Java and those other cats from the Pink House? Well, he didn't have room at the Sanctuary for all of them, so he brought her here."

Belle thunked her forehead with her palm. "That's right. Since I've just had this wonderful shock, my brains are a little scrambled."

"You can thank Shawn for how pretty she looks and how nice she smells. I am no cat groomer."

Belle laughed. "I'll thank him next time I see him. But this police business is disturbing. I—"

Candace came back into the room and said, "Chief gave the okay, Belle."

"Wonderful." Belle looked at me. "Can you take us back to my car?"

"I'd be glad to do that," Candace said. "I dropped Morris off at Belle's Beans, since he had a hankering for that red velvet cake you always have in the dessert case."

Belle smiled. "That's my granny's recipe—older than I am, if you can imagine."

As they left, Candace lagged behind and whispered, "I'll call you."

While I waited for her call, I worked hard to keep my mind off the case. I'd never thought after what I'd gone through since John's death that my emotions would come alive for anything again—but it was happening. I cared about these cats and wanted to find out what had happened to them.

I spent hours piecing quilts and listening to the Beatles on my iPod while waiting anxiously for Candace's phone call. At least the music drowned out my thoughts about murder and stolen pets, and my work soothed me as it always did.

When Candace finally contacted me, it was well past nine p.m. She explained she'd had to work overtime. I told her about the other developments prior to figuring out that the Persian belonged to Belle—about Chase and his cat, the idea I had about the cat flyers, my chat with Lydia and my thought that the woman might have actually threatened me. But I didn't get any information from Candace when I asked her what Baca said about Java belonging to Belle. She simply told me to be ready for a trip to the Pink House in the morning.

What would we be doing there? Looking for cat flyers? Or did Candace have something else in mind?

Eighteen

Candace arrived about ten a.m.—it was her day off—and she looked cranky and tired. Though I didn't want another adventurous trek in her RAV4, I was afraid that if I suggested I drive it might agitate her even more, so I kept my mouth shut. I noticed she was wearing a Sam Houston State University sweatshirt and thought asking her about that would be safe territory.

After I was sitting beside her, braced for another Indy-style race to our destination, I said, "I like your sweatshirt. That college is north of my old stomping grounds in Texas."

"Went to a three-day workshop there. They have an awesome criminal justice school. I took a forensics course, but now that you've brought that up, I'm pissed off all over again. Why do I have to practically beg to use what I've learned?"

Pissed off all over again? My guess was she woke up that way and nothing had changed. "Baca still being stubborn?" I said.

"He's saying this is a crime about money, not some silly cats," she said.

"Baca mentioned money when he talked to me too, and then Lydia brought up a life insurance policy. Is that the money he's talking about?"

"That Lydia. She doesn't know how to keep her mouth shut." This further cause for irritation made Candace press her foot down on the gas even harder, and I closed my eyes, sure that we'd end up wrapped around a telephone pole.

Hoping to calm her, I said, "You can be sure I won't be saying anything to anyone about the money. But Mr. Wilkerson could have been getting money from cat sales, right?"

"It's possible. But Baca wouldn't listen to me when I said this looked like a crime of passion, not a premeditated murder by someone cold and calculating. Wilkerson made Shawn angry enough to spit nails, and who's to say he didn't make someone else that mad?"

"He upset me, that's for sure," I said. "Not angry enough to kill him, but everyone has their own breaking point. What if someone went to the Pink House to get their cat back, just as I did?" And then I had another idea. "And what if that person became incensed when he or she realized their pet was already gone?"

"I had the same thought. The killer used a knife from the kitchen, for Pete's sake. Knives come out of the drawer when someone's in a rage. I've been out on enough domestic calls to know that much. That has to be it. Flake Wilkerson stole the wrong person's cat—someone who had a major temper failure."

Candace was really getting worked up.

"You're tired, aren't you?" I said.

"Tired of being treated like I don't know squat," she said.

"By the chief?" I asked.

"By Lydia mostly. The chief and I are cool, but he's not handing me any assignments directly related to the case aside from those evidence samples I took at the Pink House."

"Is that why we're heading there this morning? To take more samples?"

"Not exactly. We're simply paying a friendly visit to Wilkerson's daughter, like you and I discussed. She got in last night."

"She knows we're coming?" I said.

"Not really."

Candace made a sharp right onto the dirt road leading to the Pink House, and I nearly cracked my head on the passenger window on the rebound. "The chief interviewed Daphne last night, so we're not interfering with the investigation. Let's start out by saying you just want to talk to her, extend your condolences, and I'm along for the ride. She's the life insurance beneficiary, so the chief probably suspects her, but you and I don't suspect her of anything. We have no reason to, right?"

"I'll be able to respond after I recover from my broken neck," I said.

She looked confused. "What?"

"Never mind," I said.

But then she slammed to a stop behind an ancient Cadillac Seville sitting in the driveway, and this time the seat belt nearly snapped my collarbone as it tightened in response to the sudden braking.

That does it. She never drives me anywhere again.

Candace slid from behind the wheel, totally oblivious.

Rubbing my surely bruised shoulder, I got out of the car, too. Candace stopped behind the Cadillac, took a small notebook from her jeans pocket and scribbled down the tag number.

When she was done, she said, "Come on, let's go meet Daphne so you can tell her how sorry you are you walked into this house and found her father dead."

"Me? I have to start the conversation?" I said.

"Yes." She'd gone into full cop mode. And here I thought this was supposed to be a friendly visit.

"But you know how to do this stuff," I said, realizing I sounded like I was whining. I hate whining.

"You are a lot nicer than I am. She'll like you." She was walking toward the front door.

Why did I have to be the front woman? Maybe because Daphne—I didn't even know her last name; was it

Wilkerson?—would learn soon enough that Candace was a police officer? If Candace wasn't forthright, she could get in hot water again. Whereas I could say anything I wanted. Oh brother. I was beginning to think like Candace.

Though I expected a weeping, overwrought woman to answer the door, that wasn't my first impression. Daphne, petite and maybe mid-thirties, had an unlit cigarette clinging to her upper lip, wore an army green Henley and had long, dark frizzy hair. Her features were hard, her jaw tight.

"The estate sale isn't until next week. Come back then." She started to close the door.

Candace stuck her foot out and stopped this from happening. "Sorry to disturb you, but we're not here about that. I'm Candace and this is Jillian. We came to offer our condolences about your father." At least she sounded a lot kinder to her than she'd been with me all morning. Candace could do nice when she wanted to.

"Did he owe you money? Owe you a cat? What?" The cigarette bobbed as Daphne spoke, and hung precariously from her lip.

Candace gestured my way. "Jillian found your father that morning. She'd like to talk to you."

And what the heck am I supposed to say? I smiled and nodded as if this were my mission in life, to heal grieving hearts.

"If she's the one that found that bastard dead, she might need a priest for a future exorcism because his evil soul could have crawled inside her. Now, if you'll excuse me?" Again she started to close the door, but this time Candace grabbed it.

"We'd like a few minutes of your time," Candace said.

I nodded again, smiling like the fool I felt. But her calling Mr. Wilkerson a bastard at least calmed me a little. No love lost between Daphne and her father might make this easier.

"Are you from some church?" Daphne looked us both

up and down. "You're probably hiding a sheet cake or casserole somewhere, aren't you?"

"No. Jillian simply wants to answer any questions you might have," Candace said. "Just a few minutes of your time? Please?"

"Questions? What kind of questions?" she said.

I said, "I-I've been so upset since I found your father, and I thought maybe if I talked to you, then—"

"What do I look like, your shrink?" she said.

"S-sorry," I said. Gosh, I wanted to leave in the worst way. Why did Candace expect Daphne would tell us anything?

But perhaps I'd misjudged Mr. Wilkerson's daughter—I now noticed a hint of guilt in her eyes. She said, "Oh hell, why not come in and bother me? It's not like I've got anything else to do—aside from arranging a cremation and cleaning out this ridiculously huge house."

She released her hold on the door, turned and walked through that once beautiful wood-graced foyer. The uncared-for scarred oak floor, the curving banister, the window seat at the landing before the stairs turned—all of it must have once been magnificent, years ago. Why had the place fallen into such disrepair? Was Wilkerson obsessed with cats because he needed the money he would get from their sale?

As Daphne led us into the parlor area where I'd been forced to sit for hours the day of the murder, I glanced back again at the broad stairs I'd raced up as I followed the sounds of those poor trapped cats.

I expected to smell smoke from her cigarettes, but the musty odors of age and neglect overrode everything. It was stronger than the other day, perhaps because Daphne had been emptying cupboards and closets and filling boxes. At least a half dozen sat in the dining room beyond, three of them right on the spot where her father's body had lain.

I took the same seat as the day of the murder, and Candace sat beside me on the old settee.

Daphne stood looking down at us, hands on her hips.

"Out with it, whatever it is," she said. "Say your piece. I'm busy."

"I—I—" But the words wouldn't come.

Candace rested a hand on my shoulder. "She's having a hard time. We thought coming here would help her feel better about finding your father, well . . . lying there and—"

"Stuck like the pig he was?" Daphne looked at me. "Don't lose any sleep over it, honey. Is that all?"

But Candace wasn't about to let her shove us back out the door. "Jillian, ask her. Go ahead."

I looked at Candace, completely confused. "You mean about the . . . ?" *About the what?* I had no idea. I wondered if my new friend had gone off the deep end.

"Go ahead, you can say it. Tell her about your cat." Candace moved her brows and eyes in Daphne's direction, instructing me to go ahead.

And then I got it. "Yes. My cat," I said. "Your father stole my cat, and I was wondering if you had any idea why he might do that?"

Candace's shoulder was touching mine and I felt her relax a little.

"Oh, poor baby. He stole your cat, did he? Well, guess what? He stole mine, too." She looked at Candace. "Do you have a cat?"

"Not really," she said. "I'm—"

"If you did have one, he would have stolen yours, too. That's what he did. Took things people loved." The cigarette had held strong until now, but when she was finished speaking, the thing fell to the floor. She knelt, picked it up and flung it away from her. It didn't go far.

When she looked back at us, her eyes were bright with tears.

Quietly I said, "What kind of cat did you have?"

Daphne's breathing had sped up, and she took a few seconds before speaking. "What are you *really* doing here?"

"I'm trying to find answers." A little truth wouldn't hurt—in fact, I believed this woman needed some truth.

"Why do you care? I understand from the police you got your cat back. See? I know more about you than you know about me." She took a slender silver cigarette case from her jeans pocket and jabbed another white-filtered cancer stick between her lips.

"We've learned a bit about all the cats found here. Did you know your father broke a window and got into my house?" I said.

"Again, no surprise. He was good at breaking things." She began pacing in front of us.

Like your heart, I thought. "You said he stole your cat, too. Can you tell me about that?" Maybe the exotic short-hair or the Siamese belonged to her. If so, then almost all the cats we'd found would be accounted for.

Daphne didn't reply. She kept walking back and forth, apparently lost in thought.

"I have three cats," I said. "My husband named them all for different wines. We used to love to drink wine in the evening."

"Used to?" Daphne's gaze was on her feet, her combat-style boots clunking on the floor.

"My husband died. We all miss him—the cats and me."

The sound of the clock chiming the half hour broke the subsequent silence.

Daphne said, "I am so tired of that stupid clock. Either of you have a clue how to shut it up? There's no plug to pull."

Candace stood. "I can manage that. My mee-maw had a grandfather clock. Let me see what I can do."

Daphne pointed left. "It's in the living room."

I started to ask Daphne about her cat again, but she spoke first. "Did you love your husband?"

"Very much," I said.

"Is it easier to get over someone dying when you love them?" She removed the cigarette and sat on a straight-back upholstered chair across from me.

"I don't know. Are you asking because you didn't love your father?"

She was rolling the cigarette between her thumb and fingers and seemed a million miles away. "I never thought I loved him. He was a horrible man."

"How was he horrible?" I asked.

She looked at me then. "He never cared about anyone but himself. No one was good enough, especially my mom and me. How do you love someone like that?"

"Better question is how do you grieve for them when they're gone?" I said.

"There you go."

"He was your father and he's dead. You were connected enough—maybe merely by pain—to come here. To me, that means you have unfinished business."

"You sure some church didn't send you?" she asked. But the harsh tone was now subdued. "I mean, I'm not against religion or anything, but this was a house of hatred and I tried not to visit here much after my father bought it."

"So you didn't grow up here?" I said.

"No. I didn't even grow up in this town. He moved here after my mother died. Bought the place as an investment. As you may have noticed, he didn't exactly take care of that investment."

"It must have been beautiful once. Could be again," I said.

"Do you have another agenda?" she said. "Did the neighborhood improvement people send you to convince me to spruce the place up?"

"No one sent me. And by the way, this is your house now and if you need that cigarette, then—"

"I quit ten years ago," she said. "But when I learned I had to come to Mercy, first thing I did was go out and buy a pack. Haven't smoked one yet, but I think I might with every passing minute I spend here."

"I'd like to help you if I can," I said. This was a troubled person, and I felt this odd connection to her. We may have had very different ways of grieving, but I knew what she was going through.

"Okay, your visit is not about God. You've got to be a shrink." The guarded look and angry tone had returned. "But I don't need that kind of help."

I smiled. "I am no shrink. When I said I'd like to help I was being practical, not esoteric. You said something about an estate sale, and obviously you're getting ready, but this is a huge house. I'd be glad to help you sort things, trash things, do whatever is necessary."

She cocked her head. "You'd do that for a stranger?"

"Sure. I'd love to." And even though Candace might think I'd scored big-time if I were invited to hunt around in here, it wasn't like that for me. I did want to help this woman. It just felt right.

Candace returned and said, "The clock won't bother you anymore."

"Thanks," Daphne said. "Tell me your name again?"

"Candace Carson," she mumbled, reclaiming her spot next to me on the settee.

Not Deputy Carson, I thought. Wonder why. And I was also wondering why we couldn't go into the living room, where it would surely be more comfortable.

"You know," Candace said, "Shawn Cuddahee's animal shelter took all the cats your father had here, but he didn't have room for all of them. I agreed to take home a Siamese until we either find the owner or someone adopts the poor guy. Could he be your cat—the one your father took from you?"

"Or an exotic shorthair?" I said. "He had one of those, too."

But Daphne shook her head. "No. Sophie wasn't a Siamese or whatever else you said. She was a gray long-haired sweetheart. When my father came to visit me in Columbia— we were actually on speaking terms at the time—he was all over her, how pretty she was, how affectionate. Then he took off with her in the middle of the night."

"Are you kidding me?" But why should I be surprised?

"I wish I were kidding. I got in my car and drove here

when I discovered she was gone. But though he had several other cats, no Sophie. And he claimed he didn't have anything to do with her disappearance."

"Then what was his explanation for leaving your place in the middle of the night?" Candace said.

"He said he was tired of me. And since I'd heard that before, I didn't argue. And like a fool, I believed him when he said it was a coincidence that Sophie disappeared when he did, that maybe she slipped out when he was leaving. But I know different now." The more she talked, the more the contempt returned to her voice.

"What changed your mind about this coincidence?" I asked.

"This last month he's been calling me. Same old thing. He wants to make things right between us; he doesn't want to die with us being estranged. I've heard it all before."

"But that doesn't answer why you seem so sure now that he took your cat," Candace said.

"I've explained all this to the police, and it doesn't really matter now that he's dead, does it?" she said. "Sophie's been gone more than a year. I'll never see her again."

"The police?" I said. "They asked about your cat?"

"No, they didn't. I mentioned it to Chief Baca after he said my father had a bunch of cats here. He didn't seem to care."

"Yeah, tell me about it," Candace said under her breath.

"You're awfully interested in this," she said, her scorn morphing to skepticism.

"Partly because of Shawn, the guy who owns that shelter," I said quickly.

"I heard my father complain about him more than once," Daphne said.

"He's a friend of ours," I said, "and apparently the main suspect. But we're sure he couldn't have killed your father, and we wish the police chief would listen to us. We believe the cats had something to do with your father's murder."

"We? Us? What are you, conjoined twins or something?" A new cigarette came out of the case and she put it between her lips.

"No," Candace and I said in unison.

Daphne actually smiled for the first time. "Better check your hips for scars."

"We're curious types—maybe that's why we relate to cats so well," I said. "I've had a round or two with Chief Baca. I hope your experience was better than mine."

"Does he suspect you, too?" she said.

"At first he did, mostly because I . . . well, I found . . . your father." I couldn't help glancing toward the dining room.

Daphne tossed her head in the direction of my stare. "That's where he was, huh?"

I nodded, knowing that the image of him lying there would never leave me. I could picture the whole scene so clearly, as if it had just happened.

"Thanks to me, looks like they don't suspect you or Shawn as much as they do me," Daphne said.

"The chief told you that you were a suspect?" I said.

"No, but I'm not stupid. I picked up on his suspicions," she said.

"Did you come into town and go straight to the police station or did you stop by here first?" Candace asked.

"What does that have to do with anything?" Daphne spoke so quickly she lost the cigarette, but she didn't seem to notice.

Candace flushed. "I was wondering if you went to the station first and they took your clothing while you were there."

"Took my clothes?" Her eyebrows were raised and she looked completely confused. But then she got it, because she said, "You think that if I killed my father I'd be stupid enough to wear bloody clothes I wore days ago to an interview with the police?"

"No, no, no," Candace said, shaking her head. "It's about trace evidence transfer. If you didn't come here to the Pink

House before you talked to them, there'd be no cat hair on your clothing and—"

"Trace evidence? You're a cop," Daphne said. "You're a damn cop. And you think I killed him." She rose and pointed toward the foyer. "Get out of here."

I stood, palms held out in a "wait a minute" gesture. "You don't understand."

"Oh, I understand. You came here while I'm sorting through years of memories that he took from our old house, pictures and letters that only bring me pain, and you pretend like you want to help me. That's as cold as his heart."

Candace's head was down. Obviously she knew she'd screwed up big-time. "It's not like that," I said, my tone more forceful than I intended.

"Really? How is it, then?" Daphne said.

"True, Candace is a cop," I said, "but since she's friendly with me she's not officially investigating the murder. Remember, I was a suspect, too, and maybe I still am."

"You two buddies came here to find a new suspect. So she is *investigating*." Daphne stared down at Candace.

"We did not come here for that," I said emphatically. "I promise you. I'm here because of the cats. What I've learned today is that you were victimized by your father like so many others. And I want to help you."

"What about her? What's her plan, since we're getting all mushy and honest and heartfelt?" Daphne folded her arms across her chest, her lips tight with anger.

Candace's head jerked up. "I'm as pissed off as you are; that's why I'm here. At first someone had me yanked off this case for no good reason. And now I can't convince the chief your father's death might have been about more than money. That's why you're his current target. Word is, you'll inherit a pretty penny."

Daphne took a moment to think this through. Then she inhaled deeply and released the breath with her eyes closed. At last she said, "And you're saying you *don't* think I killed my father for his money?"

"I sure don't," I said.

Candace looked from me to Daphne and back to me and said, "I'm with her."

"You two swear you didn't come here because that cop sent you to see if my story's changed since I talked to them?" Daphne said.

"He doesn't know we're here," Candace said. "And if he finds out, I'm toast. I'll be answering phones again."

She stared at Candace for a long time, then me, before saying, "I may be the biggest idiot on the planet, but because of my own poor cat, and because I know plenty of cats passed through my father's lying, thieving hands, I believe you." She sat down again.

Relieved, I followed suit. For the first time I noticed how dark those circles under her eyes were, how her shoulders sagged. Now that honesty had robbed her of anger and cynicism, she looked defeated and exhausted.

"We want to find your father's killer," I said.

"I still don't get why you care," she said.

"I need to know why he was stealing cats. Added to that, I walked in here and found a dead man. And you know what? Chief Baca has no clue that a person who's had a pet stolen can become desperate and unreasonable, and maybe capable of murder."

"Then Chief Baca is plain dense, because you're right," Daphne said. "I saw firsthand how fixated the big bad policeman is on the money motive. He kept asking me if I knew how rich I was about to become. Well, guess what? I don't know and I don't care."

"What else did you two discuss?" Candace asked.

"I found out they dug up records of all the calls my father made to me. The chief asked me about those and was especially interested in the ones that started about a month ago. I told him that was how things always went. My father came into my life, usually when he needed something. Then he'd leave. This last month? It was all a bunch of new lies."

"Like what?" I asked.

"He said he was dying, for one thing. For sympathy, of course. One time he told me he was having open heart surgery just to get me here. You know what he wanted? My mother's engagement ring. The one I used to wear all the time. Said he had a use for it and that it was his property."

"Did you give it to him?" I asked.

"Yes. He did buy it originally, after all—and that made it tainted. Him reminding me of that? Well, he knew how I'd react and that I'd give him the ring. Besides, I was done arguing about every little thing. I have good memories of my mom, and that's all that counts."

"There was no heart surgery?" I asked.

"No way," she said in a scoffing tone. "He was healthier than me. I swear if someone hadn't stabbed him, he would have outlived everyone in this room."

"Back to these recent phone calls," Candace said. "What do you think his motives were this time?"

"I don't know. He said he wanted to make things right between us before he died and that he could earn back my trust by reuniting me with Sophie," Daphne said.

"Are you saying he admitted he stole your cat?" I said.

"Oh no. That would have confirmed what I knew all along—that he was a liar and a thief," she said. "He'd *never* admit to that."

"Then how did he plan to find Sophie if he wasn't involved in her disappearance?" I said.

Daphne said, "Good question. I asked him and he just said, 'Leave it to me. I have my ways.' "

"Did you believe he could make that happen?" Candace asked.

"Not for a minute. He wanted back into my life for a few months for some selfish reason and—" She bit her lower lip, her eyes filling with tears. "I've been stupid enough to let that happen over and over. Why not again?"

"Because no matter what kind of man he was, he was still your father," I said.

Daphne sniffed and swiped at her nose with her sleeve.

"Not anymore. Now, if you don't mind, I have plenty to do. I'd like to get back to it."

Candace and I stood.

"I'll stay and help," I said.

"You don't have to. I can manage," Daphne said.

"Then it's settled. I'm staying," I said with a smile. "Candace? What about you?"

"I have some errands—you know, the whole day off stuff—but I could come back later and lend a hand," she said.

"Sounds good." I was in rescue mode, just like I'd been after Katrina when so many pets needed homes. It felt good.

Nineteen

I quickly discovered why we hadn't been invited into the living room earlier. Boxes sat on the floor, on the two worn leather sofas and pretty much everywhere else I looked. Daphne must have been packing all night. No wonder she seemed tired.

"What can I do that would help you the most?" I asked.

Daphne glanced around the room. "There are frames with glass, and I brought in some of the china that belonged to my mother." She raised two trash bags. "This is shredded paper. Maybe it would make good packing material."

"You want me to cushion fragile objects with this? Seems good for sending packages, but not sturdy enough to protect glass."

"I don't have much else," she said. "Unless I want to pay for those Styrofoam peanuts at the UPS store fifty miles away."

"What about newspapers?" I asked.

"There are stacks of those in the garage. Guess we could use them."

She started to lead me out there, but I told her I could handle it, that she should keep doing what she'd been doing before we'd interrupted her. She went back to work in the kitchen while I went out to the garage.

The late-morning weather had warmed to a pleasant seventy degrees or so. I took off my sweater and tied it around my waist. Then I had an idea and called information for Ed's number. When I had him on the line, I said, "Have you collected packing peanuts by any chance?"

"Sure. People don't save nothing these days and I figured if I ever need to up and move, I—"

"Would you mind if I bought some?" I said.

"Wouldn't mind a bit. How many bags should I pull?" he said.

"Big bags?" I asked.

"Huge. How many?"

"How about three? And I have a favor to ask. Could you deliver them to the Pink House?"

A brief silence followed and then he said, "The daughter's in town and already starting to clear stuff out?"

I wondered if his mouth was watering at the thought. "Yes. I think she'll have a bunch of trash, if you're wondering. And she could use packing material."

"I'm on it. Give me thirty minutes. I'm with a customer." He couldn't disguise the excitement in his voice. This place had to be Treasure Island in Ed's eyes.

After putting my phone away, I went inside the garage. The place could have housed three cars. But there was only enough room for one late-model Lexus SUV. Hmmm. The man could afford a $50,000 car. That told me something. But it desperately needed a visit to the car wash, just as the house could have used a fresh coat of paint. Tools, fishing and hunting gear and a wall of pesticides, old paint, turpentine and other household chemicals caught my attention next. And there had to be a dozen pet carriers stacked in a corner near the lawn mower and a Weed Eater. I'd seen disassembled carriers in that bedroom upstairs, too. How many cats had passed through this man's hands for him to need so many carriers?

The newspapers were bundled, bound and piled next to a freezer. I grabbed the top two packs and returned through the kitchen. The papers smelled as musty as the house, and I'd had to brush off several clinging bugs and spiders before I brought them inside.

"This ought to work," I said to Daphne, who was on a step stool clearing out the contents of cabinets and placing jars, glasses and plates on the counter below.

An unlit cigarette drooped from her upper lip. "I haven't even touched the garage, but it seemed like there was pretty useful stuff out there," she said. "Thought the estate agent could advise me. He's coming into town on Monday."

I started undoing the twine binding the newspapers. "You'd never consider moving here?" I said.

"I have a business in Columbia—a photography studio. I don't want to relocate just because I suddenly have this big-ass house. Besides, this wasn't my beloved childhood home or anything. But the china and silver belonged to my mom, and I'm glad to have them since she picked out those things during what had to be a happier time in her life. Her engagement ring hasn't turned up so far, though. He probably sold it."

"It's good to keep a few things," I said. I'd kept John's watch and his Swiss Army knife. And his sweaters— because they smelled like him every time I walked into the closet.

"What's wrong?" Daphne said.

"Nothing. Just thinking about my husband."

Daphne made a careful turn on the narrow step so she could face me directly. "What happened to him?"

"Heart attack. He was only fifty-five."

She removed the cigarette and tossed it on the counter. "I'm really sorry."

"I'm doing so much better than even a few weeks ago. Guess worrying about stolen cats has helped." I picked up the newspapers and said, "But talking won't get anything done around here. I'm off to pack."

I sat cross-legged on the floor next to a box of china and started pulling apart newspaper pages. Then I began carefully wrapping the dishes—a gold-edged old-fashioned floral design.

I was nearly finished and ready to move on to the next

box when something caught my eye as I separated yet another issue of the meager *Mercy Messenger*. Someone—I assumed Flake Wilkerson—had drawn a red circle around a classified ad.

No surprise that it was an ad for a lost cat—a white shorthair with green eyes whose tag read SNOWBALL. I wanted to write this information down but realized I'd left my bag in Candace's car and had no pen. I'd also need one to label the boxes, so I looked around and saw a secretary-style desk nearly obscured by boxes and stuffed trash bags on the other side of the room.

I managed to dump the contents of one bag as I tossed them aside to reach the desk drawer.

I stepped over scattered paper strips and found a pen in one of the desk drawers, then hurried back to the newspaper, the pen and a small notepad from a Greenville motel in hand. The newspaper was several months old, but I thought I'd give this person a call anyway.

Now that I'd found this ad, I wondered how many other red circles there were. I groaned at the thought of all those newspapers outside. But didn't this prove that there were cats Wilkerson might have had that we didn't know about? And if Chief Baca saw this proof, maybe he'd take a closer look at other suspects—at people who'd had cats stolen by Wilkerson.

Daphne came into the room and said, "I heard you groan. Is something wrong?"

I showed her the ad. "Do you have any idea why he was so obsessed with everyone else's cats?"

"I think we've had this conversation. No." She glanced over and saw the spilled paper.

"Sorry," I said. "I was looking for something to write on and got a little clumsy."

As we both started to stuff the paper back into the bag, I said, "He had a shredding obsession, too."

"I know. The police gave me a list of what they took

from the house as evidence. They took a shredder and its wastebasket from under the desk. Didn't bother to take what had spilled out around the shredder, though."

"But what about these two bags? I said.

"I brought those from upstairs," she said. "Added what the cops missed to one of them."

"Guess they didn't care about all the shredded paper," I said half to myself. I held up a few strips. "This doesn't look like bills or credit card offers or canceled checks—the kind of things I shred. Look at the colors."

Daphne held up several long pieces as well. "Looks like pictures," she said. "Computer-generated, but still pictures." She pointed at her face. "Photographer's eye."

I explained about Ed and the cat flyers I'd collected. "I have a theory. I think your father took down lost-cat flyers before Ed could get to them. Maybe that's what we've got here—shredded posters."

Daphne squinted at the tops of a few thin strips. "But some of these came from Web sites." She pointed out what she'd seen, and sure enough, a few "http's" with forward slashes and numbers were evident at the top.

"You're right. And did Chief Baca tell you that your father's computer and keyboard were stolen?" I said.

"I didn't pay much attention to anything the chief said," she answered. "I was more focused on what in hell I would do with all of my father's crap. I'm sure you understand, now that you've been here a while."

"Totally get it. But seeing as how he shredded this stuff, I can't help wondering if the Web sites he visited could be connected to his murder," I said. "I'll have to ask Candace if the police might reconsider and be interested in these particular shreds."

"There's at least a thousand puzzle pieces if someone wants to paste strips together to figure out what sites he looked at. Maybe porn. Wouldn't that be another disgusting revelation?" she said.

"But would porn make someone steal his computer?" I said. "Maybe. If the police aren't interested in this, I might give it a shot. I'm good at piecing things together." I told her about my quilt business. And that in turn reminded me about the quilts of mine I'd seen upstairs.

But before I could ask about them, there was a knock on the door.

"Candace must not have had too many errands," Daphne said as she started for the door.

"That's probably not her. I called someone to help you out."

"What? Am I gonna have this whole frickin' town traipsing through the house?" Her pacifying cigarette was gone, but she looked like she could use one again.

Before I could explain about Ed, she was off to answer the door.

I hurried after her, worried that she would scare him off like she nearly did Candace and me. As she got to the door, I said, "I asked him to bring some real packing material, that's all."

Daphne threw open the door and Ed stood there, holding clear plastic bags filled with Styrofoam peanuts. His salt-and-pepper hair was practically standing on end. One overall strap hung down and his eyes were wide, probably in response to Daphne's commando stare.

He looked to me for help and I said, "Ed, this is Daphne, Flake Wilkerson's daughter."

Eyes down, Ed mumbled, "Pleased to meet you."

Daphne stood there, appraising him. He looked like he'd slept outdoors last night, and his overalls seemed puffy across his chest.

Since I'd left my bag in Candace's car, all I had was the crumpled ten-dollar bill in my jeans pocket. I hoped it was enough as I held it out to Ed. "I can give you more later," I said.

He dropped the bags on the doorstep and took the

money. "This is plenty." Then he reached inside his overalls and pulled out a roll of bubble wrap. "Thought this might be helpful, too."

Daphne accepted it before I could move. "Thank you. It was . . . really nice of you to come out here and bring this."

Whew. Nice response from a woman who didn't trust people and who was stressed to the max dealing with the unpleasantness of what her father had left behind.

"No problem." Ed was looking past Daphne, trying to see inside the house. "You got anything you don't know what to do with, give me a call. Miss Jillian here has my number and knows where my store is."

Uh-oh. Karen wouldn't be happy if she found out I'd led Ed to junkyard heaven.

Daphne looked out toward the driveway. "I see you have a truck. You'll need it. After I meet with the estate agent, I'll give you a call." She held up the bubble wrap. "Thanks."

Ed started to turn away but stopped when I said, "I saw computer monitors and towers in your shop. You find anything lately?"

He tilted his head. "I did, as a matter of fact. Found a tower that looked like it'd been attacked with a sledgehammer. "Don't know if I can salvage anything except the electrical cord, but you never know."

"When did you find it?" I asked, my heart speeding up.

"Yesterday. At the dump. I know it's broken, but heck, you can always save something."

Daphne and I looked at each other, and I said, "Would you recognize your father's computer?"

"I doubt it," she said.

But that wasn't about to stop me. "Ed," I said, "you save that computer for me, okay? I might want to purchase it."

"I'll tell you right now, it ain't worth much all broke like that. You'll get a fair price." He smiled.

And I was smiling, too. But not because I'd get a fair price. If that computer belonged to Flake Wilkerson, even if it was "all broke," secrets might be resurrected from the rubble—certainly not by me, but Candace would know someone skilled enough to find out what was on it and why it had disappeared from a murdered man's house.

Twenty

After Candace finished her errands and returned to the Pink House, the three of us made good progress organizing the contents of the house for the estate sale. Daphne was happy to let me have all the old newspapers, as well as the bags of shredded pictures or documents or whatever they were. When I told her about my cat quilts, she said she'd seen them upstairs and I could have them back.

Candace looked at me like I had two heads when we left the house with me carrying the garbage bags and the old newspapers along with the quilts. She said, "Your quilts I understand, but what's with this other stuff?"

Once we were on the road and I explained, she understood and said, "The day of the murder, I told Lydia about the shredded paper in the cat room. She said the most recent stuff from the wastebasket was enough, said we didn't have the resources to mess with every tiny scrap of paper."

"There's something else," I said. I told her about the smashed computer. Her mood went from interested to wary in a nanosecond. I could almost reach out and touch the tension between us.

"You can't buy that computer," she said.

"Why not? Ed found it at the dump and it could be—"

"Oh, I know what it could be. Hard evidence. The key to everything," she said.

"Yes," I said. "And that's why—"

"That's why I go to Ed's Swap Shop, secure it and call Baca."

"Did you think I planned to take it home?" I said with a laugh. "If I bought it, I thought I could hand it over to Chief Baca, no warrant attached."

"Oh. Sorry I misunderstood," she said. "But you don't have to buy the thing. Ed knows all about stolen goods. I'm surprised they haven't checked with him about the computer already. Maybe they have by now."

"And you guys will have people who could make sense of damaged computer guts? Because Ed said it wasn't in good shape."

"The county has forensic computer experts. No one in Mercy PD could begin to tackle that job," she said.

Even though it was after six and I'd had nothing to eat all day, Candace insisted we head straight for Ed's store. In what seemed like only seconds, we pulled into the tiny parking area, courtesy of Candace trying to set a world record for getting from the Pink House to the other side of town. She told me to stay in the car and she'd deal with Ed. I didn't mind. Thanks to her driving, my personal fear factor was about a ten on a scale of one to five, and I needed time to calm down.

I watched as Candace navigated through the junk in front of the building and then saw her pounding on the door. No one answered, and when she tried the latch, it was locked. Frustration was evident in every step as she stomped back to the car.

Sliding behind the wheel, she said, "The one time I need Ed to be there, he's gone. We could probably go to the dump and find him, I suppose."

"What about Karen? Remember she said they take their meals at her place?" I said.

Candace smiled. "Duh. Good thinking." She took out her phone, scrolled down in the address book, then pressed the CALL button.

But she didn't call Karen as I expected. "Tom? This is Candace. Can I have your mother's phone number?"

Wide-eyed, I said, "Tom Stewart? Are you kidding?"

Candace held up a finger to silence me. She listened intently, repeated the number he gave her and made the second call. When someone answered, she said, "Hi, this is Candace. Is Ed there?"

She listened, then politely said, "I know he's eating his supper, but this is important. I need him to meet me at the shop."

More silence as Karen spoke.

Candace said, "Yes, but—"

I could hear Karen's voice but couldn't make out the words.

Candace's shoulders slumped and she rolled her eyes. "Why, yes. We'd be delighted to join you. Be there in a few minutes." She closed the phone and slapped it down between us.

"Karen is Tom's mother?" I said.

"Thought you knew. Anyhow, the only way we're getting inside that shop without having to get a warrant—which in Mercy would be considered a rude and unfortunate course of action—is to have supper with them. Let's get this over with."

She reversed the Toyota and peeled out of the driveway. All I could think about on this leg of our journey was that I had to get the name of a good chiropractor.

In comparison to Ed's shop, Karen's cottage ranked up there with the Taj Mahal. I swear there wasn't a blade of grass out of place in her front yard. Two white rockers sat on the latticed porch, and a wind chime played its delicate tune as it swung in the evening breeze.

"How did these two ever end up together?" I whispered as Candace rang the doorbell.

"Met at church is what I heard." She lowered her voice. "She used to drink. Preferred vodka, which is kinda expensive when you're downing fifths."

Before I could respond—and God knew what I'd say, anyway—Karen answered the door. Soon we were sitting at a dining room table that looked old enough to have been handed down from her grandparents. Everything was caramel-colored wood: the chairs, the sideboard, the china hutch and the oval table.

Ed's hair was now combed and he wore a clean striped shirt buttoned up to his neck. Karen had on a peach sweater with a rabbit fur collar and pearl buttons.

When she caught me gaping, she said, "Fake fur. No animals were harmed in the making of this sweater."

I smiled. "I didn't mean to stare, but—"

"Oh, I'm sure you didn't. Now eat, ladies. Both of you could use some fat on your bones. Women are supposed to have fat to store their estrogen. Did you know that?"

And that was how it went. Ed concentrated on his pot roast, carrots and potatoes, while Karen talked nonstop, mostly offering up her fun facts. She was a wealth of information. But the last one made me set down my fork.

She said, "Did you know they kill cats in Europe for their fur? Make scarves and collars and such. Tabbies are quite popular for that, but I think that's despicable. I surely do hope that's not what Flake Wilkerson was up to in the Pink House."

"We were—I mean Jillian was there all day." Candace looked at me. "You found no sign of a cat massacre, did you?"

I felt sick at the thought.

Ed must have noticed, because he jumped in with, "Hush, Candace. And you, too, Karen. Can't you see you're upsetting Miss Jillian? She has a love of animals and you need to respect that."

I exhaled the air I'd been holding and offered Ed a grateful smile.

Karen said, "I suppose that wasn't proper talk at the supper table. Please forgive me, Jillian. The last thing I want to do is upset you. Tom has said such nice things about you. Now, time for that icebox pie I made this morning."

Candace started to clear the table, but Ed held up a hand. "Our job. Just sit."

After they took the dishes to the kitchen and we were alone, Candace said, "This is driving me crazy. There's evidence to be collected and we have to waste time being polite."

"I don't think that computer is going anywhere," I said.

"You're probably right, but I am as edgy as a terrier watching a rat hole." To prove this, she started gnawing on her pinkie finger.

I was in no hurry. The food was down-home delicious. I couldn't remember the last time I'd had mashed potatoes and gravy. I felt soothed in the presence of this odd couple, whose hospitality and concern were so genuine. I only wished it hadn't taken a murder to get me out of my house and meeting people in Mercy.

The icebox pie was like nothing I'd ever tasted, rich with lemon cookie pieces, almonds and whipped cream. I was in heaven and, to Candace's chagrin, I took my time with each bite. She'd eaten hers exactly like she drove her car: way too fast. She refused coffee, and in fear of my life I did, too, though I imagined Karen could make an awesome cup of coffee if the meal we'd had was any indication.

When Ed started to clear the pie plates, Karen waved him off. "Candace is chomping at the bit about something you've got in your shop that she sorely wants. You all go on now and I'll clean up."

We all stood and I said, "Are you sure? I'd be glad to help."

Candace's foot squeezed down on my toes, and it was all I could do not to punch her in the arm in response. But I didn't. I was forty-one years old, not twelve.

The ride back to the shop was blessedly unhurried since we were following Ed's truck. The battered, ancient vehicle probably couldn't do more than forty and, coupled with the leisurely dinner, Ed's pace was tranquil. I thought Candace might grip the steering wheel so hard her knuckles would snap.

After Ed unlocked the shop and let us in, he said, "Is this about that computer?"

"Yes," Candace said. "I may be on a day off, but a police

officer is always on duty. When Jillian mentioned your find, I thought it best I have a look since the computer could be useful in our investigation."

Ed had flicked on the lights and was leading us toward the back room. "That proves the point I've been trying to make my whole life. Trash can be treasure. We're a nation of wasters. Throw everything out before it's served its purpose. And that purpose isn't always what a thing mighta been made for in the first place."

I'd never thought about the world quite like that before, but he did have a point.

The remnants of the computer were laid out on an old carpet in the office—keyboard cracked in two with all kinds of missing keys sitting alongside what was once a tower. It was mostly shattered and the back was missing. And there was also a mass of circuits, ribbon wires and other pieces that had been rendered nearly unrecognizable by a good smashing.

Candace, hands on her hips, stared down at the mess. "Whoa. Exactly what did you think you could salvage from this, Ed?"

"Don't know," said Ed. "That's the fun of it."

She took out her cell and punched several keys. When someone on the other end answered, she said, "Sorry to bother you at home, but I might have found some evidence that needs collecting." She listened for a second and said, "Yes, the Wilkerson case. Which I am *not* working, by the way. I just happened to hear about this wrecked computer and thought I'd check it out."

Her cheeks reddened as she listened some more. Then she gave our location and hung up. "The chief's coming," she said. "He wants to see for himself."

Ed said, "The dump's a mucky place. Let me check if it's dried out enough—"

Candace grabbed his arm. "Don't touch it."

He stopped and gave her a confused look. "But there was some nasty stuff in that dump, and I wouldn't want you or the chief to get all dirty."

I said, "That's okay, Ed. Candace is worried about fingerprints and other stuff you and I probably know nothing about."

He nodded and smiled. "I get it. If you're worried about fingerprints, you won't find mine 'cause I always wear gloves when I pull stuff out of the dump. Heavy-duty ones on account of the rats."

My skin crawled at the thought.

Candace seemed pleased and said, "Ed is always careful with things. I've been here more than once looking for stolen goods, haven't I, Ed?"

"You and every officer in town," Ed said. "Hope I sometimes make your job easier."

"You do indeed." Candace knelt and stared at what she hoped was the evidence she so desperately wanted. "Wish I understood computers better. Don't know what if any of this mess will tell us a story."

"I can call Karen's boy and ask him to come over. He knows computers inside and out," Ed said.

"Tom fixed mine up with a wireless network in a hurry," I agreed.

"We have to leave this to the state computer forensic people," Candace said.

"If you say so," Ed said. "But you ask me, Tom's your best bet."

She said, "We don't need—"

I gave the still-crouching Candace a little kick in the butt and said, "I'm certain the police will call on Tom if they need help." That surely wasn't true, but Ed had been nothing but kind to us and she didn't need to be so dismissive.

She stood and looked at me as if to say, "What is wrong with you?"

I almost laughed. I wanted to say, "Payback for the toe crushing," but instead I said, "Ed seems quite proud of Tom's skills."

He smiled broadly. "Been with Karen a while now, and I've tried to do right by the both of them. He's had his share of trouble, mostly thanks to Karen losing her way for a spell, but he's a fine man."

We heard the door open and Candace called, "That you, Chief?"

Baca appeared in the office door and nodded at Ed. "Good to see you." All I got was a hard stare before he focused on the computer wreckage.

Candace started to explain, but he stopped her and began asking Ed questions. After he had the when, why, where and how of Ed's find, he looked at Candace. "You got your camera and kit?"

You'd have thought Billy Cranor had just asked her on a date. "Got my own kit and camera, so yes, sir." She was gone in a flash.

Baca turned to me. "You heard about this computer while you were visiting Daphne Wilkerson? Why were you over there?"

I should have known this question was coming, but I was woefully unprepared. I had no fantastic, smooth answer that would satisfy a skeptic like him. I explained how I'd helped her and called Ed for packing material. I finished by saying, "I—I felt like it was the right thing to do—to pay my respects."

"Really?" Baca said. "And then she asked you to find her packing peanuts? How did you two become so friendly so fast? Because, you know, she didn't seem the buddy-buddy type to me."

"She's had a rough time with her dad," I said.

"But you two are now fast friends, it would seem," he said. "Aren't you the miracle worker? Was Candace over at the Pink House with you?"

Before I could speak, Ed said, "Didn't see that station wagon Candace races around town in when I was there, Mike. Girl's gonna get herself hurt one of these days. Drives fast as blue blazes."

Baca's narrowed eyes hadn't left my face, but Candace's

return with the fingerprint kit and camera interrupted whatever he was about to say.

While Baca directed Candace on what photos he wanted, I mouthed a "thank you" at Ed. He nodded knowingly.

Soon Ed was hunting up a box to transport the computer and keyboard off the premises. Seemed Candace could not get any decent prints from what she'd dusted, but listening to her and Baca talk, I guessed there was something else they could try as far as printing the parts and pieces.

While Baca carefully carried the box outside with Candace on his heels, I looked at Ed. I didn't care what Candace said; he'd found it and he should be paid. "How much do I owe you for that?"

"Nothing. Police come and take something, I don't get a paycheck and I shouldn't. Had plenty of stolen stuff pass through my hands and I'm pretty good at figurin' out when something's not right with a swap or a sale."

"I'll bet you are," I said with a grin.

His brow creased. "This machine's not one of those times, though. I thought it got all broke because of the frustratin' nature of computers. Never woulda known it might be important if not for you askin' this afternoon."

"I hope it yields some kind of clue. Murderers should not go free," I said.

Ed checked his watch. "Man like me who gets up at the crack of dawn needs to be in bed by this time. You riding with Candace? 'Cause I'd be glad to drop you at home."

"No, she'll give me a ride." I wanted to take him up on his offer, but we had already inconvenienced him enough.

But he seemed well aware I would have rather ridden with him, because he said, "Then I wish you luck on reaching your destination in one piece." And with that he gave me a commiserating wink.

Twenty-one

I arrived home to find three unhappy cats. I'd spent the entire day away and hadn't even remembered to turn on *Animal Planet*. Though I'd checked the cat-cam several times, they, of course, had no idea I'd been checking on them. Maybe one day Tom could make the system interactive and I could talk to them, too.

After they got over their snit, which took only about fifteen minutes, we played with feathers and fake snakes and I eased my guilt by giving them some of that fancy food that costs about a buck a can. I heard purring as I left the kitchen and headed for a hot bath. I hadn't done this much physical work since John and I had moved in last year, and every muscle was barking. By the time I put my head on the pillow, three cats with fish breath were ready to settle in for the night. I don't think it took me thirty seconds to fall asleep.

When I woke up, I feared I'd gone way past my usual seven a.m., but I checked the clock and saw I'd overslept by only thirty minutes. First order of business, after coffee and cereal, was to figure out when I'd made those cat quilts and how they'd ended up in Flake Wilkerson's house. The police might not care about this—obviously they didn't, since they hadn't taken them as evidence—but I sure did.

I keep photographs of many of the quilts I make, but I'm not always good about noting where or when a particular quilt is sold. I rely on my receipt book for the IRS and usually add a quilt's description on the NCR forms I use—for instance "brown and pink Lady of the Lake pattern," with the date and price. In other words, I'm organized to a point. But the pictures might tell me precisely when I'd used the fabrics in the quilts I'd brought home from the Pink House last night.

I took the five cat quilts with me, and Merlot, Chablis, and Syrah followed along into the sewing room. How they love fabric, the hum of the sewing machine, and the chance to swipe at thread as I clip rows of quilting. When I took a photo album from the shelf, Merlot went straight to the window and jumped on the sill, his attention on birds and squirrels. Chablis plopped down in the middle of the floor, perhaps hoping she could trip me and get her revenge. Syrah sat in the middle of the room also and meowed in protest. Looking at an album was not what they'd hoped I'd be doing in here.

I sat in the comfy overstuffed chair in the corner and opened the album—this one with pictures from the last year. Only Syrah joined me, perching on the chair's arm. He seemed as interested in the pictures as I was, occasionally reaching out a paw to tap a page as I turned it.

Checking fabric patterns and colors against the quilts, I was certain these five had been ordered or purchased in April or May. Three fabrics in particular had been used in all the quilts. What had I been doing in those months, aside from making myself get out of bed and face one day at a time without John? Going to cat or craft shows? Had I sold these through my Web site?

The answer might lie in this year's tax folder. I retrieved it from its file, and sure enough, I found an almost coherent description of six quilts that matched these. They'd been sold at a cat show in Atlanta. No convenient check or credit card receipt, but I sometimes do ask for a name—in case the customer ever contacts me again. People feel good when you remember their name.

This order was purchased by one B. Smith and was a

cash payment—an order for six quilts. And yet only five had been recovered. I wondered what happened to the other one. And I didn't know if B. Smith was a man or a woman—you'd think I would have remembered if a man had bought that many quilts. My customer base is ninety percent female. But I'd been walking through life as a shadow back then. I had no memory of anything more than making the drive to Atlanta.

Surely that was where Flake Wilkerson purchased my quilts, and even in Atlanta he was being deceptive. Cash. An alias. The kinds of things people do when they have something to hide.

Knowing that I couldn't do anything more with this information than talk it over with Candace this evening, I was about to start searching through the classifieds of those newspapers I'd brought home, looking for more red circles, when my cell rang.

It was Daphne, who began talking without saying hello. "I have to go the coroner's office to pick up the death certificate. Do you know where the office is? Because the woman gave me directions like I actually knew what she was talking about, and I feel stupid calling her back. I didn't grow up in this town. I've only been to this house twice in the last five years."

From what little I knew of Daphne, who I'd decided was a vulnerable woman hiding behind an angry facade, her not wanting to call back sounded about right. "Why don't we go together?" I said. "I know my way around a few places in the county."

"I didn't call you up so you could take care of me again. But you have a computer and access to MapQuest, right?"

"Sure. Why don't I print out a map—you're headed for the county coroner's office, right?" I said.

"That's right."

"And since you probably don't know where I live and don't have e-mail access, I'll drive over and give it to you."

She wasn't fooling me a bit. Daphne was anxious and upset and doing a pitiful job of hiding her emotions.

"We could meet in front of city hall," she said tersely.

Was there something she wasn't saying? I had a strong feeling there was. "Nope. It's settled. I am on my way to the house." I hung up before she could say another word.

Once I had the map in hand, I blew kisses at the kitties and turned on the TV as well as my security system. Five minutes later I arrived at the Pink House. It didn't take much convincing for Daphne to let me drive her to the county seat.

When I hit the main road, I said, "You seem pretty upset. What's going on?"

She was gazing out the passenger window, no cigarette hanging off her upper lip today. But she was working her fingers and tapping her foot. "They said they have to talk to me, that it's not only about the death certificate."

"Really? Who called you, by the way?" I said.

"I don't know. Linda . . . Lucinda . . ."

"Lydia?" I offered.

"That's it. And she was so damn abrupt. If she treats all the families of homicide victims that way, then she needs to find another job."

"I know Lydia. Why don't you let me talk to her?" I said.

Daphne's head snapped around so she could look at me. "You do *not* need to be my savior. I can take care of myself."

"Sorry," I said. "I just thought . . . Well, when I lost John I would have appreciated a shoulder to lean on, that's all. Each loss is personal, so I apologize if I overstepped."

A short silence followed and then she said, "Figures I'd stick my foot in my mouth. I'm the one who should be apologizing. And you know what? I'm relieved you're going with me."

"There," I said with a smile. "That wasn't so hard, was it?"

Her features softened. "Yes, it was."

On the rest of our drive we talked about family and friends—or the lack thereof. Seemed Flake Wilkerson had been Daphne's only relative aside from an ex-husband she considered almost more contemptible than her dead father. Her new assignment in life, she told me, was to make sure the ex never found out about any money she inherited.

We found Lydia's office on the second floor of the county building. How could someone as flamboyant as Lydia survive in this white-walled, plain-Jane office? Perhaps she didn't want to be outdone even by a room.

She was all in black today, some of her hair beehive-like, similar to the last time I'd seen her. But she'd added the joy of side curls that bounced at her temples.

What fun she must have looking in the mirror.

She gripped Daphne's hand with both of her own, probably making up for being unpleasant on the phone. "I am so sorry for your loss." Then she looked at me, and the disdain was evident in her tone when she said, "What are *you* doing here?"

"She's a friend of mine," Daphne said. "And that's all you need to know."

What a contrast these two women were. Lydia was all painted and spandexed and bejeweled. And then there was Daphne, her natural curls untamed and her face sans makeup. But they both had plenty of attitude, and I felt like a mouse in the presence of a couple of lionesses.

We sat in plastic molded chairs across from Lydia, her cheap Formica-topped desk between us. I don't think I'd ever before been in an office where someone had actually framed and displayed their high school diploma, but there it was. The one next to it, from the community college, I could understand, and the certificate of completion from a "death investigator training school"—yes. But once I thought about it, I liked that she hadn't forgotten another important part of her education. She was a proud woman—proud of more than just her fake boobs.

Lydia said, "Sorry if you've taken offense, Ms. Wilkerson—that is your last name?"

"Yes," she said. "I never took my ex-husband's name."

"This new friend you've made, well, did you realize that Ms. Hart has been getting around town, finding bodies, making buddies with cops, cuddling up to the men? Yup, she's been really busy. And you know she found your father that morning?" Lydia said.

"Yes, I am fully aware," Daphne said. "What I am not aware of, however, is why I had to come here in person to pick up a death certificate. I'm having my father cremated, and I thought the mortuary would take care of that sort of thing."

"True enough," Lydia said. "But we did have to do an autopsy, this being a suspicious death and all—"

"Suspicious?" I said, unable to contain myself. "It was a little more than that."

"I'm trying to be gentle," Lydia said. "Anyway, I have the autopsy report right here, and you are certainly welcome to a copy. But I would suggest you allow me to summarize. These reports are—well, let's say this particular doctor we brought in doesn't always portray the victim as a human being."

"He might have been on to something," Daphne said, her tone bitter. "But you're saying you didn't do this autopsy yourself?"

"My job is to investigate suspicious deaths, issue death certificates when needed, but in cases like this the coroner calls in a doctor to perform the autopsy." She cleared her throat. "Okay, then. Do you want to read this or can I tell you the gist?"

"Gist away," Daphne said.

Lydia opened the desk drawer and took out a manila folder and a pair of glasses with bright red frames. She put the glasses on, opened the folder and stared down at the report. "Aside from the obvious cause of death—a significant stab wound to the aorta—" She looked at me. "Which is exactly what I said happened, didn't I, Ms. Hart?"

"Yes, you did," I said.

"Anyway, let me flip to the back so I can get this right." She turned several pages.

Meanwhile Daphne showed her impatience by staring at the ceiling and shaking her head.

Lydia ran a bloodred fingernail along several lines. She then looked up and folded her arms on the desk. "Here goes. Your father, I am sorry to say, was dying of pancreatic cancer. He would have expired within months if someone had not murdered him first."

Daphne's features hardened. "That's a lie."

Lydia, taken aback at this vehement response, seemed at a loss for words.

"Are you sure, Lydia?" I said.

"What? You think you can steal my boyfriend *and* do my job? Or what little is left of my job, in this particular case thanks to you," Lydia said.

Oh my God. Not only was this woman blinded by manufactured jealousy, but she also believed I had gotten her kicked off the case. For Daphne's sake, I wasn't about to respond. "Daphne's had some issues with her father not telling the truth in the past," I said evenly. "But this cancer was very real, correct?"

Lydia seemed to wake up to the fact that she wasn't exactly behaving as she should in the presence of a troubled family member. In a softer tone she said, "He had maybe six months to live."

Daphne raised trembling fingers to her lips and whispered, "He didn't lie. For once in his sorry life, he didn't lie."

"I thought you should hear this directly from the coroner's office. That's why I asked you here," Lydia said. "I've gathered together the death certificates and documents you need and will include an autopsy report if you'd like—though I wouldn't recommend that."

Daphne was shaking her head. "No. No. I don't need one."

"You change your mind, Chief Baca has a copy. You can get one from him."

"Is that all?" Daphne said.

Lydia removed her glasses and extended a hand across the desk. "Yes. And again, I am sorry for your loss."

She took Daphne's hand in both of hers again and squeezed. She looked so normal and nice I believed for a moment that I'd imagined all her silly accusations about Tom and me. But then she glared in my direction and said, "Good-bye. And remember what I told you in Belle's the other day. You stay away from him."

Nope. You didn't imagine anything, Jillian.

More important than my issues with Lydia was the fact that Daphne was struggling mightily with what she'd just learned. She seemed so stunned, in fact, that I picked up the envelope with the death certificates and led her back to my van with an arm around her shoulder.

She said nothing as we drove toward Mercy. Meanwhile, my thoughts turned to the cat that Daphne believed her father had stolen, but I decided that now was not the time to bring up her lost gray kitty. He had promised to get it back, seeing as how his attack of conscience was real.

When we pulled into the driveway of the Pink House, I said, "Don't feel guilty about not believing your father. From what you've told me about him, he gave you good reason not to trust him."

She sat, not making a move to leave the car. "Why does it have to be so complicated? I mean, I don't know if what I feel is guilt or relief or simply surprise."

"Maybe it's all those things," I said. "But this is my take. He did make it a little easier to say good-bye by being honest for once in his life."

"Yeah," she said, staring straight ahead. She took the envelope from the console between us. "I'm glad you didn't let me bully you, make you stay away from me. Thank you."

I reached over and took her hand. "Anytime. And you

better not leave town without giving me your number in Columbia."

She smiled. "I'll see you again before I leave. Promise." She got out of the van, and I watched her walk up to the front door before I headed into town.

Whew. I could sure use a double espresso about now.

After I'd parked outside Belle's Beans, I checked the cat-cam and saw all three cats sleeping, Merlot on the window seat and Chablis and Syrah curled together on the sofa. Since a stuffed mouse lay in tatters on the floor with catnip scattered everywhere, I decided they'd worn themselves out.

The coffee shop, for once, wasn't busy. But then, the lunch hour had passed. That same woman I'd sat with before, Marian Mae, was here, but this time she had a companion—Mike Baca. And with the way they were leaning so close, they looked pretty darn sweet on each other.

I ordered coffee and a chocolate biscotti to go, hoping I could sneak out before he spotted me, but no such luck. Before I made it out the door, he called my name.

I turned and smiled politely, thinking how odd it was to see him in a social situation after everything that had happened in the last few days. He looked relaxed and, well, the word *besotted* came to mind. Could coffee be besottifying? No, I surmised that the besotted part was all about Marian Mae, that attractive, elegant woman in her pale blue cashmere sweater and designer jeans.

Baca waved me over and started to introduce me.

"We've met," Marian Mae said. "You know how crowded it gets in here—we shared a table once." She rested her hand over his, a gesture I assumed was designed to explain that he belonged to her.

"Thanks for the tip about the computer," he said. "I wasn't all that polite last night and for that I apologize."

"No problem," I said. He seemed to be off the job, and

his whole demeanor was different. He actually seemed nice.

"Whatever have you two been up to?" Marian Mae said.

"Work," he said. "Join us, Jillian? Or are you headed back to the Pink House to help out again?"

Guess he wasn't off the job after all. "Would that be a problem if I did go over there?"

He removed his hand from beneath Marian Mae's and sipped his coffee before answering. "Of course not. You visit who you want. But I'd appreciate it if you call me rather than Candace if you hear anything interesting concerning the case."

"Is Candy having one of her evidence obsession seizures?" Marian Mae said with a laugh.

Baca said, "Mae, we've talked about this. She's a good cop. But sometimes—" He glanced at me. "Nothing more needs to be said—just that I'm running this investigation, not her. Got that, Jillian?"

"Got it." But I didn't exactly like it. He should be grateful he had such a dedicated and intelligent woman working for him. "Sorry I can't visit. I need to get home," I said.

I offered a polite good-bye and then turned to leave. But even with my back to the two of them, I couldn't help hearing Marian Mae say, "You need to practice being more tactful, Mike."

Gosh, wasn't that the truth?

I spent the rest of the afternoon checking Flake Wilkerson's newspapers—that is, when I wasn't removing a cat, any cat, and all the cats from the table where'd I spread out the papers. Turned out Wilkerson had subscriptions to papers in surrounding towns as well as in Atlanta. I found only four circled names, including the first one I'd already unearthed. Three ads were people hunting for a lost cat, but those were more than a year old. The one that interested me was someone who was hoping to purchase a full-grown Abyssinian—like Syrah. That ad was only two weeks old.

I sat back in the teak chair, considering this. Why wouldn't you get on the computer and search for breeders? Or put yourself on a list at the local shelters asking to be notified if any Abyssinians came up for adoption? Or even try Craigslist? There were always ads there for cats and dogs needing homes.

The only way to get answers to these questions was to phone the person who'd purchased the ad. Deep down, I wished the police would be the ones to make the call. But as long as Baca was focused on the money, that wouldn't happen. As I opened my cell to call a stranger, I felt like this was something I must do, whether it was connected to the case or not.

The man who answered sounded very old. I practically had to yell into the phone for him to understand me. Then a woman came on the line and said, "Can't you tell he doesn't get what you're saying? You selling something?"

I explained I was calling about the ad for the Abyssinian.

"We already have one on order—or so we thought," the woman said. "It was supposed to be here day before yesterday, but I'm beginning to think poor Mr. Green's been had."

"Someone sold you a cat already?" I said.

"Had to make a cash down payment. Mr. Green handed the money over before I knew it. You got a cat to sell? Because we might need a backup."

"No. But I'd sure like to talk to Mr. Green about who sold him this cat you have yet to see."

"And why's that?" She was sounding cautious now.

"There could be an explanation as to why he hasn't gotten the cat he purchased. Please? Can I come and talk to him?"

"I don't even know your name. And poor Mr. Green's so fretful, I don't think his heart—"

I heard the old man say, "Give me that phone," heard the woman protest, but seconds later, Mr. Green was on the line again. "You holding my cat for ransom or something?

You better bring me a new Banjo before the sun sets. I got that caller ID thingie, and this time your number came up. You're not—"

"A new Banjo?" I said.

"That was his name. Banjo. And like I said—"

"Mr. Green," I said gently, "I don't have your cat. I can't sell you a cat. But I might be able to share information with you that will help you understand what happened to your money—and you might be able to help me, too."

"Then come on, 'cause I've had enough of this nonsense." He rattled off an address, and it was a good thing I had the notepad with his number at hand so I could jot it down, because he hung up immediately.

Should I call Candace to go with me? I wondered, as I went for my car keys hanging on the hook by the back door. *Nah.* Surely I'd be safe with someone who sounded like he was twice my age.

But I stopped before I'd gone out the door and about-faced. I hurried to the office, where I keep my personal photos, thinking a four-by-six picture of Syrah might come in handy rather than the photos on my cell phone. I had a feeling Mr. Green might have as much trouble seeing as he did hearing.

Mercy is small enough to share an area code with Taylorville, five miles to the south. That was where Mr. Green lived, in a tiny white house between other houses that looked exactly like his.

The woman I'd spoken with on the phone answered the red-painted door at once. She was a dark-skinned black woman, and if not for her graying temples, I wouldn't have been able to venture a guess whether she was under or over forty.

She wore the sternest expression I think I've ever seen, and she didn't bother introducing herself. "You have agitated Mr. Green so much that he's refusing to take his medication, refusing to do anything but wait by the window for you."

"I'm truly sorry if I upset both of you," I said. "My name is Jillian Hart."

"I'm Alfreda, Mr. Green's caregiver. Now get your skinny self in here and calm him down. This cat business is wearing me out."

There was no question Mr. Green was old. His skin was a shade lighter than Alfreda's and his hair was a mass of pearl gray frizzy tufts. He wore thick tortoiseshell glasses, and a wool blanket with tassels was draped around his frail-looking shoulders. His feet were elevated on an ottoman, and another blanket lay across his knees. The hearing aid in his right ear explained the difficulty we'd had on the phone.

Alfreda pulled me by the elbow over to where he sat near the window in the living room. "This is that woman who called. You can see she don't have a cat with her."

Mr. Green lifted a gnarled index finger and pointed at Alfreda. "She never said she was bringing any cat. You think I can't remember what we talked about not thirty minutes ago."

"Oh, I don't think," Alfreda said. "I *know* you can't remember. She's here, so take your medicine before you have a stroke."

I believed I might have found the two crankiest people on the planet. "I don't want to upset you, Mr. Green, but—"

"My name is Cole. And what's yours, little lady?" Did I see a sparkle in his cloudy brown eyes?

"Jillian. Mind if I sit down?"

"Of course you'll sit," he said.

Alfreda said, "He promised he'd take his medicine when you got here." She stared down at her patient, her hands on her hips. "Didn't you?"

"That would be a good idea," I said. "I don't want you to fall ill while I'm here." I sat on the edge of an old leather wing chair adjacent to him.

"See how nice she said that, Alfreda?" Mr. Green said.

"You could take a lesson. Bring me the horse pills. And bring Miss Jillian here a cup of that hot cocoa you make."

Alfreda's full lips hinted at a smile. "And I'm supposing you'd like a cup of cocoa yourself?"

"You would be correct, woman. One of the few times in your life, sorry to say." But he was holding back a smile, too.

I'll bet this goes on all day, I thought. These two actually shared a fondness for each other, but they would never admit to it.

When she left the room, Cole Green said, "There's a conspiracy, isn't there? I'm not getting a new Banjo."

I almost did a "huh?" and then remembered that was the name of his cat. "Banjo was an Abyssinian?"

"Didn't know that's what he was until he took sick. Vet told me. Can't hardly pronounce it, much less spell it. Woman at the paper helped me out with the spelling when I called to say I needed a new cat."

The answers to why he hadn't used the Internet or visited animal shelters were obvious. Classified ads served the needs of his generation for things like finding a new pet.

"Abyssinians came from ancient Egypt. An Abyssinian cat was considered a child of God," I said.

Mr. Green nodded and smiled. "Banjo was that indeed."

"What happened to him?" I asked.

His eyes instantly grew rheumy. "Cancer. Cancer's gonna take over the earth. I've had it myself, but I survived. Not poor Banjo."

"I'm so sorry," I said.

Alfreda returned with a tray holding the cocoa. "Kindly help me by setting up one of those TV tables in the closet by the front door," she said to me.

Soon the folding table was between us, and Alfreda gave Mr. Green a handful of pills and a glass of water to wash them down. He grumbled but did take the medicine.

"I got laundry to do," Alfreda said. "Need anything, you holler." She pointed at Mr. Green. "And that means she can holler, not you. I've had enough of your hollering for one day."

She turned and walked out of the room.

The smell of chocolate had filled the air, and one taste of Alfreda's rich, sweet concoction soothed me from head to toe.

Mr. Green must have noticed the change in my demeanor because he was smiling. "Now, that's nature's best medicine." He nodded at my cup. "A decent dose of cocoa. I keep telling her I don't need all those pills, just two cups of this every day."

"You could be on to something." I set down the cup and leaned toward him. "Tell me about Banjo and this person who answered your ad."

"You first. What's it to you?"

"That's a long story, but I'll try to give you a quick summary." The summary took long enough for us both to finish our cocoa. "Did you follow all that?" I said, using one of the small paper napkins Alfreda had provided to wipe away my chocolate mustache.

"I may be half deaf and nearly blind, but I got the rest of my faculties," he said. "This man stole your cat, and you're on a quest for answers. That about sum it up?"

I smiled. "True enough. Was it a man who answered your ad?"

"It was, and he came with a picture. The cat was sitting in someone's big picture window. Taken from the outside, not the inside." Mr. Green stroked his chin. "Struck me as odd he'd take a picture of the cat from the outside of a house. That shoulda clued me something wasn't right."

I had a picture window and an Abyssinian. Everything seemed to fit so far. "Alfreda mentioned you gave this man money, that he came here?"

"Do I look like I could drive around town meeting up with people? Course he came here," he said.

"Was he about sixty? Messy hair with plenty of dandruff on his shoulders?" I said.

"You think these old eyes could see dandruff? I can't even tell if I have it. But the man who came—Mr. Barney Smith, he said—was gray-headed, and I had a bad feeling about him. But I was so wanting a new Banjo, I didn't listen to what my insides were telling me. And now the cat's not arrived, and I've got enough smarts to figure out this man is your corpse, Mr. Flake Wilkerson."

"That's my guess. You think you'd recognize the cat he showed you if you looked at my Abyssinian?" I said.

"Since the cat I was supposed to receive looked exactly like Banjo, probably."

I opened my bag and took out the picture. I handed it to Mr. Green.

He stared down at Syrah and then slowly his hand came to rest against his heart. "That's him. That's Banjo all over again."

"How much money did you give Mr. Wilkerson?" I said softly.

"Five hundred dollars." He couldn't take his eyes off the photo.

"And how much more were you expected to pay?" I said.

"You'll be thinking I'm crazy when I tell you. Alfreda thinks I am."

"I don't think you're crazy for a minute. Just tell me."

"Two thousand." He looked up at me then, his eyes wet with tears. "You can't put a price on getting your best friend back."

I smiled, feeling an immense sadness. "No, you can't."

"This your cat? The one he stole?" he asked.

"It is. His name is Syrah."

He handed over the picture with a trembling hand. "I'm glad he's home where he belongs."

"Do you have a photo of Banjo?" I asked.

"Got a million of them." He shouted, "Alfreda? Get yourself in here."

She bustled into the room, wiping her hands on a dish towel. "I told you not to holler at me."

"Get me the album. This lady needs to see Banjo. And you'll be happy to know that man who came here has met his Maker, as well he should have. He was a liar and a thief."

I left shortly afterward with the only picture of Mr. Green's beloved cat that he was willing to part with. The resemblance between Banjo and Syrah was amazing. Sure, there are bound to be similarities in certain breeds, but these two could have been twins. No wonder the man was willing to spend twenty-five hundred dollars hoping to replace his old friend.

Despite my sadness that Wilkerson had taken advantage of Mr. Green, I was also glad that I now had proof that this murder could very well be about cats *and* money—just as Candace and I had believed from the start.

It was despicable that Flake Wilkerson had taken advantage of the poor man. The question now was how many more desperate people like Mr. Green had Wilkerson made deals with?

Twenty-two

I drove straight to the Mercy city hall, convinced I now had proof that cats *plus* money were behind Wilkerson's murder. I had pictures of two very similar cats and a story to tell Baca. He'd better pay attention for once.

But the first person I saw when I walked into the police office was Candace. Her surprise was evident.

"What are you doing here?" she whispered, glancing back toward the hall that led to the chief's office.

"I've made a small breakthrough. Remember those newspapers Daphne gave me?"

She nodded, but before I could tell her what I'd learned, Baca walked out of his office. He was concentrating on putting on his jacket, but when he looked up and saw us, he quit halfway through the process. "What are you two cooking up now?"

I lifted my chin. "Nothing. You said to tell you if I learned anything interesting connected to the case, so here I am."

"Is this about cats again?" He seemed ready to leave and looked at Candace, not me. "Is it?"

"I have no idea, sir," she said.

"I don't believe that for a minute." He leveled a hard stare my way. "What's this about?"

"It will take me a minute to explain. Can we go into your office?" I didn't add, "And can Candace come, too?" though I wanted to.

"I have dinner plans," he said, starting past us. "But if it's that important, come along."

I hadn't expected *this* response. I was hoping we could talk here, but instead I ended up following him out.

Candace grabbed my arm and whispered, "Get with me later."

I mouthed, "I will," and hurried to catch up with Baca.

He said he was headed to the Finest Catch, a restaurant less than a block away. We walked there, and I practically had to run to keep up with him.

He asked for a table for three. Once we were seated near a window that looked out on a garden between this building and the next, he said, "Mae is always late. So, tell me this important piece of information."

I explained about the newspapers and the circled ads, my visit to Mr. Green and how the man he'd dealt with sounded very much like Flake Wilkerson. But it was the price Mr. Green was willing to pay for a cat that finally hit home with Baca.

"I had no idea cats could cost that much," he said.

"I've been to hundreds of cat shows." I sipped the white wine I'd ordered. "A champion sire cat can bring plenty. But as you see, even when a cat doesn't have pedigree papers, people might have other reasons to be willing to pay a lot."

"But what you're talking about is an old man replacing a dead pet." He'd ordered a calamari appetizer, and now he picked up a deep-fried ring with his fork.

"It's called desperation. What if Wilkerson double-crossed someone he'd promised a cat to? Took their down payment and never came through? They might be mad enough to find him. Maybe he and some angry person who'd been conned had a fight and Wilkerson ended up dead."

He chewed for a second, looking thoughtful. "I suppose that's possible. Cat fanatics like you and Shawn certainly have taught me about how obsessed cat people can be, if nothing else. I'll consider what you've told me. Maybe this motive bears more investigative work."

"Did you call me obsessed?" I said.

His ears reddened. "That came out the wrong way. Passionate, maybe? Is that a better word?"

"Who's getting passionate with whom?" Marian Mae said. She'd arrived at the table as quietly as one of my cats.

Baca rose and smiled. "Hey there, Mae. Hope you don't mind, but I asked Jillian to join us."

"Don't worry, I'm not staying." I gulped down the remaining inch of wine. "Have a fabulous dinner."

With a cup of cocoa and a glass of wine the only things in my stomach, I would need to make a sincere effort not to stumble my way out of the restaurant. But once again, before I'd gone five feet, I heard Marian Mae speak.

"What is going on between you two?" she said.

Why did she care? Or was every woman in Mercy as jealous as Lydia? I started down the sidewalk, walking carefully. I wasn't drunk, just a little light-headed, but I am clumsy enough that I could do a face plant on the uneven sidewalk even without an overload of sugar and alcohol. I was concentrating so hard on watching out for high spots that I might trip over, I nearly shot three feet in the air when Candace jumped out from between two buildings.

"You have to tell me what this is about. Right now," she said.

"Did you follow me?" I said.

"You're damn straight. Now tell me why you came in so hot to see the chief," she said.

"*Hot* is not the word I'd choose. And I need food before I can talk about anything," I said. "That restaurant smelled like heaven."

"We'll pick up something. I'll drive." She took my arm and yanked, but I didn't budge.

"No way am I riding with you. Pick up chicken and meet me at my house." I pulled a twenty from my bag and gave it to her. That was when I noticed the two pictures of the very similar Abyssinians. What an idiot. Those pictures were the reason I'd wanted to talk to Baca. If I'd remembered, maybe he would have been a little more excited about what I'd learned today.

Candace headed off to pick up the food, perhaps realizing that discussing this on the street, mere steps from where her boss was having dinner with his girlfriend, might not be such a great idea.

I'd had a chance to offer affection as well as food to my three kids by the time Candace arrived with boxed fried chicken dinners, though the offerings at the Finest Catch would have been far more enjoyable.

Once we were sitting at the counter in my kitchen and I was practically inhaling the greasy yet wonderful chicken, Candace was ready for the explanation.

After I was done telling her about Mr. Green's quest to replace his Abyssinian and my conversation with Baca, she said, "That's excellent information. But I happen to know the chief's already been persuaded by the financial evidence he's discovered that the cats might be more important than he ever wanted to believe."

"No wonder he sounded so nonchalant when I told him what I'd learned. What about this financial evidence?" I said.

"I wouldn't have known if I didn't have a partner who loves to run his mouth—especially after he's decided the boss might have this case all wrong. Morris told me some stuff that's pretty interesting," she said.

"So share." I took another bite of a chicken leg.

"Get this. Flake Wilkerson had an account with a flight shipping company. He was sending cats everywhere. It costs a lot to ship an animal across the country in this age of unstable fuel prices. Guess that's one reason he was charging an old man on a fixed income twenty-five hundred dollars for a cat. Maybe that's what he charged all his customers, and selling to locals like Mr. Green helped him make an even bigger profit."

"That's how he made his money? Stealing cats and selling them?" I said.

"After what you've learned, it makes sense," she said. "Another thing I overheard directly about Wilkerson is that he didn't have a landline. So how was he doing business?"

"Good point," I said.

"I was hoping Chief Baca's realizations would make him pay attention not only to the lack of a phone—not even a cell phone was found in the house—but I've collected cat hair samples I know could be useful. And if he would have listened to me from the beginning—"

"But he didn't. You're right about the phone, though. Mr. Wilkerson would need one, right?"

"Exactly," she said. "Or else he did everything over the Internet."

I wiped my hands on the paper towels I'd brought to the counter, and Candace did the same. "Maybe like the computer, the killer knew the cell phone could be incriminating. We should ask Ed about any new additions to his mobile phone collection—because I'm sure he has one."

Candace smiled. "Since Ed is the one who found the computer, my guess is the chief already asked about phones. He may be difficult, but he's not stupid."

"*We* didn't ask Ed. Does that make us dumb?" I said.

Candace's face fell. "Darn. Guess it does."

Leaving her to recover from the shattering realization that we'd missed an opportunity, I put the empty chicken boxes in the garbage can outside so the cats wouldn't be tempted to raid the kitchen trash. I heard thunder rumble in the distance. Another weather change was on the way.

Candace had settled on the sofa with a big glass of water, her police utility belt lying on my coffee table. She wore her gun in a shoulder holster and had removed that, too.

"I am stuffed and feeling like an idiot," she said.

I didn't like looking at a gun in my living room, so I averted my eyes from her weapon. Weapons like hers were meant to take people down. I appreciated the fact that we had folks like Candace to protect us, but that gun was plain scary.

Candace stretched out and crossed her legs at the ankles. "Know what else Morris told me?"

"Seems you have a whole lot more to tell me than I had to tell you," I said.

Her eyes glittered with excitement. "Get this. Apparently that county computer expert Baca was counting on to help with the damaged hard drive is not available and won't be for at least a month. That's where the secrets are—in that computer—and Baca's gonna need serious, expert help."

"Does that mean he'll have to wait until the computer person can work on it?" I asked.

"Maybe not. Remember what Karen said about Tom's abilities with computers? Well, I planted that seed with Morris. If I know my partner, he'll be in Baca's office tomorrow ready to persuade him to hire a consultant—Tom Stewart."

"Morris would do that?" I said.

"Any way he can play the hero is fine by him," she said.

"But won't Morris mention that you were the one who told him about Tom?" I said.

"Are you kidding? Morris isn't about to give credit to anyone but Morris." Candace intertwined her hands behind her neck. "Nope. I believe I have this all set up. Then you can grill Tom for information about that hard drive."

I'd been leaning back on the sofa myself, but that remark sat me straight up. "Grill him? What does that mean?"

"He likes you. That's as plain as day," she said. "I saw the way he looked at you when he found your cat. He was proud as punch and happy he could help you."

"Oh. So I should use him?" I was not liking this idea.

"I used Morris. Now it's your turn," she said.

"But Tom won't be permitted to talk about anything he gets off that hard drive, will he?"

"Haven't you been paying attention?" she said. "That's not how things work in Mercy."

"But I don't know Tom well enough to—"

"You could get to know him better," she said with a smile. "He treats me like I'm his little sister, but you? You could get plenty out of him."

"I wouldn't feel right about that, Candace."

"But if Tom helps the department with the computer, then Baca might be able to solve the case. And won't you be curious to find out what Tom might learn?"

"Yes, but—"

"This reluctance is coming from the woman who went to Taylorville today to question a man about a cat? Can you forget about everything you've done trying to solve this thing just because you feel uncomfortable?" She shook her head. "Nope. You're too much like me. You can't leave this alone for a minute."

Of course she was right.

Candace left about an hour later, and I closed myself in the sewing room with the bags of shredded paper. I didn't want to think about being sneaky with Tom, and what better distraction than a paper quilt? It might be a dead end, but I was intrigued.

Playing with paper, however, would be way too much fun for my cats. Any shreds I moved would become an instant toy, and soon the three of them would destroy any hope I had of piecing together even one flyer or poster. They had to stay outside the room for now—and they didn't like it one bit. Paws appeared underneath the door the minute I shut the cats out, and then Merlot started meowing loud enough for the people across the lake to hear.

Trying to ignore them, I focused on the felt design wall that I used to arrange blocks or quilt pieces. Fabric will stick to the felt all by itself, but paper would have to be pinned. Embroidery pins would do the job.

First, though, I had to find strips of paper that went together. As a longtime quilter, I have an eye for what goes with what. I sat on the floor, a pile of shreds in front of me, and something interesting popped out immediately. The rich blacks and whites of what was obviously a flyer. A flyer I'd seen with my own eyes on Chase Cook's computer.

I started searching for all the matching pieces I could find, my hands shaking with excitement. I didn't find more than a third of the picture, but this was Roscoe, all right. My first discovery was that I could recognize some of these shreds as bills and some as computer-generated flyers like my own. I decided to lay one of my own lost Syrah flyers next to me as a guide. If I did put one of those back together, it would confirm that Wilkerson had gotten his hands on one or more and didn't want any Good Samaritan interfering with the plans he had for Syrah, that being to deliver him to poor, unsuspecting Mr. Green.

After this find, I started placing other strips that seemed to go together in separate piles, a project that proved time-consuming but not all that difficult. There were plenty of colorful shreds and I actually enjoyed myself. Even though it was getting very late, I was determined to put at least one piece of paper back together.

Four hours later, fatigue finally got the better of me. But I had re-created parts of two different cats by pinning pieces on the design wall. I had half a face of one long-haired gray cat with aqua eyes as well as a chest and legs that surely belonged to a Siamese. I knew immediately that this was not the Siamese found at the Pink House and currently in Candace's care, though. The markings and colors were wrong.

Why couldn't I have been lucky enough to find the piece of either of these flyers that had a name or phone number on it? Someone could have gone to Wilkerson's house last Sunday morning hoping to pick up a cat they'd paid for. One of these two cats, perhaps. Maybe the price was too steep, they'd argued and Wilkerson died. And then the killer left with one of these two cats. It seemed possible. I needed a name and phone number, but that would have to wait until I wasn't cross-eyed from exhaustion.

I dragged myself to bed, making sure the sewing room door remained closed to keep my work safe from prying paws. The shredded paper had to yield something. Maybe then I could provide Baca with more evidence and I wouldn't have to pump Tom Stewart for information.

Twenty-three

I expected Candace to call me first thing in the morning to urge me to get busy seducing Tom. But it was Daphne who phoned as I was pouring my first cup of coffee.

After I said hello, she said, "I don't have an alibi. Have you ever needed an alibi in your lifetime?"

She sounded just as upset as the last time we spoke. "Tell me what's happened," I said.

"Apparently I was in business with my father—which is news to me. He had a post office box, and the moron used my name and my phone number when he paid for it."

"Here in Mercy?" I asked. Surely anyone with half a brain would recognize Flake Wilkerson if he came in to rent a box.

"No. In Greenville," she said. "That's a two-hour drive from here, and even farther from where I live."

"Who told you this and how did they find out?" I asked.

"Chief Baca was here bright and early. He told me he'd learned this from the bank records. And since my name was also on the bank account and there's that big life insurance payout coming in the future, the police are asking me all sorts of questions—especially about this business we were supposedly running."

"Did you sign on for this joint account?" I said.

"Of course not."

"Okay. That should help protect you. And what kind of business are we talking about?" I asked.

"There is no business, Jillian. So how the hell would I know? He asked me how many times I'd been to the Greenville-Spartanburg airport lately. But I haven't been there since I took a vacation to the West Coast last year," she said.

"But if you never signed any documents to open a bank account, it seems to me they could easily rule you out. And *do* you have an alibi for the day of the murder?"

She didn't reply, but I could hear her breathing rapidly.

"Daphne?" I said.

"Why do I have to prove anything to anyone? I didn't kill him."

"I know you didn't," I said. "Did you tell Baca what you were doing that day?"

"No. He can figure it out himself. I thought you'd understand, but apparently—"

"I do understand. Can we talk about this in person? Please?"

"If you think that will help me, come on. Personally, I doubt it." She didn't sound the least bit happy about rehashing her conversation with Baca. But of course she *had* called me, and that made it pretty clear that she wanted my help.

I poured my coffee down the drain, deciding to stop by Belle's Beans and pick up coffee for both of us. We'd had a steady rain all night, and when I'd gone out for the paper I discovered the temperature was in the low fifties, so that delicious, rich coffee might do us both some good. I put my hair in a ponytail and slipped on a sweatshirt and jeans, not bothering with makeup.

But when I entered Belle's and saw Tom Stewart in line waiting to place his order, I wished I'd at least opted for lipstick. Despite my reluctance to use him to get information, I did want to talk to him. Just because . . . well, just *because*. Reaching around the person standing between us, I poked his shoulder.

He turned and smiled when he saw me. "Hey, there. You're up early."

"You, too," I said.

He allowed the woman ahead of me to move up so we could be next to each other in line. "Making my first coffee run of the day. Got to sell my services to a couple on the lake and need to be alert and ready for all their questions."

"If they need a cat-cam, you're the man," I said with a laugh. "By the way, I met your mother the other day. Had supper with her and Ed, as a matter of fact."

We stepped ahead as the line moved.

"How did that happen?" he asked, color rising up his neck. "Because they are perhaps the oddest pair in town."

I playfully punched his arm. "Come on. They're sweet."

He looked relieved. "I like them, but I never know what people might think when they first meet them."

It was his turn at the counter and he offered to get my coffee. I told him I was buying for someone else as well as myself and that he didn't need to buy three coffees. But he did anyway, without asking who the coffee was for. Once he'd paid, he picked up his cup and seemed in a rush to get to his meeting.

"Tom, wait," I said before he reached the door.

He stood there, waiting for me to gather sugar and cream for my coffees.

I carried my drinks over to him and said, "Remember the other night when you asked me to get a bite to eat with you?"

"Yeah," he said warily.

"Can I change my mind?"

He glanced down at the two coffees and pointed back and forth between the two cups. "Those aren't for some guy you've met since I last saw you?"

"These? Oh, no. These are for Daphne and me."

He looked confused. "Wilkerson's daughter? Oh, wait. That's right. I heard she was staying at the house." His shoulders relaxed and his engaging smile appeared. "Tonight good for you?"

"Perfect," I said. "How about the Finest Catch? I've been dying to try that place."

"Pick you up at seven," he said, and hurried out the door.

I gave him some lead time before exiting. That had been tough, but I realized I liked this guy and wanted him to trust me. I would figure this out—maybe just ask him straight out if he would let me know what he learned from the computer. That seemed simple enough. But what if he wouldn't tell me? Then I'd have to contend with Candace.

Daphne, I discovered when she answered the door, had gone back to the unlit cigarette trick to calm herself. She took the coffee gratefully and led me through the house. Neatly stacked and labeled boxes lined the walls in the living and dining rooms, and I decided she must be exhausted after all the work she'd done, even with the help of Candace and me. We went into the kitchen—I could still picture that apple sitting there on the butcher block island, the one Daphne's father had probably been about to eat right before someone killed him.

Daphne held the cardboard cup to her nose and said, "Heaven."

Thank goodness she had to remove the cigarette to drink.

We sat at the small round table in the breakfast nook area. Even though a nook by definition is small, this one had been built for much larger furniture. The table, not to mention both of us, seemed lost in the space. Rain had started up again, and it pattered on the roof and meandered down the windowpanes surrounding us.

"Tell me about Baca," I said. "Why did he come here this morning?"

"I told you most of it on the phone. He said I could have come here to kill my father. He said our—what was his word?—*estrangement* was well-known."

"Well-known? I don't suppose he mentioned who told him that?" I said.

"No answer except to say he had reliable sources," she said.

"So this information came from someone your father knew. Who were his friends?" I said.

"That's the problem. I have no idea."

"I've learned he was a regular at Belle's Beans and spoke to people there. But from the few folks I talked to, he didn't seem to have any true buddies."

But I was thinking of Chase and how he and Wilkerson had frequented Belle's Beans at the same time every day, until Chase's cat disappeared. Was this the friend that Wilkerson confided in about his problems with his daughter?

"What are you thinking?" Daphne wanted to know.

"I've met a few of your father's acquaintances. Chase Cook and Belle—the owner of the coffee place. She thought your father might want to take her out. But then he stole her cat instead . . . and Chase's, too."

"He only made friends with people so he could steal from them," Daphne said. "Figures."

"Yes," I said. "It's a pattern. It's what he did. And that's what got him killed, not any money he might have left to you."

"I told that cop I don't want his stupid money. I want to clear this place out and get back to my studio." She took the lid off her coffee and inhaled again.

"You're convinced Baca suspects you?" I said.

"Duh, yeah. He's asking me for an alibi. He told me my father was shipping cats all over the place."

"I wish Baca would have believed me from the beginning," I said. "This has always been about the cats."

"You were right. But since my name was obviously used to set up the shipping account, I guess I'm involved. Maybe I have a multiple personality disorder and one of me came to town to ship cats out every now and then. And maybe I have another evil personality that came here and killed him."

"Just because he's asking you for an alibi doesn't mean

he thinks you're guilty," I said. "Maybe he's trying to rule you out."

"That's what he said, but I watch the news. One minute the police are claiming a person's not a suspect; then, next thing you know, that person is under arrest."

"Again, you have to have some sense of why Baca came here first thing this morning," I said. "Did he get some new information other than—"

"Other than the fact that my father was using my name for no good and that I needed to come up with an alibi?" she said, her voice strained by anger and what also sounded like fear.

The cigarette would reappear if I didn't calm her down. "Sorry. I know this isn't easy. But I need your help to understand it better."

She closed her eyes, took a deep breath. "I know. None of this is your fault."

"Tell me one thing," I said. "Did you tell Baca that your father took your cat?"

"Yes, but he stole Sophie over a year ago. The chief wasn't interested. But now that I think about it, when I mentioned Sophie he said the evidence told them that many, many cats had come and gone from this house. I guess that's why she wasn't important—because she was just one of many."

"If he'd shown that same attitude toward Syrah, I might have socked the man in the nose," I said.

Daphne smiled. "I'm glad someone understands."

"They found the insurance policy right after the murder," I said. "Did he show you the paperwork?"

"No," she said.

"Guess it might be evidence. That's why he can't show you," I said.

"Why would I want to see the policy? I keep telling everyone I don't give a flip about his money." Daphne was hunting for her cigarette case again.

"I believe you, if that means anything," I said.

She stopped short of taking out a cigarette. "It means a lot."

"I still think the police are missing something, though. They have some of the shredder contents, but I even wonder if anyone's working on trying to piece flyers back together—maybe to get names of possible new suspects. I'm working on what you gave me in those bags, and it's not difficult but it sure is a time suck," I said.

"You haven't uncovered some amazing revelation about who killed my father or you would have told me." She sighed and began turning the silver cigarette box over and over. "That leaves me first on the suspect list."

"Why not tell the police where you were when your father was murdered?" I said. "They can rule you out and—"

"There's a problem with that," she said quietly.

"Why? You don't remember? You were alone? What?" I said.

"You really want to know?"

"Of course," I said.

"Okay . . . I was here."

Twenty-four

My *"What?"* came out as a whisper. The pounding in my chest felt like a small bomb about to go off.

She put her head down and her wild hair spilled around her face—creating a convenient mask.

"Daphne, look at me," I said.

She didn't, but she did speak. "They know I was here, too. They took my fingerprints as soon as I arrived in town, and today Chief Baca says they matched them to a glass found in the sink the day of the murder."

"But they didn't find your prints on the murder weapon." I said it as a statement, not a question.

She jerked her head up, her dark eyes filled with anger and disappointment. Despite my effort to show her I believed her, she wasn't buying it. "No, not on the murder weapon. But they have a witness."

A *witness*? Just when I thought it couldn't get any worse. I willed myself to remain calm, but I was stunned and even a tiny bit frightened. I'd been so sure this woman wasn't a killer and yet . . . "Tell me everything," I said. "Otherwise I can't help you."

"That man who saves cats and dogs—what's his name?"

"Shawn?" I said.

"The chief told me Shawn saw me here—through the window—and he kept quiet about it until they brought him in for questioning again. But apparently Shawn finally admitted he saw me and my father having a disagreement."

It would be like Shawn not to give that up easily. Probably why he was mad at me for so readily telling the police things about him. "Since the police didn't ask him directly about anything he saw through the window, he didn't offer it willingly. He's not a fan of the police force."

"You must know Shawn pretty well," she said. "He apparently only gave up the information when they told him about my fingerprints and they pressed him for anything he might have seen."

"What in God's name were you doing here?" I asked.

Her turn for a deep breath before she spoke. "My father told me he had Sophie. He said I could pick her up. But when I got here—"

"When did you get here?" I said.

"It was the day before the murder, Saturday afternoon. But Sophie wasn't here. He'd lied, and I'd fallen for it again." She was shaking her head, tears welling.

"Why did he lure you here if he didn't really have your cat?" I said.

"Oh, he stuck to his story. Told me to be patient. Someone would be bringing her to me. Like a fool, I waited, and he kept leaving the room to make phone calls. By ten that night I was so angry I was about to burst. He said there'd been a delay and if Sophie wasn't here in the morning, he'd personally go and pick her up."

Phone calls. What happened to Wilkerson's phone? "So your father did have a phone."

"Prepaid cell. He said it saved money. But since he was doing illegal things, I guess that's the real reason he needed something untraceable."

"Did you mention at least that much to Baca?"

"No. He didn't ask about the phone."

I steeled myself for my next question, knowing I might not like the answer. "Did you stay the night? Wait until the morning your father died before you left?" I hated myself for thinking it, but this could be how it all happened. An angry daughter and a mean old man got into it when he failed to come through on a promise yet again—a last argument that ended in tragedy.

"Did I wait?" she said, incredulous. "Are you crazy? I drove home that night. Got there in record time, too. For the first time in my life, I wish I'd gotten stopped for speeding. At least then I'd have the precious alibi I so desperately need now."

"Wow," I said. "And you told everything to Baca?"

She looked at me like I was an idiot. "Come on, Jillian. I hated my father, I was here close to the time he was murdered and we argued—and there's a witness who saw me. Plus there's the insurance policy naming me as beneficiary. No, I didn't say much of anything. I told the chief I needed to speak to my attorney—and by the way, I don't have an attorney." She finally stuck a cigarette between her lips.

"You can't trust Baca with what you've told me?" I said. But she didn't answer, just rolled her eyes, so I said, "I don't know any lawyers, either. I could ask Candace. She'd know who's the best in town."

"Have you forgotten she's a cop?"

"But she's also—" I stopped. Knowing Candace and knowing that real evidence pointed straight at Daphne, she was right. I couldn't ask Candace for help. "Okay. Not a good idea."

"Don't worry about it. I'll figure it out." She swiped at the tears on her pale cheeks. "Right now I just hope you believe me."

"I do." And that was the truth. I started to ask her to come to my house for supper, because if anyone needed a friend right now, it was Daphne, but then I remembered my "date" with Tom. "Your estate sale is set for Monday, so you'll be staying here." *If you aren't in jail*, I thought. "Why not spend the day with me tomorrow? Stuck here alone, you'll have nothing to do but think. And that's not good."

"Maybe I'll take you up on that. And as for the estate sale? Postponed. The chief saw everything boxed up and wondered why I felt *compelled*—that's his word—to get rid of my father's things so fast." Her cigarette bobbed as she spoke and I almost wished she'd just light up and get it over with.

"Baca told you to postpone the sale?" I said.

"He said another warrant might be issued. That means he thinks I've hidden evidence that proves I killed my father." She shook her head. "All this because I was sure I'd get Sophie back."

"Tell me about her." I wasn't sure if talking about this would help calm Daphne, but it was worth a try.

She pushed away from the table and got the cell phone that had been charging on the counter. She flipped it open and held it out for me. The wallpaper on her small screen was of a gray long-haired domestic cat sitting on a pillow.

Uh-oh. I squinted and studied the screen. This cat looked an awful lot like the half a cat I'd pieced together last night But I wasn't about to mention that. Not until I'd put the whole picture together. I didn't even know if it was simply a computer-generated picture or a lost-cat flyer right now. But what if it was a picture of Sophie, one Wilkerson used to show her off so he could sell her to a grieving person— the same approach he'd used with Mr. Green? Only that time, a year ago, it was not an Abyssinian but a gray cat. I had to finish that picture. And now I had something to compare it to.

"She's beautiful," I said. "Did your father have any pictures of Sophie?"

"Not that I know about, but since he took her, he could have taken pictures. Why are you asking?" Daphne said.

"If your father was supplying cats to people, wouldn't he need pictures of what he had available to sell?"

"I suppose," she said. "But that won't help me get her back, will it?"

"Maybe not. But we know your father really was dying and maybe he did intend to reunite you with your cat. It's not like he provided any other reason, right?"

Sounding disgusted, she said, "You mean besides telling me he'd switched beneficiaries on his insurance?"

"Switched? I thought this was a new policy and you didn't know about it," I said. What else was she holding back?

"I've been racking my brain, and now I do recall him telling me he had life insurance, but I totally forgot, probably figured it was another lie. Apparently I wasn't the original beneficiary, though. So I guess that's why when I learned about the switch, I swooped into town and killed my father first chance I got." She bent her head and pressed her hands against her temples. "Joking aside, I realize this looks bad for me, but I swear I didn't kill him."

"You were upset about Sophie. You say you don't care about any money, and I believe you." I rested a hand on her arm. "Listen, if your father did steal Sophie—and he most likely did—he knew what he'd done with her; he knew where she was. And maybe whoever he sold her to was unwilling to return her. Maybe that's the person he kept calling over and over the night before the murder."

The cigarette dropped when Daphne looked up. "You think his death really was about my cat?"

"Like Candace always says, evidence is the key, and right now I'm only guessing. I don't have any proof. But it seems plausible after all you've told me. Think about it. Not only did the killer take the computer, he or she apparently took your father's phone, too."

"Plausible to you and me," she said. "Chief Baca might be hard to convince."

"That's why we need evidence." I thought about that half-completed puzzle of a gray cat on my design board again. Was that picture the key to everything? "Text me that picture of Sophie right now," I said. "I gotta go, but I'll call you."

I started for home, anxious to transfer Sophie's picture from my phone to my computer. If I could prove Wilkerson had a cat flyer that resembled Sophie, then Baca might be compelled to consider that he had stolen his daughter's cat, which in turn might help him believe that Daphne was really only in town in hopes of getting Sophie back. But I swallowed hard, thinking that it could offer Baca an even stronger reason to suspect Daphne of murder.

I pushed that thought aside as I slid behind the wheel of my van. *That's not what happened.* I wasn't wrong about Daphne. I turned the key in the ignition and went to put my phone in my bag and was again confronted by the photos of Banjo and Syrah, those twin Abyssinians. I didn't care if Baca laughed me out of the police station—he should see these, maybe even talk to Mr. Green himself. Maybe Mr. Wilkerson said something that day he met with the old guy, something about other customers. I drove into town and parked outside the city hall. I opened my phone and stared at the picture of Sophie that Daphne had just sent. Maybe talking to the chief might not be the best idea after all. Daphne had told me things she should have told Baca herself. Did I trust myself to go in there and not spill every-thing? Heck, I didn't even know what Baca had on her, at least not everything. If Daphne got arrested because of my mouth, I'd never forgive myself.

So I dialed Candace instead.

She answered on the first ring. "Hey. What's up?"

"I need you to give the pictures of Syrah and Banjo to Baca," I said quickly. "Maybe after he sees how closely the two cats resemble each other he'll talk to Mr. Green. Mr. Green knows firsthand what Wilkerson—"

"Can I call you back, Mom?" Candace said.

Damn. She must be with someone—probably Morris.

"If you get a break, I'll be at home." I snapped my phone shut and backed up, thinking. *Why didn't Daphne tell Baca everything? And has she told* me *everything?* All I knew was that I believed her, but I could see that Baca and even Can-dace might not.

I was aching for the comfort of a cat in my lap and a mind free of questions. I got half of that. All three cats sensed my tension when I came in. I made a cup of tea with honey to rid myself of the chill of a cold day—so cold in so many ways. When I sat on the sofa, Chablis crawled into my lap, her long champagne fur spilling around her. Merlot and Syrah jockeyed for space beside me and soon settled down. There is nothing so calming as the music of three cats purring in unison and a cup of tea on a dark, damp day.

By the time Candace arrived at my door, my mind felt clearer.

My three friends greeted her, and when the petting was over, she straightened and said, "I have ten minutes. What's going on?"

I handed her the pictures of Syrah and Banjo. "Take these to the chief. Tell him to talk to Mr. Green, and maybe then he'll pursue a course other than the one he's chosen." As soon as the words left my mouth, I cursed silently. With all the evidence against Daphne, Candace would surely see where he was going with his investigation.

"What does that mean?" Candace said.

"All I know is I can't talk to him again and—"

"Why, Jillian? You know something and you're not willing to tell me. That's not good."

The tension that had eased in my neck returned with a vengeance. Pursuing answers together, we'd developed a true friendship and I couldn't keep Daphne's secret from Candace. She would never forgive me when she found out. And she'd surely find out.

"This might take more than ten minutes," I said.

"Then give me the speed-dating version."

I told her about Daphne being at the Pink House the day before the murder, how she'd come thinking she was about to get Sophie back.

When I was done, Candace said, "Holy crap." Her follow-up was, "And you weren't going to tell me?"

"You have an obligation as a police officer," I said. "Baca knows she was in the house, but he doesn't know why, and if he finds out she was angry and disappointed, left in a rage, then, well, you know what will happen."

She chewed on the inside of her cheek and finally said, "This is all hearsay. Not even admissible in court. I'd suggest Daphne get a lawyer and we both forget you told me anything."

"Um . . . yeah. What were we talking about, anyway?" I said.

She smiled for the first time. "See what I mean? Shawn Cuddahee is the one who set the chief onto Daphne when he admitted he saw her at the house the day before the murder. The chief knows she lied about being in town, so he's keeping a close eye on her. He'll find out what's what without any help from us."

"You won't tell him I was there this morning?" I said.

"I don't think I heard you mention that," she said, her jaw tight.

Twenty-five

I spent most of the afternoon piecing paper on my design board. Finding matching colors was the easy part of this re-creation project. Numbers, letters and other printing, I learned, were difficult to put back together, and I was having little success discovering what "lost" or maybe even "found" message went with the picture.

I'd printed out Sophie's photo, and though the similarities between her and whatever cat was on this flyer were real, obvious differences had begun to appear. But maybe it was just the difference between Sophie posing on a pillow and the cat I was putting back together, who was sitting by what I'd decided was a fireplace. Finally, my eyes burning, I stopped working.

All three cats were waiting as I cracked the door. I pushed interested noses aside with my palm so I could get out of the room without them slipping inside. They weren't happy about that. If there's anything a cat hates, it's a closed door.

But they were happy to follow me to the bathroom and watch from a safe distance as I took a bath. No splotches of late-afternoon sunlight coming in through the window for them to enjoy today, but the steam from the hot water created a comfortable kitty spa. Merlot spread his huge body out on the marble vanity, not caring that he knocked off toothpaste, cotton swabs and moisturizer as he made space for himself.

I had to laugh at Syrah, who found the cotton swabs wonderful for tossing and carrying off to far corners. Yup, a bath with my friends was just what the doctor ordered. Chablis joined me as I blow-dried my hair. She's the only one unafraid of the dryer, which always made me believe she might have been a show cat and thus used to being groomed. Who knew what homes these three had lived in before?

Tom arrived at seven on the dot, and I had to admit it felt nice when he told me I had a glow about me despite the rainy, gloomy day.

His driving—he'd arrived in a Prius rather than his van—was nothing like what I'd had to endure with Candace. When we parked a block down from the Finest Catch, Tom said, "You've gone quiet on me. Was it my driving?"

I had to laugh at that one. "No. You have no idea how much I appreciated your driving. I'm a little tired, that's all."

"I think that's the first time I've heard you laugh," he said as we approached the entrance to the restaurant. "What a great laugh you have."

He took my hand as we went inside, and though my first instinct was to withdraw, I didn't. His touch felt warm and strong. I liked it.

After the waitress took our drink order, Tom said, "If you favor bass, they do an amazing job with the largemouth from Mercy Lake."

"That was easy." I closed the menu. "Is that what you're having?"

"Yes," he said, "but the coffee here sucks. We'll go to Belle's after dinner and have a cappuccino, okay?"

"Sounds good. I noticed you say 'dinner,' not 'supper,' and the way you talk—"

"I was born here, but I left with my mother when I was in grade school. We lived in New York, New Jersey, New Hampshire—all the *new* places. I truly believe my mother thought about that word as she dragged me around with each *new* boyfriend."

"How did you end up back here?" I asked.

Before he could answer, our drinks arrived, white wine for me and Scotch for Tom. The waitress then took our order.

Tom looked at me after she left and said, "All this first-date business is awkward."

The memory of his hand clutching mine reminded me that despite being urged on by Candace, I felt as if this actually was a date. I liked what I was seeing across the table from me and felt the heat on my cheeks as soon as that thought crossed my mind.

"You feel guilty, don't you? Like you're cheating on him?" Tom said.

I nodded. "That is such a cliché. But it's true. To help me get past it, you have to tell me as much about yourself as you know about me."

"I already have." He slugged down a hefty swallow of Scotch. "But I'll go on. You asked why we came back to Mercy. Because my mother finally found that the twelve steps worked for her and it was time to come home. She'd gotten some money when she divorced her third—or maybe fourth—husband. She bought that little house you've been to. I was grown by then, but I have worried about her all my life. I decided I should be close."

"Sounds like you love your mom a lot," I said. "She's an interesting person, that's for sure."

"I do love her," he said. That brought out his smile.

Once we'd moved past conversation about his mother, he opened up about his current job, about how he'd never thought he'd enjoy working for himself but he did, and about how he finally felt, after five years, that he was fitting into the community.

The fish, as advertised, was delicious. Tom had ordered his blackened, while I'd chosen mine broiled with lemon and wine sauce. Unfortunately we never reached a point where I felt comfortable asking him whether he'd been consulted about that wrecked computer. He kept talking about his job and the great fishing here and how he loved the weather while I kept listening.

The rain had slowed to a drizzle as we took the short walk to Belle's Beans. I decided I needed to give a little information since he'd completely opened up, so I told him about meeting my husband, how we rescued the cats, moved here and thought everything in our little world was perfect.

"Life has a way of doing that—screwing up the perfect times," he said.

"I was finally getting past the grief and then what happens? I find a body. Never had that on my to-do list."

He said, "Never thought of it that way, but I understand."

I said, "I was talking with Daphne Wilkerson today and—"

"Ah, Daphne," he said. "From what I've heard she's a nutcase."

I stopped. "She lost her father. I think that's an especially unkind way to portray her."

Tom held up his hands in surrender. "I didn't say she *was* a nutcase. I said that's what I've heard."

We started walking again. "You did. Sorry. I happen to like her, though."

"You're getting to know the neighbors, then." He pulled open the door, and the smells of roasted beans rushed out to greet us.

"I hope it doesn't take me five years to fit in," I said with a laugh.

"It won't. You're a lot sweeter than me. Cappuccino okay?"

The weather had brought the town in for coffee, but I was lucky to nab a table just as a couple left. When Tom brought our coffee in real china cappuccino cups, I was surprised. "I didn't know you had a choice between paper or the real deal," I said.

"You do, but it's a poorly kept secret—just like everything else in town." He offered me a choice between a rock candy stir stick and a tiny chocolate spoon. Guess what I chose.

We both paid attention to our coffee for a few seconds, and finally he said, "Seems I have a new calling—police consultant. I think that's pretty hilarious." He stirred the rock candy stick a little faster.

"Why?" I said. I'd been tense all night about this very topic and now he'd brought it up himself. Amazing.

"Because Mike Baca, even though we're friends, doesn't exactly think I have many skills. He thought all I could do was install cameras. So he was surprised to learn how much I know about computer forensics—but any decent PI has to know that stuff."

"Baca asked for your help?" Gosh, I felt like such a fake. And I didn't like that one bit, so I said, "Actually, let me correct that. I heard he asked you to help. I, too, listen to the Mercy grapevine."

Tom laughed. "Did Candace encourage you to accept a date with me to find out what I learned? Because I know that girl, and she is steaming mad that she's been pushed aside."

"She may have encouraged me, but it didn't take much convincing. I wanted to go out the first time you asked," I said. "Although maybe I should be worried about Lydia finding us together. You sure she's not waiting outside?"

His jaw tightened. "I cannot shake that woman. Did you know she and Mike Baca were involved once? She was on him like a fly on sticky paper the first time they met. He's since dumped her for Marian Mae Temple, the reigning queen of Mercy. Lydia's left those two alone, so why won't she give up on me?"

"I got nothing for you," I said with a laugh, "except that she maintains *she* dumped *him*. I wish Lydia wanted Baca back rather than focusing on you. The elegant and rich Marian Mae is a much better target of her derision, don't you think?"

"Not in my book. If Lydia thinks she can compete with

you, she's completely deluded. But don't be fooled by Marian Mae. I installed her security system and she's as fake as that red-colored crabmeat at the supermarket."

"You're kidding. Fake how?"

"I shouldn't be saying anything about former clients, but since her check bounced and I never collected near what she owed me—mostly because I can't seem to escape being Mr. Nice Guy—I don't feel I need to keep secrets about her."

"She's not rich? She sure dresses and acts like she is," I said.

"Rough divorce. Money troubles. I felt sorry for her, I guess. Baca's taking care of her now, so she'll be fine."

"Okay, enough about the Mercy-ites," I said. "Can you muster a little Mr. Nice Guy and pacify poor Candace? Is there anything you can tell me about that computer?"

"Mom told me that you had Ed open the shop after you heard he'd rescued it from the dump." He rested a hand on mine. "Even if you're using me to get information, I don't give a crap. It's fine with me."

"Hey. Don't think like that. You're easy to talk to, easy to look at and I'd like to get to know you better," I said.

"Good. What do you want to know?" he said.

"You're willing to tell me if you found something on that computer?" I said. This was so much easier than I'd thought it would be—and much more fun than I'd had in the last year.

"Sure, because there isn't much to tell. Looks like Wilkerson was running his cat business off a MyFriend page. That's not good news for Baca."

"MyFriend?" I said.

"Sort of a MySpace and Craigslist rolled into one. But though I reconstructed enough of the hard drive and memory to figure that out, it's too late for a preservation order. The page he was running—called Match-a-Cat, by the way—has been taken down already."

"What's a preservation order?" I asked.

"An order from a judge not to destroy any account access records to the pages a user has created," he said. "That computer is a challenge all by itself, but then you add the complication of a business run off MyFriend? Tough stuff. Figuring out where the Internet traffic to that site originated is nearly impossible."

"Why?" I asked.

"Traveling on the Internet is like traveling on any highway. The more turns you take, the harder it is to follow your trail. You log on through your provider, you go to, say, Yahoo or Google or Hotmail, wherever you pick up your mail, and there are passwords at each stop. Using a server like—"

"I got it. It's sort of like peeling back an onion to find out who's been logging on. Lots of layers."

"I'll quit with the geek speak if you want," he said.

"If I wanted that, I'd just say, 'Shut up, Tom.' "

He laughed. "I like the direct approach."

"Can you tell when the page was taken down?" I asked.

"Baca sent a request to the MyFriend owners asking about any sites recently dismantled that had to do with cats, pets, cat breeders, any combination that might offer a clue as to what to look for. He could have been running more pages than his Match-a-Cat. Cheesy name, but probably has good search engine productivity. I don't expect an answer soon. But whoever dismantled the site had the password, and if it went down after the murder, that's good information."

"Meaning the person who shut it down was probably the one who murdered Wilkerson? And perhaps they were in business together?" I said.

"Seems likely, doesn't it? And probably that person hoped to obliterate all the evidence by smashing that computer to smithereens."

"Are you sure it's okay to tell me all this?" I said.

"What am I disclosing? That I did computer forensic work on a battered hard drive and got next to nothing?

That's no state secret. I was glad I got to show the big man I know a few things he doesn't, though."

"It's a competition, then?" I said.

"With men, life's mostly about competition," he said.

"And you're sure the gorgeous Marian Mae Temple has nothing to do with this competition between you two guys?" I said.

"No way," he said emphatically.

Perhaps a little too emphatically, I decided.

He brought me home not long after, and we spent another couple hours getting to know each other better. Merlot stretched out between Tom and me on the couch. He'd never done that when John and I sat side by side, and I wondered if my big Maine coon was making sure I stayed a respectable distance from this man. But when Merlot turned over for Tom to rub his belly, I figured it was more about getting some affection.

The conversation finally came back to the murder, and I decided to show Tom what I'd done with the shredded paper from the Wilkerson house. Three cats knew what was up and followed us, hoping to get into that darn closed-up sewing room. But they were shut out again.

I flipped on the lights and Tom stared at the pinned-up pieces on the design wall. Finally he said, "All the talking in the world couldn't tell me this much about you."

"What does that mean?" I said.

He waved at the wall. "You are a persistent, precise woman. Actually, you should work in a crime lab. They have to do stuff like this all the time. Put pieces of paper back together, look at bugs and dirt and all sorts of crap people never think is important. You've gone above and beyond here, Jillian."

"Funny. Ed said how we throw stuff away before we even know how important it might be," I replied. "I guess this is an example of how what Flake Wilkerson saved might be important."

"Good old Ed. He is one cool dude and the best thing

that ever happened to my mom—even though he looks like the Unabomber."

"I'm fond of Ed myself. But back to this." I waved at my work. "You've been inside plenty of Mercy houses these last few years. Do you recognize this gray cat?" I said.

He tilted his head one way and another, looking at the half-constructed pictures. "Doesn't look like any of the cats Wilkerson had. But why are you even doing this?"

"Because . . . This may sound silly, but I know this is important to finding out what happened last Sunday. And I may not be a policeperson, but I do know how to piece things together. Here, check this out." I pointed at the photo I'd printed of Sophie that was pinned next to the piecing project.

He stepped closer to the board, and since they were stuck up there at my eye level, he had to bend to compare them. "Similar," he said. He rotated a finger around where I'd pieced the cat's front left leg together. "This looks different than the printed-out picture, though. Or is there some trivia about cats changing their spots that I'm unaware of?"

I laughed. "You're just confirming what I thought. Two different cats." I pointed at Sophie. "This is the cat Mr. Wilkerson stole from his own daughter. Does it look like any cat you've seen, say, in the last year?"

"Cats hide when I work in someone's house, so I'm not a source of useful information, I'm sorry to say. I might have seen this cat, but that's like asking me to pick out a specific banana I saw in a bowl on someone's counter two weeks ago. No can do."

"Okay," I said. "It was worth a shot." I glanced at my watch. It was past midnight.

"Time for me to go?" he said.

"Yeah. But thanks for being so open with me. And for understanding about, well—"

"You hoping to get information from me?" he said. "Anytime."

His smile was so infectious, so honest, I grinned back.

But the major blush burning my cheeks? I had no control over that.

I'd been energized by our evening together, and after he left I returned to finish the gray-cat puzzle. This may not be Sophie, but my gut told me it was important.

Obviously Wilkerson was using every available resource—newspapers, the Internet, postings of lost animals, shelter visits. And no doubt he bought cats at shows if someone had sent him a picture looking for a cat to replace one they'd lost or that had died. This gray cat could belong to someone way under anyone's radar. Finding a name or phone number connected to this particular cat, or one I hadn't pieced together yet, could provide an important lead.

Returning to the project at hand, I clicked my gooseneck quilting lamp on so I'd have plenty of light and began the search for the right puzzle pieces to finish this picture.

Two hours later I'd put together enough to know it was definitely not Sophie—even though there were even more similarities than I had seen initially.

Not about to let a little fatigue keep me from smiling, I stood back and admired my work. This was indeed a flyer for a lost cat. And I'd put together every shred. I had the name and phone number I'd been hoping to find.

This lovely, long-haired gray cat was a Mercy-ite—a cat that had once, or perhaps still, belonged to one of the few people in town I knew.

Twenty-six

The next morning, still in my pajamas, I snapped off several photos of my design wall creation while Merlot, Chablis and Syrah sat in a row staring at my work like patrons at an art gallery show.

"It's fantastic, isn't it?" I turned to smile at them and saw that Syrah had disappeared. *I get no props around here*, I thought. But I saw one of the garbage bags filled with paper move, and then a brown nose appeared at the very opening of the bag. Syrah was probably thinking, *Just let those other two try and share my new playground.*

I ran down the hall with the camera, ready to print pictures. Chablis thought this was great fun. She raced after me, and when I bent to dock the camera, she jumped on my back.

Even with claws digging into me, I managed to press the right buttons. While the pictures printed, I carefully removed my cat from my skin. Then I lifted Chablis so we were face-to-face and said, "Someone else had a missing cat last year. I need to see about this."

She began to resist our conversation, so I put her down. She sat by the computer table, watched the pictures appear in the tray and lifted a tentative paw. But I snatched them up before she could further explore the magic of the amazing paper so I could examine my work.

I nodded. "Good job, Jillian."

An hour later I was in the minivan and off to Marian Mae Temple's house. I got her name and phone number off the flyer and found her address in the telephone book, but she hadn't answered her phone. Maybe she was in the shower; maybe she wasn't even awake yet. Strange, because it was well past nine a.m. and everyone in this town seemed to be early risers, judging by the line to get inside Belle's Beans when I drove past.

The pictures of the pieced-together shredded flyer lying on the seat next to me told me that Marian Mae had lost a gray long-haired cat last year, if the date at the top of the computer-generated flyer was correct. Since I'd mentioned my plight to her and she probably knew about this whole Wilkerson investigation via her boyfriend, Mike Baca, why hadn't she said anything?

I had a guess. She'd done business with Flake Wilkerson, maybe paid a pretty penny for Sophie as a replacement for her lost cat, a cat named Diamond, as I'd learned from the once-shredded flyer.

And then, before I made it to Marian Mae's house, the commonsense button clicked on. Hadn't I speculated that whoever had Sophie didn't want to give her up and might have killed Wilkerson? Duh, yeah.

But Marian Mae? She didn't fit my image of a knife-wielding killer. She struck me as someone who would be annoyed if she got dirt on her shoes. All that blood? Nope. Couldn't be her. There had to be a different explanation.

Maybe she and her boyfriend were getting coffee together this morning? *Her boyfriend.* That was who I needed to talk to, not her. But did Baca even work on Saturday? Candace could tell me. Besides, she would want to know what I'd found out.

She sounded tired when she answered her phone. "Carson here."

"Is Baca at the office today?" I said.

"Huh? Only a few of us work on the Saturday day shift. And one of the 'us' would be me. What do you need?"

"I need to show him something. Can you give me his number or tell me where he lives?" I said.

"You can't go to his house." She sounded mortified that I would even consider this.

"Maybe you wouldn't go there, but I'm one of those tax-paying citizens who provides his salary. Tell me where he lives. I can find out myself, but—"

"What's going on? Maybe I can help," she said.

"Know who lost a long-haired gray cat last year?" I said.

"What is this about? And talk fast before Morris gets back here with our coffee."

I explained what I'd learned from Tom and about Marian Mae's lost cat.

Candace said nothing for several seconds. When she finally spoke, she sounded none too happy. "Wait on this, okay? She and Baca are probably going to get married, and if she needs investigating, then—"

"I only want to call him. What's wrong with that?" I said.

"This may be nothing. Marian Mae lost a gray cat just like Sophie. Can you spell coincidence? How many gray cats do you think passed through Wilkerson's slimy hands?"

"Yes, but—"

"This is not how to go about this. What if Marian Mae no longer has a cat? What if it's permanently lost? What if she's a victim of Wilkerson just like you and Mr. Green and Daphne and who knows how many more? What if she got so upset about losing—Diamond, is that right?"

"That's right," I said morosely.

"What if she was so devastated by losing her cat that she decided to never talk about Diamond again. Hurtful chapter closed. We know Sophie's female, but what do you know about Diamond? If someone like Marian Mae used Wilkerson's Match-a-Cat service or whatever he called it, she was paying big bucks. She'd want a close match. And you told me there were plenty of differences."

"Not that many, but I get what you're saying." I felt completely deflated. Here I thought I might have found Sophie right here in town.

"I'm not saying you're wrong," she said. But her tone more than implied that I was. "I'm only saying that you can't bring my boss's girlfriend into the picture based on theory and coincidence."

Candace was putting me down and I felt awful. No one likes to be wrong, much less have someone hammer home just how wrong she might be. I couldn't think of anything to say that might convince her this was important.

After a strained silence she said, "Jillian, I'm sorry, but—"

"I'll talk to you later." I closed the phone and tossed it on the seat next to me. Was I really as stupid as she made me sound? Maybe. But here was a lead, and I wanted to get to the bottom of it. I'd spent two nights piecing together what I thought was an important clue, only to be shot down by one of the few friends I had in this town.

I'm overtired, I thought. *Not thinking straight.* But no matter what Candace said, no matter how many hours of sleep I'd lost, I had to tell Baca about this. He would know about Diamond and if the cat had ever been found. Of course, he might not be happy to have me asking questions about Marian Mae, but a lead is a lead. Now all I had to do was find out where he lived. No phone book to offer an address this time.

I stopped at the grocery store, hoping that David the bagger could help me. I was completely surprised when he blurted out, "Michael Baca, phone number unlisted," followed by his address. It was as if he'd memorized every name and address in Mercy.

Baca's house wasn't far from downtown, in a quiet, tree-lined neighborhood. He answered the door so quickly after I knocked that my heart skipped. It was like he was waiting for me to show up or something.

Oh boy. Had Candace called him?

If so, he wasn't giving anything away. He said, "What are you doing here?"

He was wearing blue jeans and a Carolina Panthers

T-shirt. Seemed fitting he'd be wearing a shirt bearing a cat—albeit a very big, snarling cat—this morning. His sandy hair wasn't combed and he hadn't shaved yet. This casual look made me hope he'd be less uptight—like the Mike Baca who'd talked to me at the Finest Catch.

"Can I come in?" I said. "I have a few things to run by you."

He glanced back over his shoulder and showed no sign he was ready to invite me in. "Can't this wait until I'm at the station on Monday?" he said.

"I don't think so. Candace says police officers are never off duty. Is that true?"

He opened the door wider and stepped aside. "Did she send you here? Because if she did, this better be important."

"She didn't. I promise," I said.

"Let's go into my office." He led me through a small foyer, past the living room and down a hall.

As he opened his office door, Marian Mae appeared at the end of the hall wearing a terry-cloth robe and with a towel wrapped around her head.

She said, "Honey, who are you talking— Oh. Hello, Jillian."

"Work, Mae. Sorry," he said.

"No problem," she said cheerfully.

Baca practically pushed me into an office that revealed a new side of the man. What a mess. Books piled waist high, folders covering a love seat against one wall and a computer desk buried under a mass of papers with Post-it notes stuck everywhere. And here I'd taken him for a neat freak, the way his office at the police station looked.

He removed a stack of files from a padded chair so I could sit and took his desk chair, swiveling to look at me. "What's so important?"

"Did Candace show you the photos of my cat and the poor deceased cat that belonged to Mr. Green—that man I went to see?"

"She dropped them off here last night. As I said yesterday, I'm willing to concede that the cat business the victim was running is more important than I previously believed and could have played a part in Mr. Wilkerson's murder. I've received confirmation of this through a second independent source."

He was talking about Tom's forensic work on that hard drive, but I wasn't about to let him know I was aware of that. I'd gotten Candace in trouble with this guy, and I didn't want to add Tom to the list.

"I'm glad to hear that straight from you. I know you've been thinking I was a pain in the butt, and now I hope you realize I've been trying to help. I also wanted to make sure you got those pictures of my cat and Mr. Green's. Those two Abyssinians could have been twins."

"You came here for that? I'm not buying it, Jillian. What's really going on?"

I felt nervous. And dumb again. He and Candace were right. This could have waited. But I was here and I might as well say what I came to tell him.

I pulled the computer-generated photos of the gray cats from my pocket. "Were you aware your *friend* lost a cat last year?" I handed over the picture of Marian Mae's lost-cat flyer.

He looked at it, held it closer, then turned on a light above his computer. "What is this? Some kind of screwed-up attempt with Photoshop?"

I explained about the shredded paper from the Pink House.

He said, "How long did it take you to put this back together?"

"A long time. Do you know anything about her cat?"

He smiled, and I could tell he thought I was being ridiculous. "You think Diamond was stolen by Wilkerson?"

"It's possible." I handed him the other picture—of Daphne's cat. "You recognize this cat?"

"That's Diamond, too. I still don't—"

"Look closer. You really think I'm showing you pictures of the same cat?" I said.

He squinted, looking back and forth between the two photos. "There's hardly any difference. Why don't we ask the expert?"

Before I could speak, he got up and hollered out the door. "Mae, can you come here for a sec?"

Marian Mae was dressed now, her blue jeans creased, the buttons on her turquoise sweater revealing a hint of cleavage. "What do you need, Mike?" she asked, ignoring me.

"Look what our concerned citizen Ms. Hart brought to show me." He handed her the pictures.

She glanced back and forth between them. Her eyes rested on the flyer. "Where did you get this, and why does it look all fuzzy and wavy?"

"Doesn't matter where she got it," Baca said. "Tell her about Diamond, because I think she'll listen better to you than to me."

Marian Mae cocked her head at Baca as if to say, "What does this have to do with anything?" but then she looked at me. "I lost Diamond last year, put up a few flyers. That's what people do when something they love disappears."

It sure seemed like plenty of cats had disappeared around here—and Shawn was probably the only one who'd cared. "And what happened? Did you get Diamond—is it a him or a her?—back?"

"Diamond is a beautiful little girl. But she did get herself lost for a day. She came home right away, though," she said.

"Good news," I said. "So this is her, too?" I held out the picture of Sophie.

Marian Mae looked at me as if I'd lost my mind. "No. That's not Diamond. Can't you tell the difference?"

"I can," I said. "But Chief Baca didn't seem to have the same keen eye as the two of us. Of course, I have the advantage of knowing these two are *not* the same cat."

"Is this some kind of game?" Marian Mae said, her sky blue eyes darkening. "Mike tells me you keep sticking your nose in police business, but that's for him to handle. Just don't bring me and my cat into this."

I plucked the pictures away from her, not sure if I was irritated with her because of her attitude or upset with myself.

Baca put a hand on her shoulder and massaged the muscles. "It's okay, hon." He turned to me. "When Diamond disappeared, Mae was beside herself. I guess I should have been more sympathetic to your own situation with your cat, should have recalled how Mae reacted last year. So, please, take this as an apology."

"Apology accepted," I said. "Thanks for your time."

Baca walked me to the door, but before he opened it, I said, "Know who that unidentified cat belongs to?" I said.

"As Mae pointed out, this isn't a game. Just tell me," he said. I'd bothered him on a weekend and upset his girlfriend. He was probably past exasperation by now.

I handed him the pictures. "These are for you to keep. See, that other cat, the one that looks so much like Diamond? She belonged to Daphne—before her father stole her. This has something to do with her cat, Sophie. I'm sure of it."

I opened the door and walked out, but as I headed to my car I heard Baca call, "Stay away from the Pink House, Jillian. That woman could be dangerous."

Twenty-seven

As I drove away from Baca's house, I realized that mentioning Daphne hadn't been the smartest move, since Baca already suspected her. And then I'd gone and asked questions about Marian Mae, the woman he loved. So what if I'd pieced a shredded flyer back together and it had me wondering about Marian Mae? I wasn't accusing her of anything. But you'd have thought I was. The chief was practically living with a woman who'd lost a cat, and her flyer had ended up in Wilkerson's shredded pile of paper. Wasn't that important enough to question? Maybe not. Maybe Candace was right. How many other cat flyers had Wilkerson torn down and shredded? How many other people had the man stolen from? How many other suspects were there in Mercy?

Feeling low, but still not completely beaten into the ground, I decided to visit Shawn, find out what he might know about lost gray cats. If Marian Mae had done the same things I had when I lost Syrah, she might have gone to the Sanctuary hoping to find Diamond. Maybe she did get her cat back right away, but Shawn or Allison might know about the loss, could help me get a better read on Marian Mae Temple. Because despite only a flyer and two gray cats that looked a little alike, I couldn't help but still suspect her, even if I didn't know why. It was just instinct, and even Tom had said that instinct shouldn't necessarily be ignored. Or maybe I was going to visit them because I needed to talk to people who understood how important this mystery was to me.

There was another car in the minuscule parking lot at Mercy Animal Sanctuary. I walked into the office and found a couple and their young son adopting a kitten. *This is what's good for the soul*, I thought. *This is what I need right now.*

Snug the parrot seemed to mirror that idea, because he was bobbing and talking up a storm. Bringing a new pet into your life is one of the most special times ever, and the positive energy in the little room was almost palpable.

Shawn was attempting to coax the kitten away from the little boy, while Allison was taking care of the paperwork. She looked up and said, "Hi, Jillian. Be with you in a minute."

"You know how you have to wear your seat belt?" Shawn said, kneeling in front of the child.

The kid nodded.

"Well, we have to keep your new kitty safe in the car by letting him ride in the box your mom and dad brought," he said.

Safe. That reminded me I hadn't checked on my crew in a while, so I opened my phone and brought up the cat-cam feed. I ended up nearly laughing out loud. I'd tuned in on a game of chase. I swear, those three could be the inspiration for a cartoon series. I was so intent on watching them that Allison had to ask me to move aside so the family could leave with their new baby.

"Sorry," I said, stepping to my right. I looked at Shawn while Allison walked the family out to their car, motioned for him to have a look at what was happening at my house. He was smiling, too, after watching a few seconds of cat play. Syrah, as usual, was winning the race around the house.

"Fast cat," Shawn said. "Handsome guy, your Syrah. Bet you're relieved the Mercy catnapper is dead. I know I am."

"Maybe relieved," I said, "but sad, too. His murder was pretty darn brutal."

"What goes around, as they say," Shawn said. "What can I do for you?"

"I'm not completely sure. Mr. Wilkerson's daughter is in town—but I think you were aware of that. Did you know her father stole her cat, too?"

"Oh yeah. First thing she did was rush to Mercy hoping to get Sophie back. She came here straightaway when her father told her he hadn't taken the cat. We knew that wasn't true. Anyway, I didn't have the heart to tell her that a couple days before I'd had to call animal control for a dead gray long-haired. I figured Sophie escaped from Wilkerson—cats know when they need to get out of a situation—and got run over."

"Wow. That's not good." My heart sank. Seemed simple explanations often escaped wannabe detectives. I'd brought in a set of my computer pictures and showed him Sophie first. "Was this the cat that you found, um . . . you know?" I didn't even want to say the word, much less think about poor Sophie like that.

He glanced at the picture. "Daphne showed me a picture, too. Could be the cat in the road, but it was kinda hard to tell. See, I don't take close-up looks at animals that have died for whatever reason. Can't take it. I called that stupid, good-for-nothing animal control officer. It's his job to take care of that kind of problem. I sat in my truck waiting five damn hours for him to show up."

"You waited that long?" I said.

"You bet I did. He shoulda gotten his butt to town and picked up that cat right away. As it was, I had to steer cars around the poor thing more times than I want to remember."

Hoping to distract him from the lazy animal control officer—who might not really be lazy but could have been extra busy that day—I showed him the pieced-together picture of Diamond.

Shawn looked at it for several seconds, appeared to be

focused on the "lost cat" plea. He said, "Marian Mae lost her cat? Wait. Better question: Marian Mae *had* a cat?"

"Obviously you don't recognize Diamond, and I take it Marian Mae didn't come here looking for her last year?" I said.

"Nope. But the date on this flyer is right around the time I found that gray cat in the road. Could have been Diamond." He held up the picture of Sophie. "Or it could have been her."

Great. That helps complicate matters.

"How can you be sure of the timing?" I said.

"Because of the damn restraining order. I can tell you the when, where and how of the document that dumbass served on me. I don't care what the judge said. I had every right to go off on that fool when he finally showed up to take care of the poor cat."

"You went off on him how?" I asked.

Shawn hung his head. "There was some pushing. But I never hit him, even though he claimed I did."

"And you're sure that Daphne came looking for her cat around the same time that Marian Mae apparently lost hers?" I said.

He took a deep breath and gave me back the pictures. "That's about all I'm sure of. Wish I could help, but Allison will tell you, I'm a wimp when it comes to animal deaths. If we have one that's so sick it has to be put down, she's the one who takes it to the vet."

His eyes had filled, and he blinked hard to fight the tears.

I squeezed his arm with what I hoped he knew was sympathy. "I'm sorry I even brought this up. I'm heading over to see Daphne. I was thinking that the little domestic shorthair taken from the Pink House might find a good home with her."

His jaw tightened. "Don't make any promises. That lady is plain weird, you ask me. She could be an apple that didn't fall far, much as I hate to say it."

Once I'd climbed back in my minivan, I sat for a minute.

Two men in the last hour had warned me about Daphne. Should I keep my promise and pick her up for a day away from that stuffy, cluttered old house?

Gripping the steering wheel, I put my head down and fought against logic, tried to drown out the warning voices. My gut told me Daphne wasn't a killer. She might be depressed and troubled, but I understood how that felt. Understood too well.

I opened my phone, called her and then was on my way to her place. When I got to the Pink House, Daphne tried to convince me to stay there rather than spend the day at my place. But I won out. I showed her the cat-cam and my three babies, now stretched out in the living room, completely worn-out. She couldn't resist my invitation to meet them in person.

On the drive I talked nonstop about them—their unique personalities, how Chablis had the human allergy, how smart Syrah was and how Merlot was more watchdog than cat.

I was starving, and since Daphne was so thin she could have been the inspiration for the hangman game, I put a frozen pizza in the oven as soon as we got to my place.

While we waited for the pizza to bake, Daphne sat in the middle of the living room floor and let the cats come to her. And come they did. There is no doubt pets can heal, no doubt my three knew she needed them, but the transformation I saw in Daphne was remarkable. Her face lit up; her shoulders straightened. She looked like a different person. I wondered why she hadn't gotten another cat or even a dog since she'd lost Sophie.

But people must grieve at their own pace. I only hoped that this playtime with my three might make her realize she was ready for a new cat. If she didn't end up in jail, that was. Baca wasn't done with Daphne. In fact, he might only be getting started where she was concerned.

Daphne shared strings of mozzarella with Merlot, the only cheese-taker today. The other two curled up together near her since she'd stayed on the floor.

I didn't want to bring up the investigation, not today, so we were sharing stories about our pasts when the doorbell rang. *I sure hope this isn't some policeperson looking for Daphne*, I thought as I went to answer.

Not a policeperson at all. When I opened the door, I saw that Marian Mae Temple had come calling. What was this all about? Whatever it was, I had a bad feeling the minute I saw her.

I invited her in, and she stepped into the foyer, at first glance seeming as collected as usual. She held a handbag over her arm and her makeup had been applied to perfection. But her cold blue eyes belied calm. This was an unhappy woman. But why was she so upset? Had my coming to Baca's house created tension between her and her boyfriend?

Syrah came into the foyer, probably curious about yet another visitor. And then he did something I'd never seen him do before. He arched his back and hissed loudly through his open mouth at Marian Mae.

"Syrah," I said, "it's okay."

He turned his gaze on me before he bounded down the hall.

If Syrah's behavior wasn't unsettling enough, Marian Mae confirmed my earlier thoughts by saying, "You, Jillian, have created problems for me. I came here to tell you to keep your nose—" Her gaze was drawn over my shoulder and she said, "What are you doing here, Daphne?"

Whoa. Another surprise. How exactly did these two know each other?

"Who are *you*?" Daphne said, as only the well-guarded and paranoid could.

And the flustered look on Marian Mae's face told me more than words.

"Let me get this straight," I said. "You know Daphne, but she doesn't know you. How do you explain that, Marian Mae?"

The answer didn't come fast enough. She was thinking

too hard. Finally she said, "Mike showed me her picture. He thinks—well—" she said, seeming to regain her composure, "Perhaps I shouldn't say what he thinks."

"You know what?" I said. "He doesn't strike me as the kind of officer to discuss a case with his girlfriend, much less show her photos of someone he's interviewed. I mean, what did he do, show you the whole murder file?"

"Of course not," Marian Mae said, switching to indignation. She was good at sounding indignant.

I looked at Daphne. "Chief Baca take any pictures of you?"

"Not that I know about," Daphne said.

I returned my attention to Marian Mae. "Better answer would have been to say that Flake Wilkerson showed you his daughter's picture when you two shared a table at Belle's Beans," I said. "I might have bought that explanation, since you've already told me you and Mr. Wilkerson were acquainted."

Marian Mae ran her tongue over her upper lip, those baby blues dancing left and right. "I'm not a liar, if that's what you're implying."

"Then finish telling me why you're here. Something about me keeping my nose out of your business? Problem is, I'd about convinced myself this had nothing to do with your business—until you showed up here. How do you know Daphne? From seeing her picture at Flake Wilkerson's house?"

When I saw Marian Mae's hand dart into her bag, fear struck me like a small electrical shock, shooting up my arms and nearly making me jump.

And when the gun appeared and she pointed it at the two of us, I felt as if my legs would give out. Now I understood what Syrah was trying to tell me. He knew this woman—he'd met her at the Pink House. And he didn't much care for her.

I took a deep breath, held my palms up and facing toward her. "Please. You're scaring me," I said.

Marian Mae looked past Daphne again and into my living room. "Go in there."

I didn't like the way she waved the gun in that direction, as if she couldn't care less if the thing went off. And that unflinching stare. Obviously she hated me. "Sure," I said. "Whatever you say, Marian Mae." But I walked backward, not wanting to give her a target as inviting as my spine if she went completely loony.

The way I was walking, with my hands half raised, must have blocked Marian Mae's view of Daphne, because when we got into the living room, my friend had already pulled her cell phone from her pocket.

But Marian aimed the gun at her and said, "Put that on the coffee table, you idiot."

Daphne complied, but I noticed she didn't look the least bit afraid. Her eyes were a little chilling, too.

A shiver climbed my spine as I focused again on that gun. I'd never been so terrified in my life, but I had to hold it together. I took a deep breath and tried to make sense of this.

Marian Mae comes to my house carrying a gun. Why? Obviously my visit to Baca this morning changed her world.

But was Daphne's surprise presence in my home so unsettling that Marian Mae might be vulnerable? It was two against one. Well, two against two, if you counted the gun.

What are you thinking, Jillian? You can hardly pull Chablis out from behind the armoire. Your cats are stronger than you are.

And with this thought Merlot decided to show his face. He sauntered into the living room, completely unbothered by an additional stranger. And I spotted Chablis curled in front of the entertainment center a few feet from Marian Mae. Chablis's eyes were intent on that gun, though. Cats smell danger—and that was why Merlot's nonchalance was so confusing.

Marian Mae ignored the cats, turning her attention to me again. "Get rid of your phone, too."

It would have been easy to speed-dial Candace if I

didn't have a flip phone, but I had to open mine to use it. With a trembling hand, I set the useless phone on the table alongside Daphne's.

Her tone even, Marian Mae said, "Daphne's going to do to you what she did to her father—stab you with a kitchen knife. But you'll try to fight her off. And after this little spat, you'll both be dead. Case solved, but with a tragic end."

Okay, the woman was certifiable. How was she going to orchestrate this? But my pointing out the implausibility of her plan wouldn't help Daphne or me right now.

"What are you talking about?" Daphne said, her voice cold. "I never killed my father. Seems obvious you're the one who killed him."

How I longed to tell Daphne to hush up. Instead I said, "This is pretty complicated, what with two of us to deal with. Maybe we can call Mike, you can explain and—"

"No," she said sharply. "Get me two big, sharp kitchen knives. Now." But her eyes were unfocused, and I was betting she was racking her brain for a better way to deal with this situation.

I had a feeling Daphne wouldn't cooperate in any way, shape or form, and she confirmed this by saying, "Why should she do that? We're not going to make this easy for you."

I closed my eyes. Why wasn't she scared of that gun?

Without warning, Marian Mae sidestepped and as fast as light, reached down and grabbed an unsuspecting Chablis by the scruff of the neck and pointed the gun at her. "If you don't get me those knives right now . . . well, you get the picture."

Poor Chablis was struggling in the air, trying to turn this way and that to free herself. My mouth was dry, my stomach tight with fear. Chablis was unable even to cry out because Marian Mae was holding her so tightly.

Merlot's "I couldn't care less" act—and it had been an act—was over with this new development. He leaped from what had to be five feet away. Being the big strong cat he is, and with surprise on his side, he knocked Marian Mae off balance.

This is your only chance.

I was across the room in a second and rammed Marian Mae against the wall. She let go of Chablis, but not the gun.

I gripped her right wrist, and when she tried to twist free, we both ended up on the floor. But I had the advantage. She was on the bottom, and I was able to press my knee into her gut.

"Daphne, call 911," I shouted.

"Already did," Daphne said calmly.

Marian Mae released her grip on the gun, but as I shoved it away, I must have let up on her. That allowed her enough freedom to grab my hair. She pulled my head back until I feared my neck might break.

But suddenly Marian Mae was screeching and she released her hold. At first I thought she'd finally lost it because Daphne, thank God, was holding the gun on her. But that wasn't the entire problem.

Syrah had clamped down on her ankle with his very sharp teeth, and he wasn't letting go. I could almost hear him whisper, "Revenge is so sweet."

To add to the confusion, not to mention the noise coming out of this lunatic woman, someone knocked on the door. They must have heard Marian Mae's continuing wails, because that someone invited themselves to the party by bursting in.

Candace had her gun drawn when she rushed into the living room.

The very agitated Marian Mae was pretty well pinned, but I thought it only right to say to Candace, "A little help from a friend would be appreciated."

Twenty-eight

The number of people in my living room was making me claustrophobic. But we were waiting for Mike Baca to arrive. Seemed odd he would take his sweet time getting here.

Candace had cuffed Marian Mae, and Morris, who had also responded to the 911 call, was sitting at my dining room table with Marian Mae, trying to get her to explain her behavior.

But she'd clammed up, hadn't said a word. Billy Cranor and his firemen friends were here, too. I was beginning to accept the fact that everyone showed up everywhere for emergencies in Mercy.

Marian Mae had needed the puncture wounds on her ankle cleaned and bandaged. The paramedics could have left right afterward, but they hung around. Each emergency was a potential story to be passed along at Belle's Beans.

Convincing Daphne to give up the gun had been interesting. She hadn't wanted to part with it. Trust issues, I'd decided. I was the one to convince her the gun was evidence and Candace couldn't make a case against Marian Mae without it.

The wait for Baca was an agonizing thirty minutes. But when he arrived wearing golf spikes and a ridiculous argyle sweater vest, I understood. He took the shoes off at my front door before entering the living room.

When he saw Marian Mae sitting across the room in handcuffs, he said, "What have you done, Mae?"

Seemed she'd been thinking hard during her prolonged silence. "I came here to tell Miss Marple to allow you to do your job and this wacko"—she pointed at Daphne, who was sitting in John's recliner—"this woman pulled a gun on me. It's obvious they were in on Mr. Wilkerson's murder together."

I think my jaw dropped to my knees, but Daphne responded by jumping up from the chair in an instant. I believe I heard her say, "You lying bitch," before Candace grabbed her from behind with some kind of fancy police maneuver.

Candace whirled Daphne around so they were nose to nose and said, "Sit down or I'll have to cuff you, too."

The two of them stared at each other, with Candace's grip on Daphne's upper arms so tight her knuckles were white.

I stepped toward them. "Do what she says. Please?"

Once Daphne reluctantly sat back down and stuck a cigarette in her mouth, the tension in the room lowered a few notches. Not taking any chances, Candace positioned herself between Daphne and Marian Mae, who sat at the dining room table.

Meanwhile, Baca took a seat next to his girlfriend. The three extra police officers and the four firemen edged closer in unison so they could hear the conversation that was about to take place.

Baca may have been blind when it came to Marian Mae, but not to them. "Everyone but Morris, Candace, Ms. Wilkerson and Ms. Hart can wait outside."

"Does that mean *I* can leave?" Marian Mae said with the sickest, most smug smile I believe I have ever seen. But Mike's look kept her in her seat. As people filed out of my house, grumbling all the way, Mike Baca leveled a stare at Marian Mae Temple that was filled with both shock and disgust.

He said to Marian, "You're saying Ms. Wilkerson pulled a gun on you?"

Marian Mae lifted her chin. "That's right."

Baca looked at Candace and said, "Can I see the gun, please?"

Candace being Candace, she'd already bagged the weapon as evidence. She'd put the Ziploc holding the gun inside a large brown paper sack, and now she lifted the gun by the corner of the plastic so Baca could see it.

He rubbed between his eyes with his thumb and index finger. "That's my service revolver, Mae."

She said, "That Daphne person must have snuck into your house and stolen it before—"

"Did anyone tell you that you have the right to remain silent?" Baca said.

"Yes, but—"

"Then I'm reminding you again of your rights," Baca said wearily.

"But I have to tell you what happened," she said, sounding a tad desperate now. "These women attacked me and that awful cat bit me." She seemed to be working hard to summon up tears, but it wasn't happening, so she extended her ankle for some sympathy. "Look at this. I might get rabies. Now take off these silly handcuffs and we can go to the hospital where I can be adequately treated. And get Candy and Morris to take these two violent people to jail."

He ignored the speech by saying, "You're waiving your rights?"

Marian Mae stared at her once-future husband for several long seconds. Finally she said, "Should I do that? You're the policeman; you tell me."

"That's not how this works," Baca said. "It's your decision. We need to search your house, Mae. Do I need a warrant or do you give me permission?"

"You've been in my house, for heaven's sake. What could you possibly expect to find there that you don't already know about?"

I pulled the picture of Sophie from my pocket, held it up and said, "A cat that looks like this. This cat may not be proof of murder, but if it proves to be Daphne's, it will explain why you might have been angry with Flake Wilkerson when he told you he wanted the cat back."

Those frigid eyes narrowed, a look from Marian Mae I'd seen way more times than I'd wanted to. She said, "You'll need a warrant, then. And get me that lawyer, Mike."

Candace and Morris took Marian Mae away on Baca's orders. Once he'd placed a call to a judge for his warrant, he addressed Daphne and me.

"I'm sorry about all this. Neither of you were injured, I hope?" he said.

I would certainly feel the effects of the scuffle tomorrow, but that didn't matter. "I'm fine, Chief," I said.

"She never touched me." Daphne's cigarette danced with each word.

"Good. Right now I'm at a loss to understand how a person I thought I knew so well could . . ." His words trailed off. "Anyway, about your cat. If Mae does have—what's its name again?"

"Sophie," Daphne said. "You want me to spell it?"

"No. And I apologize again for coming in late on the cat angle. Maybe if I'd been on it sooner, this confrontation today could have been avoided," he said.

"Confrontation? You mean the attempted murder, don't you?" I said. I was thinking more about poor Chablis as well as the two of us. She'd run off once Marian Mae let go of her, and I was sure it would be a while before she came out of hiding.

"Assault will be on the table," he said, "as well as your father's murder, Ms. Wilkerson. As you know, a few things only came to light yesterday. The online cat business, for example. I would have seen things differently once—"

"Seen things differently? You mean realized you were wrong about Daphne? Wrong about me?" I was upset at Baca's offering up what seemed like platitudes.

He took a deep breath. "You're right and I'm sorry. Anyway, I've been examining your father's financials, Daphne. Most of what you inherit will come from the rather large insurance policy he took out a year ago. That change in beneficiaries is more important than ever now."

Daphne said, "Tell me about that. Who was the original beneficiary?"

"That's a problem," he said. "The insurance company is not cooperating. I had to ask the DA to subpoena them, and we don't have the name of the original beneficiary yet. See, they're dragging their feet, probably because if you went to jail for killing your father, the company wouldn't have to pay."

"But if that previous beneficiary killed him, they will," I said.

Baca nodded.

"You had to know Marian Mae was acquainted with Mr. Wilkerson," I said.

"She never mentioned him. But once we get the information from that insurance company subpoena, my guess is I'll find out they did know each other well enough that he was ready to take care of her for life. Why, I don't know. They aren't exactly two folks you'd expect to be friends." He sighed. "We will get the whole story, though. From what Candace described to me on the phone when she called, Mae terrorized the two of you. I apologize."

"And she terrorized someone else," I said. "Excuse me if I don't see you out. One of my cats needs me."

Twenty-nine

I found Chablis hiding under my bed, and it took some serious coaxing to get her to come out. I soothed her for several minutes, and she seemed relieved that I, rather than some crazy woman, came to find her.

I took her into the living room and asked Daphne if she'd sit in John's chair again and hold Chablis for a while. I thought it would be good for both of them. Daphne was more than happy to comply and so was Chablis. Meanwhile, I called the other cats, and soon they ventured into the living room, checking every nook and cranny for signs of strangers.

I sat on the floor, tickled to congratulate my heroes. Merlot immediately plopped down beside me and turned over for a tummy rub, while Syrah found a comfy spot in the center of my crossed legs.

"Do you really think Marian Mae has Sophie?" Daphne asked.

Before I could answer, someone knocked on the door. Merlot and Syrah took off, ready to lie in wait for another takedown, perhaps. Chablis was happy right where she was.

"Who could this be?" I rose. "The local reporter? Is there even a local reporter in Mercy?"

Daphne laughed. "You're asking the wrong person."

As I went to answer, relief washed over me when I saw how calm Daphne seemed. Chablis was a hero, too.

I opened the door to find Tom holding two steaming cups of coffee from Belle's Beans.

"Thought you could use a fix. What in heck's been going on, anyway?" he said.

"As if you haven't heard," I said. "This is Mercy, after all. But Daphne's here, so you didn't bring enough java."

Daphne ended up with Tom's latte while he warmed up what was left in the bottom of my pot for himself. When I protested that I could drink the old stuff, he said, "Not if what I heard is true. You *need* the fresh stuff."

As Daphne and I related all that had gone on, he kept shaking his head in disbelief, occasionally interjecting, "Unbelievable."

"The chief is waiting on his warrant, but I have the feeling that will be all she wrote for Marian Mae," I said. "I'm betting Baca wants to take a very close look at Marian Mae's cat. Maybe her computer, too."

"Ah," he said. "She's the one who took down the Match-a-Cat site."

I blinked. "I never thought about that. But yes. She was probably in business with him."

"That's why she took the computer from the crime scene and tried to destroy it," Tom said. "She knew there were links back to her. Her home computer will probably finish off any hope she has of denying a relationship between her and Daphne's father."

I said, "Though why a woman who the chief seemed to be taking care of would sign on with him is baffling."

"Remember? I had to sic a bill collector on her to get paid for her security system," he said. "She could have plenty of debt Mike didn't know about."

"Must have been in major debt to do what she did," I said.

"So she actually needed money," Daphne said, "and my father was her go-to guy? She must have been desperate."

"Still," I said, "why would he take out a life insurance policy with her as beneficiary—? They couldn't possibly have been involved romantically, could they?"

"Marian Mae is by no means stupid," Tom said. "He was a frail-looking guy, and if they went into business together she might have insisted on life insurance. You mentioned that the insurance company wasn't exactly cooperating. I'll bet we'll soon discover that Marian was the original beneficiary."

"And she killed him in a rage when Mr. Wilkerson told her he'd made that switch," I said, half to myself. I didn't say aloud my other thought—that this might have had nothing to do with Sophie. Daphne would be so disappointed if the gray cat called Diamond really *was* Diamond.

Tom said, "If Marian Mae's as smart as I think she is, she'll make a deal with the prosecutors. It didn't look like a premeditated crime to me, and it probably wasn't."

I looked at Daphne and said, "Tom used to be a cop," like I was his proud mother or something. I wondered if I sounded plain silly to him.

"You think she has Sophie?" Daphne asked. "Because I'm too afraid to hope."

Yup. Here it was. And I felt a little sick to my stomach.

"We'll know once the warrant is completed," Tom said. "Bet they turn over whatever cat they find to Shawn."

But a call from Candace an hour later surprised us. She asked us to meet her outside Marian Mae's house, so we all piled in Tom's Prius and hurried over there.

We had to park on the next block, and we saw why when we walked up to the crime scene tape tied to several trees. The search warrant was being executed, and gloved police people were removing items from the house. I saw a laptop in one officer's hands. And Mike Baca standing well away from the house, hands clasped behind his back, head hung.

And then I saw why. Lydia emerged from the house, her hands gloved, her hair piled high. She wore purple today, but the satisfied smile on her face was more prominent than anything else. She was in charge again and loving it.

Candace came down the walkway and approached me

from the other side of the tape. "This is pretty awesome, huh?"

"Very," Daphne said. "That woman was crazy."

I had to smile at that one.

"One thing I didn't get to tell you back at your house was that I'd gathered a little more evidence," Candace said. "We might not need it now, though."

"But tell me first how you answered the 911 so fast?" I said.

"Um, you've driven with me, right?" She grinned.

"Oh yeah. Guess I do appreciate your timing." I pulled my oversize cardigan tighter around me, thinking that didn't mean I wanted another ride with her in the near future.

"Is my cat in there?" Daphne was wearing my jacket, which hung on her thin frame. She was looking past Candace toward the house.

"Let me explain about this evidence," Candace said excitedly. "I noticed the chief had gray cat hairs on his coat yesterday—not the suit jacket he was wearing the day he came to the crime scene, either. So when he left for a bathroom break, I took some Scotch tape and grabbed a sample off the coat he'd left on the back of his chair."

"What does that have to do with Sophie?" Daphne said.

"Here's the deal," Candace said. "I took many cat hair samples from your father's house, but I also took some from his clothing—what he was wearing when he died. That gray hair on his pants legs didn't appear to match anything in the house—and believe me, I examined a ton of cat hair under the microscope. See, cat hairs are pretty distinctive, and—"

"*Please*. What about Sophie?" Daphne said.

"The cat hair on the victim's pants appears very similar to the cat hair I pulled off the chief's coat," Candace said with a smile.

"I'm confused," I said. "What does that mean?"

"I think I follow," Tom said. "You took a sample from

the gray cat that I assume you just found in that house. You think it matches those other two samples?"

Candace leaned back, pointing at him. "You got it. We know the chief has been inside Marian Mae's house before, but now we know either Wilkerson was at Marian Mae's house the morning he died or she transferred her cat's hair onto him when she killed him. My guess is the latter. It's proof. Animal hair has been used over and over in court and—"

"Is my cat in that house?" Daphne said tersely. She had the silver cigarette case in her hands, and from the look on her drawn face, she'd had about all she could take of Candace's enthusiastic explanation.

"There is a cat in there. Lydia says that since we've taken the hair samples, there's no need to keep her. We can turn her over to Shawn if she's not yours—but there is a little surprise. Wait right here." Candace took off running back toward the house.

Like she was worried we'd leave if she didn't hurry? Candace was something else.

But Daphne wasn't amused. She didn't take out a cigarette, but she kept turning the case over and over as we stood there.

A minute later Candace came out carrying a cardboard box with my missing sixth quilt covering it.

"Oh no," Daphne said, as Candace approached. "Is she hurt or something?"

Candace ducked under the crime scene tape and set the box on the grass in front of us. "Check this out," she said, lifting the quilt.

Daphne's hands flew to cover her mouth and she knelt in front of the box. "Sophie. Oh my God, Sophie."

I went on my knees beside her, my smile so big it hurt.

Daphne only had eyes for her kidnapped cat and was gently petting her head.

But I was melting at the sight of four beautiful silver kittens suckling at their mama's teats.

Thirty

It was closing in on six o'clock and I was sitting in my living room with Chablis, Merlot and Syrah, waiting on Candace and Tom to arrive. The three cats had me surrounded—Chablis on my lap and Syrah and Merlot on either side.

Tom, Candace and I were headed out to dinner for a celebration. A week had passed since Marian Mae Temple's arrest for murdering Flake Wilkerson, and evidence of her guilt had piled up. Her lawyer made a deal by Wednesday. Seemed her computer showed she'd accessed the Match-a-Cat Web site too many times to count.

And the e-mails exchanged between Wilkerson and Marian Mae explained their relationship—one created when Marian Mae mentioned her lost cat at Belle's Beans and Flake Wilkerson came up with a plan to replace Diamond with his daughter's cat—for a price.

Trouble was, Marian Mae didn't have much money. But she'd had a plan. They'd become partners. If Marian Mae wanted a cat exactly like her lost Diamond, then there were probably others like her. Yes, there was a market out there, and she and Mr. Wilkerson would take advantage of it. Their plans were detailed in those e-mails, right down to their mutual insurance policies. She'd insured Flake Wilkerson, just as he had insured her. But the last e-mail from Flake was the most telling. He was dying and he owed his daughter not only money but the truth. And he wanted to give Daphne her cat back.

Marian Mae had bills—more than fifty thousand in credit card debt alone. No wonder she needed that insurance payout, one that she'd been counting on since she'd learned of Flake's illness. She must have been enraged when she found out he'd switched beneficiaries. My guess, however, was that Flake's demand to return Sophie was the straw that led Marian Mae right to a knife. The gray cat found in the road by Shawn a year ago must have been hers, but Marian Mae wasn't about to give up Sophie, a cat she'd loved as her own for more than a year. That might be the one thing I understood about Marian Mae Temple. Her love for a cat.

Though Tom had called me every day, I wanted to wait on another date alone with him. I was more at peace than I had ever been since John's death, finally understanding that he wouldn't want me to shut my life down even though I still missed him so much. But I needed to go forward with baby steps. Tom and I would go out again, but for now, after all that had happened, I was glad to share an evening with both Candace and him.

The three of us had become good friends in the last week. Many secrets had come to light and a mystery had been solved. I only wished I hadn't ignored Syrah's warning when Marian Mae walked into my house with a gun. I would never doubt his people skills again.

As for my other new friend, Daphne—she had survived the estate sale and taken her new little family back to Columbia. She was a different person when I saw her off. Smiling, happy to be mothering Sophie and those gorgeous babies. The fate of the Pink House was yet to be determined. She said she had to give herself time away from the place to figure out what she wanted to do. Made sense to me.

When I heard the knock at the door, I had to extricate myself from my three cats. I snatched a pet roller on the way to answer and was getting rid of the cat hair on my jeans when I opened the door.

"Ready?" said Tom.

"Where's Candace?" I said.

"She's keeping the car warm for the cat. Shawn's okay with the plan," he said. "He's tried everything to find the owner of that Siamese and has had absolutely no luck."

"And Shawn would know how to do a thorough search." I grabbed my jacket, but when I saw the RAV4 sitting in the driveway, my stomach sank. "She's driving?" I wanted to add, "How could you let this happen?"

Since the crate with the cat was on the front seat with Candace, Tom and I sat in back. We had an important stop to make before we headed to dinner—we had to see a man about this cat.

I was already gripping the door handle as we left, wondering if this kind of car had backseat air bags. But I was unprepared for the almost placid driving on Candace's part. Finally I had to ask.

I leaned forward and said, "Did you take defensive driving this week?"

She glanced at me in the rearview mirror, her eyes showing her amusement. "I have an important passenger. Boy doesn't like to drive too fast."

Boy. I sure hoped the Siamese that Shawn had rescued from the Pink House would soon have a better name.

We pulled up to Mr. Green's house a few minutes later. Alfreda knew we were coming but had advised us against telling her boss. She'd told me he'd "get all stubborn" if we told him about Boy ahead of time, since he wasn't an Abyssinian, and we'd be told to stay away.

Candace had toyed with the idea of keeping Boy, but said her mother was too allergic. Even though Candace had her own apartment, cat hair clung to everything. During the last two weeks, that had proved valuable. But not for someone who sneezed and wheezed like Candace's mom. Besides, Boy demanded plenty of attention.

Tom carried the crate, and Mr. Green was completely surprised when Alfreda ushered the three of us into his tiny living room.

He smiled when he recognized me and said, "We havin' a party or something? I hear that police business you came to see me about the other day is all resolved."

I introduced Tom and Candace to Mr. Green and Alfreda. Tom set down the carrier without Mr. Green seeming to notice. But when Boy decided to make his presence known with a loud meow—the kind Siamese cats are famous for—Mr. Green sat taller and looked around.

He then met my gaze. "What you got there, missy?"

"Not exactly a new Banjo. But I think you might like this guy." I knelt and opened the crate.

Boy stuck his head out to check the place out, but according to Candace, he wasn't a stranger to anyone. He loved people, and the blanket across Mr. Green's lap was just the kind of thing he lived for.

Boy walked out of the crate, took one look at Mr. Green and hopped into his lap.

Let the purring begin, I thought with a smile.